# she's gone

# she's gone

## KWAME DAWES

AKASHIC BOOKS
NEW YORK

This is a work of fiction. All names, characters, places, and incidents are the product of the author's imagination. Any resemblance to real events or persons, living or dead, is entirely coincidental.

Published by Akashic Books
©2007 Kwame Dawes

ISBN-13: 978-1-933354-18-7
ISBN-10: 1-933354-18-6
Library of Congress Control Number: 2006923120

An excerpt of *She's Gone* appeared in a different form as "Marley's Ghost" in *A Place to Hide and Other Stories* (Peepal Tree Books) and in *Iron Balloons* edited by Colin Channer (Akashic Books).

First printing

Akashic Books
PO Box 1456
New York, NY 10009
info@akashicbooks.com
www.akashicbooks.com

*for Lorna, Sena, Kekeli, and Akua*
*for Gwyneth, Kojo, Aba, Adjoa, and Kojovi*
*for Mama the Great*
*and remembering Neville*

## Acknowledgments

Special thanks to Colin Channer, dub organizer and great reader and guide for this book. Thanks to Katie Blount, for her sterling edits and passion for these characters. Thanks also to the Department of English at the University of South Carolina, for giving me the space and support to work on the novel.

*Oh mocking bird*
*Have you ever heard*
*Words that I never heard*
—Bob Marley

# BOOK I

# Chapter One

They came across the border like a band of bearded outlaws, eight reggae rockers in a black tour bus that smelled of chewstick, garlic, and marijuana, three months after starting a U.S. tour, three weeks away from going home to Kingston.

A trooper had escorted them from Georgia. Pedro, the lanky bassman, had counted his change inside a convenience store and thought he had been shorted; after that the clerk fell into character and a tragedy was averted by Kofi, the shorthaired lead singer, who strode across the parking lot in tie-dyed jeans to interrupt his bredren's exposition on civil rights and slavery with a simple observation: "If they call the cops they'll search the bus. If they search the bus they'll find the weed. If they find the weed we going to jail. If we go to jail we'll miss the gig. If we miss the gig we miss the chance to spread the word. This country needs salvation."

They spent the next half hour concealing guns and ganja and shouting at each other, Kofi and Pedro almost coming to blows. But nothing happened. The flashing lights did not appear. Then just outside of Columbia, the trooper showed up. No siren. No lights. And they held their breath until I-20 delivered them to South Carolina.

The performance in Columbia was going to be the twelfth gig of a Tidewater tour of small clubs and universities. The idea was to use the tour to hammer out the dynamics of the songs they were going to record in New

York for their fourth album—the one they expected to bring them stardom. The first three were successful but sold well only in Europe and the Caribbean. America was not an easy market. Even though their appearance on *The Grammys* was a blip showing Kofi scowling and holding the Grammy that he had been handed during the sloppily organized and unglamorous pre-televised ceremony, the fact that they could stick the words *Grammy winner* beside their name had to count for something. Of course, critical success did not pay the bills. But with heightened interest in Marley thanks to the Marley children, and with the sweet marriage taking place between hip-hop and reggae, Pedro was convinced that something could happen.

Kofi was not convinced. He did not rap. Hip-hop rhythms were different, and hip-hop ruled black sensibilities in America.

As Pedro snored and tossed and muttered in the bunk below, Kofi tried to use his mind to trap the sound of the engine in one part of him and hold it just there. He was working to discipline his wandering mind, to get it to serve him only.

He held the sound of the engine in his bones until they arrived at the Governor's House, a small hotel in downtown Columbia. The lobby had the look of a once elegant home with a carefully arranged library of books and dull oil paintings of fruits and decanters. The carpeting was a mixture of crimson and tan.

At the marble counter, Kofi said he had to have a room to himself, muttered something about needing to write, and left his bandmates giggling at the sign that they had pasted to his back: *Reggae Virgin*.

In his room he undressed to his dull white briefs and sat on the edge of the bed. His head hung low, and his fibrous beard tickled the coils of hair on his chest, which was broad but soft, with nipples that would not seem out of place on a pair of women's breasts. He was a big man, bearish, with a proud stomach that would contract itself as soon as he stood up, though it was sagging now. But he assured himself that he was fit and that was enough. Fitness showed best from his waist down. From dancing every night on stage his legs were tight and muscled.

*Reggae Virgin*. He crushed the note. So he didn't pick up women on the road. He flopped across the duveted double bed, his head hanging off the side, the whole world topsy-turvy. A week ago Pedro had given him a batch of letters from Dorothy. Should he read them now?

He pictured her sitting like a dowager on her front verandah in Jamaica, swathed in her golden kimono, waiting for him to arrive, sipping gin and smiling like a mother would. The night he left, she was standing in the same kimono, drunk, crying, for the first time looking like fifty-two. She swore at him, cursed him, punched him, pushed him, and then held him close, the sea wind tossing her gray highlighted hair.

*How sad*, he thought, as he felt the weight of blood against his brain. *How sad. How did it come to this?*

When the voices had convinced him that he could fly, she did not release him in fear for her own safety. Instead she clung to him, and he had dragged her along the graveled road of her beach cottage on a sun-drenched morning, the screaming gulls and the grumbling sea drowning the sound of cars and people from the village across the cove.

It was all coming back now . . . clearly but upside down . . . he was running, telling her he could fly, pumping himself into a sprint, knowing he could lift his body and fly over the twisted sea-grape trees and beach bramble, over the cottage, over the beach with the overturned canoes of fishermen, over Dorothy and the small, dumbfounded audience of the short fat cook, the tall skinny helper, the ancient gnarled gardener with his machete, and the perfectly proportioned black teenaged boy who stood shirtless and in awe at all that was going on.

How he had run. How had she kept pace with him? Crushing his bandmate's note into a plug, he thought about the force of Dorothy's hold as she pleaded and screamed as if she thought he could actually take off. Now leading him inside she nursed him, fed him his medication, her concoction of herbs, and her whisperings of assurance. He liked being mothered. It was impossible not to feel as if he owed her something after this, and she knew it. He called that feeling love until he felt more himself and he wanted to play music again . . . then the fight . . .

Would he be coming back? He told her he didn't know. She called him ungrateful. Reminded him that he was leaving with more than when he came—hand-dyed cotton shirts, Russell & Bromley shoes, silk boxer shorts. It was a younger woman. She knew. But what did she know? What the bomborassclaat did she know? She knew everything except the truth—that she loved him more than he could imagine loving her, he had been living with a constant sense of guilt, and he had felt the guilt souring into anger. He had to leave before it curdled and became disgust.

Should he read the letters now? Or would they spoil his mood? If they were like the rest, they would.

She had a way of reminding him of his perversions, his attraction to a woman who knew her own desire and used him as a tool. She would remind him of those moments when he was weakest emotionally—of the fact that she had seen him weeping like a child, hopeless and weak under the weight of his depression. She would remind him that not many women could give him what she had given him. And yet her letters were laced with a terrible quality of sadness and hurt.

He rolled onto his belly and allowed the room to settle. He dug through his bag for the zip-locked bundle, opened one, and sat on the edge of the bed to read.

The letter began quite cunningly: *By the time you get this letter, Aunt Josephine might be dead.*

She knew how much he loved his aunt and she knew that this threat would bring him back. He crushed the letter like his bandmate's silly note and made to fling it at his image in the mirror, but instead he unfolded it and placed it in his lap.

Nothing was free of complication with Dorothy. She should have been simply an aunt, the best friend of his Aunt Josephine who had raised him as her son. But it had never been quite that way with Dorothy. She had made her home a refuge for him. Unlike his Aunt Josephine, descended from old Jamaican free coloreds who became wealthy merchants and crusaders against slavery at the dawn of the nineteenth century, Aunt Dorothy had come into her wealth late. She began as a secretary for an old lawyer and brilliantly orchestrated her way into his bed and then into matrimony. She was twenty-three and he was sixty and sickly with no apparent heirs.

People thought the old man was gay, as he kept his long-term liaisons with prostitutes in downtown Kingston discreet. But Aunt Dorothy was proud of what she did for him, of her calculation that he would need her, and of the way she protected him from people who tried to discredit his name with lies and innuendo. He died one morning while they were walking around the Mona Dam, a large reservoir tucked into the side of the mountains that surround Kingston.

He left a decent fortune to her, and Dorothy began her new life as a shrewd investor in the garment industry and several businesses, including a printing company and a recording studio. She was a committed patron of the arts—especially the modern dance movement—and she gathered around her a retinue of male dancers who protected her fiercely and made everywhere she went something of a party.

Kofi had gotten used to it, and she had sensed that for him to continue to be happy with her, she would need to keep a space for them alone. It worked for a while—she reminded everyone that Kofi was different, and her dancers grudgingly stayed out of his way. But he still felt closed in, scrutinized. He knew he had to leave. And now he imagined her walking through the rooms, picking at the things he had left there, contemplating how to bring about his return—using everything in her, every predatory power she had, to get him to come back.

He could read no more.

Can't let her get under my skin.

Kofi closed his eyes. The darkness was complete. He wanted spots of light—moments of lightness that would confound the gloom.

# Chapter Two

He slept into the next afternoon, on his side, his body balled into a fist. At 4:00, he went out to the balcony and looked out on the city of gray wet walls, the streets festooned with carefully placed elm trees that were, here in the last days of October, already dressed in Christmas lights. From the balcony, he could see the dome of the State House where the Confederate flag—a stunningly lovely banner with its crimson belly, navy blue slashes crossing each other like swords, and the jewelling of white stars—still flew defiantly, reminding Kofi where he was.

In Jamaica there was racism. It just had a different language. Whiteness was not a pure entity, not like he sensed it to be here. The lines of racial definition were blurred. Aunt Josephine was a white woman, born in Britain to Jamaican parents. She had some black blood, she must have. But she was, for all useful reference, a white woman. Yet it did not seem a contradiction to him that she was the woman he loved more than anyone else in the world.

He thought of her that night. Wondered if she would have laughed. For he had arrived at the club in paratrooper pants and army boots and a smock handprinted with Nkrumah's visage to see a college crowd in sandals lining up for a concert billed as *Island in the Sun*. Free hula hoops for the first two hundred women. The men were wearing floral shirts and chino shorts from Banana Republic. As he entered through the stage door he overheard a woman tell her boyfriend, "This better be as good as Jimmy Buffett."

Inside the spectacle continued. Sand had been trucked in to fill the dance floor, and volleyball nets had been installed for atmosphere. The waitresses were dressed in key lime string bikinis, and all the drinks they carried were either pink or tangerine and topped with orange wedges stuck up next to cherry red umbrellas. The low, broad stage was fringed with bamboo fronds, and the ambient music was calypso. Only a few black faces were in sight despite this being a city with a forty percent black population. But that was reggae in America. Clubs in cities with a large West Indian population transported you to Jamaica—the smells, the voices, the energy, the easy vibe of people who knew how to move to roots reggae. But the mainstay of the tour were college towns where rich white kids crowded the shows to hear music that spoke to them only of sun, sand, and weed.

The band rearranged the set that night and opened up with Marley covers. It was Pedro's idea, and the band agreed, the logic being that Marley tunes would get the audience into a sing-along, priming them to hear the original songs. Kofi did not agree. Pandering was a slippery slope. He had scripted an introduction, had calculated what to say between the songs, had found the perfect words with which to use the Confederate flag to dust off the elemental truths that had been mucked up by white people. But the other members took Pedro's side— the band was guaranteed a percentage of the bar take, and Bob sell nuff Budweiser.

As they took the stage to open up the final set, Kofi

raised his arms to calm the crowd, pointed backward to the band, and began to scratch a riff that matched his mood, and scuffed out a line that communicated to the band exactly who was in charge of this crusade: *Two bull cyaah reign inna one pen, Pedro. This is my band, Pedro, my band.* The first to fall in line was the drummer, who began to swish softly on the high hat until he found the sweet spot, into which he punched a one-drop, driving the riddim, and the bass and keys and horns came in, dragging like a chain gang. A hush fell over the room when the keyboards found a voice and the Hammond organ began to churchify the sound, calling forth the spirits of slaves and angels who had ascended from the ends of ropes, and the horns began to bleat in lamentation.

A gasp went up when the engineer put some extra echo on the riffing guitar and cut the lights. Kofi opened his eyes to see the world in blackness, until the Zippos began sparking one by one. He felt his nostrils flaring as he saw the beach that babylon built being transformed into a sea of light as the stage lights came back up again, softer now and different, the band in blue behind him, the key light silver, coning him, Pedro's bassline roping his waist and twisting him, unfurling him to skip toward the crowd before it dragged him back to plant his feet and drop into a concentrated grind, a meticulously focused movement, as if he were shining up a door knob with his crotch.

*This is how it should feel*, he thought, when the sound that filled him up began to raise his arms. Deadly. Deadly like a Kingston street at night. And a refrain began to play inside his head as he high-stepped inside his cone of silver light, and his mouth, drawn into a scowl beneath his smiling eyes, shaped the words into the ritual lament of a righteous killer:

*Oh, I killed a cowboy today*
*Thought they was dead, you know;*
*That old generation of pale face*
*With their trinkets and guns and forked tongues*
*But I know down there in Oka*
*I shot one of dem boys today*
*I killed a cowboy today,*
*I shot John Wayne . . .*

He turned around and Pedro nodded. *Gwaaan, man.*
*Gwaan.* And he began to dart from side to side now and
pump his fist, and the crowd began to cheer and pump
their fists and jump with him, high-stepping.

He glanced behind him at the band again, and as the
boy-faced guitarist began to play a looping, bluesy run,
Kofi scanned the audience for the first time.

Perhaps it was because she was one of the few black
faces, or it may have been the way she moved, but she
caught his eye like an old friend in a strange place would.
She moved toward the stage in a flaming yellow dress.
Low waist, slightly bowed legs, upright broad shoulders,
the elegance of her small round head balanced on a long
proud neck. He stared hard, trying to make out her
features, but it was too dark.

She was dancing, now ten rows deep. He nodded his
head and smiled. She waved and smiled and slapped her
face and blew a kiss at him.

Dancing slightly off the beat, she squeezed toward the
front, her breasts appearing to him like an offering as he
looked down at her. The spill of the stage lights caught
her face. He could see her more clearly now. Her features
were more African than he had expected, her eyes wide
with questions—she was beautiful in a new and startling

way. She smiled like someone who knew him and she opened up to dance with him.

He began to dance with her, began to challenge her with his moves, and she dared him to follow hers. She moved as if possessed by some shameless old Jamaican woman at a rum bar, strutting, gyrating her eyes closed tightly. She rolled her waist, smiling at this game of impressing herself. Then she turned her back to him, her waist rolling. With this woman in his head, Kofi began to sing with a jazzlike sense of improvisation and variation. He signaled to the soundman to go to town with the echo and reverb so that his voice went forward and then twinned on itself.

Kofi took his time to walk toward her. At the edge of the stage he put his foot upon the monitor and let his shadow fall on her face. She laughed, acknowledging the game. And she began to move to his voice now, abandoning the music. Only the words.

She was a deep mellow brown, with long cascading hair. Her entire face was a query—the thick yet neatly arched brows, the glint of teardrop jewel on her right nostril, the perky ears that had been studded with a line of silver roses.

The band riffed on a version break, counting time to segue into the next song—a rehearsed tight shift that they were quite proud of. Kofi turned to Pedro and shouted, "Virgin!" Pedro nodded, and communicated this to the rest of the band before smoothly slowing the tempo and shifting the key into a minor groove. The band followed delicately, and into this well-made bed, Kofi, looking at this woman, began to sing "Dream Virgin":

*She's a priestess, bearing her chalice*
*Chalice to the altar, body to the altar*

*She's a virgin in her dreams,*
*Constantly warring with her karma*

Kofi rushed toward the congas and began to beat out a frantic tattoo. And Pedro ran over and began to do elaborate knee-lifts on the spot beside Kofi, urging him on. He liked to see Kofi like this, animated, driven, full of purpose. He smiled at the woman who was turning Kofi's performance into an event, trying to tell her *thank you*. The reggae Virgin might commit a sin tonight. It would be good for him. He needed something to pull him out of the morass of despair that was sucking him downwards since he left Jamaica, since he left Dorothy.

But Pedro also knew what happened when Kofi became the prancing, animated prophet. The giddiness was always inspired, always a flame that caught everyone around him on fire. But it would never last. Afterwards there would be the crash. Then he would vanish for a few weeks, only to return escorted by Dorothy, who would hover over him like a hen.

Pedro grinned at Kofi and then jerked his head to the woman. He had never seen a woman affect Kofi this way before. Kofi grinned back. He ran away toward the drummer, leaving Kofi behind to beat a mating call.

Backstage in the dressing room, Pedro said to Kofi: "The nice ting out dere waiting for you. Dat woman want yuh bad."

"True words dat," Pudgy, the drummer, said.

"The gyal well phat," Simon, the guitarist, whispered. "Oonoo sight de batty-jaw?"

Kofi nodded. She had held a door open, but he knew enough to know that a woman sometimes just wants to dance before she goes back to her normal life. On tour these stage connections happened, but afterwards they fell flat. He had learned to let them stay on stage. He sat with his eyes closed while the others congratulated themselves on the gig and then started to argue about money, beer, and food. Kofi's eyes stayed closed. In his head he was thinking of the show and the woman, the gleeful and unself-conscious way she applauded after he had beaten bruises into his palms on the congas and wiped sweat from his face; the way she had then looked downwards and held her fisted hands to her chest and began to grind, slow, easy. No one troubled her, none of the guys dancing in the front attempted to dance with her—they watched, they smiled, but it was as if they had assumed she was his woman. He heard a white man's voice cutting into the chatter.

"Hey, man. I have some nice herb for you guys, man. Sensimilla, colly, you know?" He was trying too hard—the inflections were all wrong, very white. "Really nice stuff."

"So why you feel we need dat, bredda?" Pedro asked aggressively. It was his usual test.

"No, no, him cool. Ah know de bredda," Pudgy said.

"Hey, you think the singer there would want some? He is wicked, man. Wicked," the white man said.

"The man a rest off, man. 'Low him," Pedro replied.

"No, he might want to rest, you know. Unwind. He looks tired." This was a woman's voice, a white woman— a hip Southerner. Kofi imagined a thin woman in an extra-wide flowing dress of tie-dye, her fragile straw locks bundled up in an untidily wrapped cotton cloth, and her skin smelling of hemp perfume.

"Yeah, man. Leave the man. Come, we go out to the back alley," Pedro said. "Soon come, Kofi, yuh all right?"

"Yeah man. Yeah man," Kofi said, his eyes still closed. He heard the door slam with a thud and then the silence.

He kept his eyes closed until he heard feet scratching the floor and the slight shuffle of fabric. He opened his eyes.

"You noticed me?" she asked with her smile. He glimpsed at once the glittering knob of gold on her right nostril.

"You were fidgeting," he said.

"I couldn't let you fall asleep on me," she grinned.

"It's been known to happen," he chuckled. He was glad she was there.

"Shame, shame," she reprimanded him playfully. She gave him a bottle of water—cold water. "Here, I know you roots guys like water first." Her accent was clearly Southern, but she had been around, or planned to be around. She had weaned some of the earth from her tones—the effect was to sound almost white urban Southern.

He took the water bottle.

"I want to talk to you. Buy you a drink and chat. Interested?" she asked, still standing at a distance and sounding like she had rehearsed the speech.

"You dance nice," he said.

"You want to stay back here?" she asked with a hint of uncertainty. What she was doing, he could tell, was difficult for her, but she was working hard to make it seem light. She laughed a little too loudly.

"Yeah. Come, we go to the bar." He got up. His clothes were soaked with sweat. He was cooling.

"By the way, my name is Keisha," she said, holding out her hand. He reached for it, self-conscious of the damp in his hands.

"Nice—very Negro," he said, testing how she would handle the tease.

"We don't choose our own names, honey. Anyway, I like it," she laughed, and he liked her more for the irony in her voice.

"Kofi," he said with a smile.

"I know. Remember, I am the groupie."

"Ahh," he released her hand and rubbed his right palm on his left arm.

"Kofi, eh? Very, well . . . Negro . . ."

"Touché."

Loud calypso was booming through the club. People were dancing. The bar was busy. The smoke. The smoke. He felt a burning in his chest, as if he himself was smoking. People touched him and smiled at him as he walked through. White women winked at him; some came forward and spoke quickly and intensely, staring at him, shouting so he could hear. Kofi suggested they go outside instead of heading to the bar.

Keisha walked with a high-breasted assurance. But when she saw him staring, she folded her arms.

It was beginning to happen, he thought—the promise of connection, and then the more we start to talk, the more she changes, starts to get impatient, starts to realize that hanging with a reggae-singing Jamaican is not as exotic as she had thought it would be. Soon it will end with a complimentary screw, some awkward parting. This one won't even stay that long, she is prepared to bolt already, like she is already ashamed of being so bold. But as he thought this, she said, "I want to dance with you," and embraced him before he could answer.

The music had changed from Arrow to the Rolling Stones' "Angie." They held each other lightly, her face on his collarbone, her hands on his shoulders, his hands on her arms, the trucked-in beach sand *crunch-crunching* underneath their feet.

"You guys are killer," she said when the song was done. Around them other couples danced. "I love reggae. Been to lots of cool reggae clubs in New York."

"You from New York?" Kofi asked. He drawing her into his chest again.

"No, from right here. But I know New York."

He led her to a table in the corner. The table was wet with spilled beer and dew. She took a fistful of napkins from another table and sopped it up.

"You know, I am waiting for your man to come and give me a hard time now, right?" He said this while pretending to search out this man in the crowd. "It is that one, isn't it?" She followed his gaze to the only black man dancing near the bar—tall, athletic, very young looking.

"He is cute but not my guy," she said, fiddling with the row of thin silver bangles on her arm. "I came alone."

"You do that a lot?" He looked directly at her.

"No, not a lot. But I heard you guys were good. I just felt like hearing some good reggae, to dance. It gets like that sometimes, you know?" And she meant it, he could tell—that soft appeal in her eyes—she trusted him.

"Yeah, I know. And you dance sweet; made me feel I was in Jamaica. Where you learn to dance like that?"

"Here and there . . ." she said, waving her hands in front of her.

"Your boyfriend is a Jamaican, right?" He leaned back, trying to look cool about the question.

"Now isn't that a cliché?" She leaned toward him. He looked down to avoid the full confrontation, but met the round tender glow of her breasts, soft against the white fabric. He could see the brown shadow of her right nipple.

"You are avoiding my question—a little red Jamaican man from Miami whose family escaped socialism in the '70s, and he only uses his Jamaican accent when he wants to turn you on, but talks like a true Yankee with the other insurance executives he works with. He is traveling on business this weekend, and you miss him, so you came to get a lickle Jamaican vibe in the club, just to make sure your dreams are righteous tonight . . ." By the time he was finished, he had her right hand between his palms. "Right?"

"All that to explain why your music made me move like waves were swaying me," she said slowly. "Man, you have no idea how good you are, do you?"

"How good?"

"You saw me dancing . . ."

It was easy, this banter. An open door. He was starting to relax.

She maneuvered her hand around his and got up, pulling him up gently . . . "Come, I want to dance."

Sade's husky whisper thickened the air, the bass rumbling underneath it. Keisha found a comfortable place against his chest to rest her head, and they moved easily, allowing the raw honesty of Sade's passion to carry them:

*You think I'd leave you down when you're down on your knees?*
*I wouldn't do that*

They danced themselves into a corner. Slower. Tighter. Nice.

# Chapter Three

At 2:00 they left the club to get some air. They stood on the parking lot looking out at the river beyond a row of trees. Kofi was feeling a curious sense of elation. He felt the return of the man who used to live inside him, the man who enjoyed the freshness of a new person—a whole new history to discover in another person. He felt also the anticipation of watching her discover him, of him perhaps remaking himself in the stories that he could tell her. For a long time, he had lost interest in his own story, and he was not convinced that the women he met on the road really wanted to know it. Dorothy knew everything. She knew so much that he had begun to depend on her for his understanding of himself. The boredom was thorough. Now he saw a chance to retell the story of himself.

"I can't shake that Sade song," Keisha said, looking toward the sky. "You guys should do that one."

"It is a great tune—fat sound. Great lyrics, yes," Kofi said, bending down to pick up pebbles. He tossed them toward the river, but they fell short into the thick vegetation at the edge of the water.

He watched as Keisha raised her hands over her head, causing the hem of her dress to run up her thighs. She stretched her body and then let it fall. Her hair fell forward, revealing her nape, a tiny dimple covered by the tight shrubbery of her tiny curls that had defied the chemicals. There was something intimate, almost sexual about that instant. She reached to hold her waist and slowly lifted her torso upwards, vertebrae by vertebrae.

"Your back?" Kofi asked, resting his palm in the soft of her back.

"All day staring at a computer will do that to you," she said, dropping her torso again with a sigh.

"Slowly, now, vertebrae by vertebrae," Kofi said softly, walking his fingers up her spine. He settled himself behind her and began to knead her shoulders. She allowed her neck to roll around.

"Oh God, that's good," she breathed.

"Tight, tight, tight," Kofi said, working his thumbs deep into her muscles until he felt them loosening. Her bottom pressed into his groin as she relaxed some more.

"Gooood," she said as if to herself. Then she reached her hand to her shoulder and rested it on his. "Let's walk. It is a nice night. Walk and talk, 'kay?"

She took his hand and led him, and he followed dutifully. They walked out to the main road, falling into an easy pace as they headed deeper into Columbia.

Keisha made silly jokes about the displays in the windows of the chic boutiques and antique stores, and shops that vended art supplies and gadgets for the serious kitchen. The fall air was clean, slightly chilled, but comfortable—the best of seasons in the South. The rain clouds from the night before had hurried across the state toward Charleston and the Atlantic, leaving a gentle vacuum of tender air in their wake.

The sky was clear, starry, and as they moved through waves of laughing students, some of whom were staggering home, he linked his arm in hers and did not let go.

Up the grade ahead of them began a residential area, and they could see the moon-washed purple tint of the broad oak trees that in daylight shaded stately homes.

As they walked under the darkened awnings of a flower shop, he noticed that she limped slightly on her right leg.

"Dancing too hard, eh? Maybe you should take off your shoes."

"Maybe," she said, but continued to walk.

"How you hurt it?" he asked.

"Tae Bo," she replied simply. Looking ahead.

For a second he paused, trying to see if he had heard right. Then he burst out laughing. She turned on him with a mock serious glare.

"What is so funny? I am limping and you think it's funny."

"Tae Bo? You mean that kicking thing?" he sputtered. Then he started to laugh again, leaning against a parking meter. Her look of hurt was too much for him.

"You are not a nice person," she said. "Tae Bo ain't easy, now. Ask Oprah." She started to smile.

"So you do Tae Bo? Why?" he asked her.

"To keep fit. Lose weight. Learn to kick punk-ass fools like you to the curb."

He lifted his arms in a karate gesture, turning on her.

"I will hurt you, fool," she said.

"Not wid your bruk foot," he said, slapping her softly on the shoulder.

"Don't play with me now, boy. I've been doing this for two weeks. I could lethally harm you."

"Yeah, yeah. Mash me down," he said.

"I thought you would be nicer. You should feel sorry for me. I'm in pain, you know."

"Tae Bo," he said with some disbelief. "You watch Oprah, too?"

"And read E. Lynn Harris, yeah. All the stereotypes.

And I like chitlins. My name is Keisha, for God's sake. You said it."

"What is chitlins?" he said, laughing more heartily.

"Part of the Tae Bo diet. Will you stop laughing?"

"I wish I coulda see yuh bruk yuh foot . . ."

"Tae Bo ain't for e'rrbody, I will tell you that much," she said.

There was a rut in their way but she passed it with ease.

"Did you hurt it bad?" he asked her, looking at her ankle.

"Nah, nah. I was just playing. Just playing with you. It's an old thing, that's all. Sometimes it hurts like this when it rains. I am getting old, you know. You hit fifty and the body starts to go."

"You are only fifty? God, you seem so mature—"

"Fool," she said, slapping him in the head.

He looked at her and grinned. She shook her head and touched his arm and then looked ahead again. "I think you're crazy," she said.

Kofi drew a hurried breath. Couldn't let it out. *Crazy*. Maybe he was a bit crazy. For the last several weeks he had decided to fast from relationships, from dealings with people. He wanted to be free, to think in an uncluttered way about what he was doing with Dorothy. But he knew he was starting to like this woman. He was already starting to over-think things, trying to read her, to read himself. Where was he going? What was he doing? He thought of the pills in his suitcase. He always had them. And he hadn't been taking them. Had not been feeling the need. Perhaps he should go back to the hotel. Just kiss her cheek and say goodbye and have her wonder. Have her wonder.

They walked in silence for a while. But as he thought

of how their dance had brought him peace, and as he felt the coolness of the night against his skin, and saw how her limp gave her hips an extra roll, he heard a man say, "I like you very much," and he realized it was him.

"Thanks," she said. She stopped and drew him close. "But we should part ways now. I should quit while I am ahead."

He should have felt relieved, but he didn't. "I'm thirsty," he said in a courtly way, stepping back to draw a line with his finger from behind her ear, along her neck, to the dip beneath her throat. "And I would like to drink some water from the cup in which you make your coffee in the morning."

"I . . . drink . . . tea," she mumbled. She looked away, down the grade, and then up toward the moon, whose light was confettied by the edges of the shimmering leaves. The hairs around her nipples were on end. A block of ice within her had begun to melt. Kofi followed her along a darkened residential street whose houses showed as brooding shadows.

She talked quickly, about herself, about South Carolina, about work, about anything that would stop him from doing what he just did again. Kofi listened, enjoying the dance of her accent, chuckling at her jokes.

By the time they arrived at her house, he knew a lot about her—that she had fallen in love with Marley's music in her teens, that she had gone to university at Vanderbilt and had moved around a lot . . . Chicago, Detroit, Atlanta, Miami . . . or, as she put it, "wherever the work is." As they walked across her lawn, which was strewn with pine needles, she told him that she worked in research down at the University of South Carolina . . . sex research.

Through the lining of his pocket, Kofi became aware

of the hotness of his palms. She was playing with him, dangerously.

"Don't think I'm a pervert," she said, laughing loudly.

Her laughter made him laugh. As they doubled over on her stoop, she added: "Liar, you do, you do. Don't worry."

"Nah, nah, nah," he said, like a man who is trying not to lie. Then he added, "But you can't blame a man for hoping . . ."

"I really do legitimate research," she said, giggling lightly. "I work with a woman at Columbia University in New York who is doing research on women's sexuality. Nationwide study. Means I have to go around the country and interview people. Me and a crew of other women. I am doing South Carolina because I know the place. My folks are from here."

It was a three-story house owned by her cousin Leonora. Keisha lived on the top floor. The other floors were furnished but not occupied. Although she did not yet let him in, he felt a sense of inevitability. They sat on the porch, which was in darkness while the porches of the other homes were lit. The lawn was thick with tall pine trees, some live oaks as well, and the shadows of trees he could not know. The yard and building appeared to be a bit unkempt.

"Whole heap a tree," he said, quietly sketching out a riff he hoped she would read and follow. She stood behind him by the door.

"I love trees," he heard her say above the jangling of her keys. "That is why I took this place."

She was fidgeting.

"Whole heap a work with all them leaves," he said, half smiling.

"I want to hire a good-looking gardener to clear the

leaves up. Know anybody?" She continued to fidget with the keys.

"No, no. Don't know a soul looking for that kind of work. How much you paying?"

"Don't worry, I will make it worth his while."

"Mmmmmm."

"This is my place. I make the rules." Her arms encircled him and he felt self-conscious about his weight.

Pressing against his back, she nuzzled her face into the slight give of his armpit and breathed him deeply. She held the keys now at the zipper of his pants, and jangled them again. He wanted to turn around, but she was pressing him against the railing and he was slightly off balance. With his hands in his pockets, he could fall. There would be no charm in that.

He was hard—he could feel himself against the wood.

As her breathing warmed his skin, he thought of making love with her, began to wonder how her loving would be different. It had been five months since he had been with a woman—since he had left Jamaica, since the argument with Dorothy and his departure for the tour. For three of those months the quiet felt good. He felt no hunger. He dreamt of Dorothy for a while and then that too faded. Sex seemed complicated to him, and the fact that for the first time in years he seemed able to do without it, seemed able to handle small pangs of desire, was attractive to him. But that quiet period had passed. The last two months had brought back the familiar desire. He was waking up mornings with a strong need for release, images of sexual positions spinning in his head. At night he took showers, masturbating with a mechanical efficiency that left him drained but comfortable. Tonight he felt desire. He knew that sleeping with this woman whom he really did not know would bring confusion, but he wanted her. He was in a bad state.

"Them chairs strong enough for a big man like me?" He took his hands out of his pockets and the gesture signaled that she should let him go.

When he turned around, she seemed relieved but disappointed.

"Yes, yes, they are," she said. "I will get some tea. Tea for you, or water?" She bit her lower lip and put the key into the door. She said quietly, "You want to come . . . and do it yourself? . . . I don't know how you like it."

"No, I will wait out here," he said, looking at the trees. "I like it. Cool, quiet. Hot tea, yeah?"

She returned with a throw around her shoulder, a tray with two mugs of herbal tea, and a pot of honey. She was slightly shorter, and more compact, the shape of a sprinter, the bow in her legs more pronounced. But she still had the tall upright bearing and the poise of a dancer. He looked down. Instead of her pumps she was wearing slightly tattered slippers.

"This is for you," she said. He took the throw. It was a soft chenille.

She sat across from him and placed the tray on a green aluminum table and crossed her legs.

He glanced at her slippers and smiled.

"Sentimental attachments," she said.

"From your man?" he fished.

"I have no man." She sipped the tea. "You don't want honey?"

"Your ex-man, then." He rolled the wooden orb in the honey pot and dripped it slowly into his cup.

"Maybe," she said, holding the cup in both hands and sipping, her eyes squinting slightly.

"That is a yes. Him live roun' here?"

"I don't kiss on a first date, and I don't talk about past lovers, ever."

"This is not no date. Just strangers trying to pass the night. The best kind of friendship." He leaned back and relaxed. "So you can tell me your business now."

"You will tell your wife about this?" she asked after a pause in which the sound of crickets overrode the creaks and groans of the aging house. Somewhere in the distance, a truck trundled by. "About meeting me, about drinking my tea and honey, about our dance . . . ?"

"Yeah man. I tell her everything," he deadpanned.

"You are married?" She covered her mouth.

"I look married?"

"Well . . . how does . . . ?"

"One day, when I am with my wife," he said, leaning forward, "she and I will sit on a porch and look out into the Blue Mountains, and we will remember this story of me and this sweet-looking dawta meeting and drinking hot tea late at night right in the heart of Dixie. But my wife will have on a new pair of puppy slippers instead of the old mangy one weh I personally dispose of on the night that we met."

She closed her eyes and laughed softly.

"You are completely idiotic," she said. "You had me."

"Keisha, Keisha, Keisha," Kofi said. Her name in his mouth was giving him the pleasure of kissing.

"Yes, Kofi?"

"I am just saying your name. I like it."

"I like Kofi. It's a nice name, too. A noble name."

"It's from Ghana. I don' sound Ghanaian, but I am. I moved to Jamaica with my parents when I was four. So I sound Jamaican but I'm not. Although I am."

"I wouldn't have guessed, but I wondered. You know how our people take on names . . ." she said.

"Yeah, this was honestly acquired," he said, smiling.

"Ghanaian," she said, smiling to herself. "Exotic."

"Don't ask me to say anything in my language now—please, don't let me down like that."

"So how many wives do you have?"

"Cute, cute, Sister Keisha, real cute," he chuckled, rubbing his neck.

She stood up and walked to one end of the porch with her cup in her hand. He watched her back, liked the way her bottom seemed to assert itself—from her waist down, she was full. She spoke with her back to him.

"Sometimes, on stage tonight, it was as if you were not there. You were in a kind of trance. Like a preacher." Her voice was soft, as if weighing the words.

"I *am* a preacher," he said. He felt a start at the thought that Keisha might have seen into that other self. Then, to avert suspicion, he began to orate exaggeratedly—feigning the kind of madness that sometimes consumed him. "I come to save the heathen from this barren and godforsaken Babylon system, this place full of careless Ethiopian and parasite, saprophyte. I come to take captivity captive and burn away the chaff, the dross, weed, and bush!"

"You are crazy," she laughed. "I'm trying to be serious and you're trying to save the world."

"Well, I could start with you," he bluffed. "I see that inside you are a sweet lickle child. I could save that child."

She turned around, then turned away, and he saw that he had stepped into a private space. She turned around again, her voice harder now, but flippant.

"I am saved, honey. Born again and everything."

"Yuh serious?" He looked at her intensely. "Yuh sure?"

He should stop, he knew. She was a kind woman and she liked him. But he allowed himself to press.

"Hey, I was just joking," she said, pulling back into herself.

"So you not saved then?"

"I may be. I mean, I am saved, but . . . but I was joking. I mean I—" She stopped, clearly embarrassed at her befuddlement. "It was a joke."

"I know." He was grinning now. "But I need to practice my sermons, you know?"

"I don't think I want to hear a sermon tonight, to be honest." She returned to the seat. "You want some more tea?"

The mood had changed and he blamed himself.

Lost, they began to talk about trees again. She asked him if he liked them. He said he thought trees were fine. She asked him what kind of tree he would be, were he a tree.

"A woman asked Lee Scratch dat one time," he said, laughing.

"Who?"

"Lee Scratch Perry. Reggae godfather. No, she ask him if he was a bird, what kind of bird he would be. You know what he said? I am *a bird*." Kofi was laughing hard. "*I am a bird of the sky—I fly above all creation. Seeth thou not I and I wings? And I shall beak yuh wid I and I beak.*"

"I suppose you had to be there." Keisha smiled because he was laughing. She did not understand.

"No, it was a fool-fool question, so that is how Scratch handle fool-fool question. Ananse, you know?"

"So you are saying my question was stupid?" She seemed genuinely hurt.

"No, no, I just remembered Scratch. No. I would be . . . Let me answer," he said. She was not smiling. "Keisha, Keisha, Keisha, you are frowning. Look, look, your lip is pouting."

She turned away from him, trying to keep her serious temperament.

"You know, if a fly pitches on your face while you're frowning, your face will stay that way forever?"

"Pitches?" she asked, still looking away, but there was a smile in her voice.

"That is what we say in Jamaica: pitches. Maybe we mean perches, but pitches sound better."

She said nothing, her back still toward him. So he began to speak slowly.

"A ficus berry tree. They are dense trees that spread like the peepal tree. Tendril like roots that twist and turn and are exposed above the earth, and then the trunk is a convolution of thick branches that spread wide and far, flat over a wide space. It is like the branches are mirroring the roots. The leaves are fat, almost plastic things, and they shed an orange berry that when you squeeze it, something white and sticky comes out. When you shelter under a ficus tree, rain don't touch you. But when you look at this dark tree, you see strength, but a crippling muscularity— so strong and yet so twist up, so locked up in itself, like it wants to break loose and dance, but it can't. Roots tied up. We had one at the university I went to in Kingston. I would sit under there for hours in the shade and look at the tendrils. Sad tree. But a strong, hardy tree. That would be me. People love to sit under that tree, sit in the limbs. Pickney love to climb a ficus tree because you can grab onto something every time . . ." He stopped talking, sensing himself going beyond the experiment. Her back was to him, but he could tell she was listening. He sipped from the cup. "Is a quiet tree, really."

"That is sad," she said softly.

"No, not sad. Just a tree. You know. I *am* a tree," he added, laughing slightly.

"Funny," she said, turning around. "You just shift from one mood to another. It's hard to keep up with you."

"Maybe. But no law says you must keep up. You know? What about you?" he asked.

"The ginkgo. A Japanese tree that grows here. Sometimes I feel I came out of a ginkgo tree, like that tree was my mother. Just pushed me out at the height of its spring flowering. We had one on my road. I always used to go and stand under it, and it was like the only peace I could feel. It turns such a flaming yellow color in the fall. You stand under it and it's like a light is raining on you— warm light. Before it turns, it is just a normal big, strong tree, and then it turns, and for a short time it is a beautiful thing. Just for a short time. Nobody expects it to turn on you like that. Then it goes back to being a normal big, tall tree."

"That's you?" he asked

"No, I just like the tree," she said.

"Beautiful. Beautiful. Ginkgo. Yeah."

The darkness, the unspoken agreement that they were simply going to talk, not touch, not make love, the pleasure in the serendipity of their meeting—all these things conspired to make them talk, make them open up. They were passing each other and might never meet again.

# Chapter Four

She woke up after the third ring, the light spilling in through the dense yellowing leaves of the live oak tree that loomed over the back wall of the house. She was still in a daze of half-sleep, sweetened by a fuzzy sense of pleasure and anticipation. She decided to let the answering machine take the message.

Then she heard the modulated and intentionally sensual Jamaican voice intoning: *This is Keisha's answering machine, she is rather indisposed at the moment, so if you leave a name and number and a reason you called, she will hit you back with her loveliness soon as she can. One love.*

She sprinted across the room, tottering to find her balance after sliding on the throw rug on the glazed wooden floor, but by the time she reached the phone that sat precariously on the edge of her computer desk, Troy had begun to curse into the phone.

"What the . . . ?" he was sputtering; she imagined the tight muscles in his jaw flexing. "Keisha, you need to tell me which nigger you have up in your house. Keisha, you better pick up the damn phone. Who you got up in there?"

At first she had thought to pick up the phone, but his tone—like he still owned her—made her stop. He was pissed, and even though she had meant the message for her cousin Leonora to hear, she relished Troy's annoyance.

"Keisha, Keisha, answer the damn phone, woman. I know you are there. Don't play with me." His voice had already reached that high falsetto pitch he soared to when he was angry, and his accent had slipped from Southern urban hip to plain old country. "This is some shit. This is some shit!" he said, almost to himself, and then hung up.

Somehow she knew the phone would ring again. It did. This time Kofi's voice managed a few words and then the receiver clicked off.

Keisha threw herself back on the bed, and groaned. *Oh, drama. That fool better not come here today. He better not,* she said to herself. It had been bold to ask Kofi to record her new answering machine message before he left. It was only partly her idea—they had been in a giddy enough mood and wanted to prolong the time together, even though he kept saying he had to take off before the sun came up. When he was leaving, she said she wished she had something of his, just to keep. He promised to send her one of the band's T-shirts.

"I will wear it first, for five days without bathing," he said.

"Oh joy," she groaned.

"Well, what do you want then?" he asked.

"I don't know," she said, trying to think of something playful, funny, but sincere—something that would tell him that she really appreciated the company, that his coming over, the time together, the laughter, the stories, they were a gift that she needed.

"So what do you like about me?" he asked, looking directly in her face.

"You are a vain man, you know?"

"No, no, I mean, there must be something. Something you like about me, something that would make you serve me tea on your porch."

"Your voice," she said quickly.

"Okay, you want a free CD."

She slapped him on the shoulder.

"Not the way you sing, fool. I mean your voice, the way you talk, your—"

"Accent. The island talk," he said with mild sarcasm.

"Yeah, that too, but I like the way you say things, the way you stress certain words, the way you mix up your lingo with some kind of English accent and, you know, normal talk. The way you say my name. You have a nice mellow tone. You know it, too."

Then he came up with the idea of leaving a message on her answering machine so she could have his voice. They recorded the message and laughed at their silliness. They did several versions of it. She liked his use of the word *indisposed*, she said.

"Keisha is indisposed at the moment, please leave your name and number . . ."

"Too funny," she laughed.

"Yeah, you would like that. Makes it sound like Bob Marley is keeping you busy so you can't come to the phone," he laughed.

"Exactly," she said, staring him directly in the face, her hands on her hips. "Exactly."

She kept calling her home number on her cell phone and they laughed as they listened to the message.

"Sweet savior, people are going to think I have gone all Stella on them. My cousin Leonora will be scandalized. She is going to want to know all your details. That woman will come looking for you," she said.

"She good looking?" he asked.

Keisha pushed him playfully to the door. "Get out of my house. You need to go. It's late. People will start talking."

He stood on the porch looking out. She was behind him. Then he turned and opened his arms. She fell into his embrace. They held each other. He could feel the pulse in her chest, the increasing grip of her arms. After over a minute, he leaned down and spoke softly.

"Thank you, thank you, thank you, Keisha. I like you."

When he left, she called her number on her cell and listened to the voice several times over. She liked this guy. She had wrestled with the idea of asking him for his number. But she didn't. She wanted him to make a move that would tell her that he wanted to see her again. But she felt silly. He was a singer, a reggae singer, on the road. He met women on the road all the time. He could not stay in touch with all of them. If he did not ask for some way to stay in touch, it couldn't have been an oversight. He had his reasons and there was no point making more of their time than it was. She went to sleep with him in her head.

It would have been easy for her to forget him if they had made love, if they had gone through the awkwardness of waking up the next morning wondering what stupidity had happened, if she had held him close and said goodbye and promised she would keep in touch while deep down being grateful that their paths would never cross again.

If this had happened, she thought, as she showered the following day, she would have managed to reduce him to a moment, because he would be like all other men . . .

But they had not slept together. They had stayed up all night talking and sipping tea. They had parted with a wave and more laughter—him telling her that she really needed to do something about the slippers she was wearing.

And now he had been admitted to the place where she kept moments of beauty and grace: a sunset that had enveloped her on a summer's evening on Folly Beach, or the afternoon in Sumter when some ginkgo leaves had set her face aglow.

She collected such moments, and this would be one of them.

As she put her feet up on the toilet tank to clip her nails, she held onto little parts of him and tucked them deep inside her mind . . . Kofi on the stage, the white cotton shirt soaked with his sweat, making his dark nipples show through the fabric, his beard glistening in the light, his husky voice . . . his laughter . . . his playfulness . . . the shape of his hands, the long fingers wrapped around the mug while he sat back and stared into the night grinning at his own jokes . . . his decency, his kindness . . . his eyes, the dark irises, the corners pleated with laugh lines, the way they sometimes grew so weary, so old, so sad.

She had already missed the early-morning service. It was almost noon, and if she hurried she would arrive in time to make her offering and then continue with her Sunday ritual—visiting her aunts and cousins down in Kingstree, explaining why she had arrived too late— again—to get her full dose of Holy Ghost blessing, acknowledging to herself that she had failed God again, and then driving back to Columbia to spend the rest of the evening punching in data on her home computer.

Of course, now there was Troy and this answering machine. He was likely to come by at some point. She would have to talk to him, let him vent, and maybe, if she felt like it, just ease his mind. She would call him as soon as she got back from church.

She showered and dressed quickly. As she hurried outside in her blue skirt suit and broad-rimmed hat, she saw a package leaning on the azalea bush at the foot of the porch step. On top of the package was an envelope.

She went back inside and sat in her living room. With the package beside her she opened the card. On the cover was a print of "Jubilation," a Jonathan Green painting that she had seen at the university's small museum. It showed a black girl in a white dress waving a scarf in a field of grass. From the scarf there flew a bird—an ivory dove. Her mind cast back to the time that she had first seen the work, and as she crossed her ankles on the table, she remembered that she had been drawn to the strange disproportion in the girl's body—her raised arms seemed too strong, too muscular, like a man's arms or the branches of a tree, and yet the sense of her vulnerability was always there. A woman as child, she had thought at the time.

The inscription in the card was simple: *To my Black Cinderella—thanks for last night.*

She smiled, uncrossed her legs, and folded them beneath her. Her heels felt nice and hard against her softness. She set the card beside the vase and rubbed her palms against her thighs to dry them.

The package was a simple box, unsealed but with the flaps cross-folded. Inside the box was a shopping bag from Sears. Inside the bag was a pair of fluffy slippers, Hush Puppies in a mongrel brown. The tag was still attached. Between the facing slippers was a CD, the case cracked slightly, titled *Meeting of Minds*. It was Kofi's new CD. On the cover was a faint bas-relief on dark brown wood of a pair of merging faces. The texturing was beautiful. On the back there was a picture of the band—Small Axe—the members crowded into a tiny car driving through the streets of Kingston. Kofi looked distracted in the picture. She wondered what had happened at the shoot.

She read the letter while she curled up on the sofa on her side, her skirt tucked tight between her knees, her hat perched on the table.

*Dear Keisha,*

*Maybe we won't see each other again, but you never know. Still, people come and go like that. I just want to thank you for last night. I needed the attention you gave me. I wish I could give back more, but . . .*

*My Black Cinderella. Southern hospitality, nuh? I like it. Take care, sweet woman. Rasta love. Your love. My love.*

—Kofi

*p.s. I hope your boyfriend has heard that recording and decided to drop your two-timing ass. If so, let me know. (Smile)*

*p.s.s. Left the tags on the shoes in case your foot too big.*

She was grinning broadly and shaking her head. *I swear, he really thinks I have a boyfriend. But why would he think that? I told him I didn't. Or did I? Maybe I made him think I did. But he wants to stay linked, which can't be bad.*

He had thought of her. Considered her. Devoted time to doing something to make her smile. This man was either the most calculated charmer in the world or perhaps the kind of man who drew his pleasure from making women feel confused. *Or maybe I seemed really pathetic. No, he is a sweet guy. And yet, he is playing with me. "Let me know. Let me know?" How am I supposed to let you know? The man left no address, no telephone number, no nothing to tell me I should call him. Of course, I could try. Just to say thanks for the slippers. That would be polite—very Southern. He is playing with me. He is.*

She stood and walked to a window. The funny thing was that even though she really was free—single and somewhat disengaged—she felt like she was considering cheating on somebody. Maybe that was Troy's fault. Over the last two months, he had started to call regularly, and she would chat with him casually about small things. And when she thought to ask him about some problem with the filters in her car, he was over there the next day to swap cars so he could fix hers She drove his silver Mercedes CL500 for three days—leather seats, a wonderful sensation—and each night he would ask, as if tempting her, "How it ride, baby? How you like the ride?" It rode well. She knew he was giving her much but she tried to be casual about it. Soon he was bringing the draft of a birthday letter he and his brothers wanted to give to their mother. He asked Keisha to fix it, make sure it read well. Which she did. She liked his mother. It was all harmless. And then three weeks ago he sent her flowers with a small card that was scrupulously free of any love statements—just a *Glad you are still my friend* card. It was "innocent" enough to make it hard for her to toss the flowers. But she was done with Troy, despite what Leonora said to her every time he performed another act of kindness.

"You are an intelligent and educated woman, you studied abusive relationships, you know all of this, and yet you can't see that the son of a bitch is still trying to work his way back to you," Leonora had almost shouted over the phone a week ago.

"I have no interest in Troy, Leonora. So don't even start all that mess," she said impatiently.

"Your problem is you so damned arrogant, you think you above all of that. Don't forget it's your ass called me when that fool beat you down the other day." Leonora was now actually shouting.

"Two years ago, Leonora," Keisha said, not wanting to think of it. "That is history."

"History knocking on your door, baby, you better ask somebody."

She hadn't had a man since Troy and had always assumed in the two years since their break-up that her feelings for him, as painful and wrong as they had been, were the only complicated feelings she could harbor for a man. She had stopped explaining to Leonora that when you have been with a man for such a long time, and when there was a time when you really loved him, the best you can do afterwards is to accept that, mixed with the hate, anger, and resentment, is a whole set of strange feelings that don't just go away. And Troy knew things about her, about her body, about her secrets, that nobody else did, and that made things difficult. But she was not going to go back to him. She knew that.

She laughed when she thought of how Troy would feel if he knew that in some weird way, he was responsible for her meeting Kofi, the first guy since Troy who she had even thought about like that.

She discovered reggae music because of Troy. She had moved to New York to get away from him. While living in Brooklyn, she had finished up her master's degree in public administration at N.Y.U., whose FM station played Jamaican music on Friday evenings. She had come back to South Carolina six months ago because she believed that time had cured her.

She stepped away from the window remembering the final time, the four open-handed slaps that had sent her into flight, how he had shattered the television with a baseball bat when he found out she'd been taking contraceptive pills in secret. And as she reached out for Kofi's card, she heard the distant echo of Troy's big mitt against her cheek.

She had left him late that night while he was sleeping.

Had walked to the Hess gas station on the corner of their street and called Leonora. She had three dresses and two pairs of jeans and all the panties and bras she could stuff in his gym bag. Tall Leonora with half her hair rolled in curlers, the other bushy like a jungle, had pulled up in her four-wheel drive, and they sped away along the interstate in silence.

Two days later Leonora drove her to New York—before Keisha could change her mind and call Troy to come and get her, before Troy could honk his horn and Keisha could peep out and walk down the drive to meet him and kiss him and promise to go back if he promised to be good. Leonora was taking no chances. Keisha asked if she needed to get the rest of her stuff. Leonora said no. They left Columbia as fast as Leonora could arrange things.

In New York, Leonora found a place for Keisha with some cousins, stayed with her a week to settle her and then went back to Columbia to get the rest of Keisha's things from Troy's place. With backup from old Aunt Rose, who stood with her husband's shotgun over her shoulder, Leonora boxed Keisha's belongings while Troy watched, smiling stupidly and saying, "C'mon, Miss Rose, ain't no need for none of that now," and asking them to remind "his boo" that she could call him collect.

She called him six months later. It was a lonely night, she needed him, and he was gentle, whispered sweet things to her, encouraged her to touch herself and come loudly as he listened. The conversation left her wanting, wanting him, and she called again the next morning, hoping he would ask her to come home. A woman answered. And she stayed.

Now the phone startled her from her thoughts. She did a quick calculation as to who it could be. Leonora would still be in service, although she would have grown sick of the preacher's reprimands about sexual sin and gone outside to find out where Keisha was. Or perhaps it was her Aunt Rose asking if she was planning to come by as usual. Rose did not like to use the phone, so Keisha ruled her out. Kofi? She wished. It was Troy. He was probably parked on the road. She picked up the phone. She heard his voice. She instinctively went to the front window to look. No silver Mercedes coup humming in the road. But it was Troy.

"Who the fuck was that?" he said. She could see the scowl on his face.

"Please tell me that you are not calling me on a Sunday morning to use that kind of language with me." Keisha spoke in tones that she knew he would understand.

"Well, I want to know who the fuck was . . ." he began.

"Troy, have a good afternoon—"

"Keisha, don't you hang up on me, now . . . Keisha!"

She held the phone away from her body as she waited.

"Keisha?" His voice was more tentative now.

"What do you want, Troy?" She spoke calmly, almost sweetly.

"I just want to know who you have up in your house. I didn't know you . . ." he was beginning to stammer.

"Troy," she interrupted him again. "You know it's none of your business who I have here. You know that. And it's none of your business whose voice answers my phone. You know that. So if you don't have anything else to talk to me about—"

"He one of them guys you was messing with in New York, right?" Troy spoke quickly, trying to stop her from hanging up. "So, you told him about me?"

"You are such a clown," Keisha laughed dryly. "Troy, I got to go to church, okay? Got to go—"

"Okay, okay, so it's like that then. Okay." He was changing tactics. "So how them flowers doing?"

"Just fine, Troy. Got to go," she said, wincing at the sly way he was reminding her of her mistake of accepting the flowers.

"A'ight, a'ight. Listen, you want us to go somewhere to eat tonight? They got a nice spot in the Vista, now, a new restaurant—"

"Troy, we are not like that no more. Don't start that, okay? Got to go . . ."

"Okay . . ."

"Bye." She hung up the phone. Breathed.

He was still in her blood, like a persistent, low-grade viral infection.

When she dreamt at night of lovemaking, she dreamt of Troy, with his hardened muscular body, his short squat torso, his bald head, and the intensity of his deep-set eyes. Troy was a good-looking man who took care of his body. Military service had taught him how to stay fit, and after he retired he had continued his daily routine of running and lifting weights.

Like so many things in her life, Troy had begun as a casual idea and then became a habit. He was good at that. They had met in line at the DMV in downtown Columbia. She was getting her license renewed and he was taking a test for a motorcycle license. He was confident, smiled a lot, and wore his uniform with that cocky, good-natured pride that soldiers had. For some paradoxical reason, their clean-shaven faces, their neat hair, their neatly rolled sleeves, and their difference in a world of civilians made them seem safe. Troy talked quickly, hands moving, full of suggestions. Soon he had chosen the perfect new car for her, promised to have a look at her brakes, and made arrangements to hook her up with his mechanic. It began like that, them meeting for some reason related to what he could do for her. And she had let him lead—it was what he did best, and she was in a place where a man leading felt right. Soon the only way she could describe him was as a habit, a fixture in her life. His help painting the window frames in her house got him into her home. His hearty appetite and love for soppy movies got him into her bedroom. Habit got him into bed with her. Habit, comfort, and the absolute shallowness of the man. He went no deeper than his clean look. She thought she would discover something deep, something profound in him, but it never happened. Troy remained exactly as he had appeared at first.

His only surprise, his only complexity, was his temper, which flared for the first time suddenly and startlingly one night, three months into their friendship, after she had danced with an old friend at a club. He slapped her. She asked him *why* some days later, having spent the intervening days first planning her departure and then trying to work out why he was behaving as if nothing had happened. He apologized. There was nothing there, no good reason, just his temper. "I just lose it sometimes, baby, but you know I don't mean it. You know that."

And it may have been this disarming simplicity that made her see nothing diabolic in his violence, in his control—that made her stay with him even when it became dangerous. He seemed to carry no grudges, and this almost childlike quality made it hard for her to carry a grudge. When she hurt him, which she often did by insulting him about his poor English or his ignorance about world affairs—and this always in public when he could do nothing about it—he seemed to forget every bit of viciousness and would crawl back into bed with her as if nothing had happened.

Beyond that, he was reliable. On Leonora's list of things that trifling black men did, Troy was guilty of only one. He was not a "cheap-ass free-loader and moocher"— he made good money and was generous to Keisha without making a fuss about it. He was not a "baby father several times over to some surprise hoochies who call up to cause drama in your life"—if Troy had a baby mother, he kept her under wraps. Besides, he was not the type to lie about those things. He was not "doing time, just done time, or about to do time," he was not a "ho," and he had a job. Troy was someone to profile with, and despite her complaints about the way he talked or how country he could be sometimes, Keisha knew she could rely on Troy to look good and to make her look good in public. Troy's one sin was that he beat her.

Soon she began to believe that she had mastered strategies of curtailing the violence. Soon she was the only one who did not realize that Troy could easily kill her and apologize sincerely for having done so. Soon she was the only one who did not realize that Troy had managed to convince her that the way they lived was normal. When she called Leonora that night, she had every intention of going back with Troy. Leonora saved her life. But back in Columbia, Keisha was slowly admitting to herself that there was a certain comfort in familiar habits.

Her strategy for dealing with life after returning to Columbia was to treat such things as men, relationships, that kind of thing, as distractions. She would focus on work. She would develop a routine and avoid situations that would make her think too much about men. Which is how she handled Troy. He was outside of the important things in her life. He could not affect her because she was not thinking about all that. Leonora warned her about how she tended to slip into bad habits out of carelessness, but Leonora was also a woman who believed that every healthy woman had to have a man. If she said she didn't, she was lying to herself. Leonora was already calling Troy her "crazy-ass" man—as in "That crazy-ass fool come by today?" or "You wouldn't believe what that crazy-ass man of yours called me to ask me!" or "You fucking that crazy-ass man of yours yet?"

If Troy was a habit waiting to happen again, Kofi was a choice. He presented himself as something she had to decide about. But she knew that if she were to fall asleep right now, she would will herself to dream of Kofi. It would be a nice dream. She would rehearse the whole night, the moment she walked into the club expecting to hear reggae but not being entirely sure of how good the band would be. She had heard some of the band's music on the radio while in New York, and she liked their mix of roots lyrics—a social consciousness and a dark flirtation with pained love—with the very hard-nosed dancehall feel to their rhythm section, the kind of sound that demanded dance, a bouncing kind of hip-shaking dance. She had seen the pictures of the band—the lead singer always hovering in the back, a brooding presence. So she had not expected to see the man in a white shirt that flowed like water down to his knees, to see the complete intensity of his face as he raised the microphone high to chant. The music, the energy, the body—a full, strong body, sweating—and the wide-open emotion of his performance made her want to get closer to the music, to him, to the force coming from the stage.

But to have found that quick connection with this guy was something she had not been prepared for. That dancing, that way in which he seemed to be directing her body from the stage, that grin of his when she slowed her movement to a slow grind, put her in a mood not to care whether or not he told her to go to hell when she went backstage to meet him. Perhaps it was the fact that she was one of only a few black women in the club, or that she really felt as if he was telling her to come back to talk— whatever it was, she wanted to meet him and to thank him.

Every detail would come to her in a dream. In the best of her dreams, she found ways to turn short narratives of pleasure from her real life into epics of sweetness. She had enough from Kofi to dream for several weeks—several good weeks. His voice, the way he sipped tea, his laughter, and the hug, the hug, the hug. But what would be the point of dreaming of him and waking up alone?

Driving back from visiting her relatives that Sunday night, she felt a certain excitement about going home. Much of the time she would forget what was making her feel that way, but she would pause and think and remember that she was heading home to listen to his CD and to reread his note. She had her evening planned out by the time she walked into her home. The shower—hot and quick—the cream on her body, the towel around her head, the candle at her bedside, the glass of iced tea chilling, the CD, the half light, the bed duvet pulled aside, the pillows. She lay there and listened to his voice, the CD player locked on auto-replay. She fell asleep with Kofi in her head. It was her choice.

# Chapter Five

The next day, Keisha took the CD to work, slipped it into her player, and turned up the volume. No Lauryn Hill or Mambo Kings this morning.

Her office was located in a small brick cottage in an older corner of the campus where nineteenth-century buildings evoked the exclusive white college the university had been for the first 100 of its 250 years. Forty years ago she would have been the cleaning lady in the building she worked in. Now she had her own office.

She knew the choruses and hooks from Kofi's songs by heart now, and as she booted her computer she sang along with Kofi's grainy baritone:

*Drifting on an angry occasion*
*A dream-like quality*
*I reach out to you you're drowning next to me . . .*

The new sun was gleaming through the long bay windows that overlooked the curving wooden steps. The music flowed along the corridor, whose walls were covered up with posters, notices, and folk paintings in bright colors.

Down the corridor and back for water in her jeans and orange cotton shirt, bobbing her head to the music and doing that hip-only grind that she knew had impressed Kofi in the club, she pulled some files from the bottom drawer.

Today: more transcriptions.

If she continued to work like this, she would be finished with the project two weeks ahead of her deadline. She calculated that the rest of the transcriptions would occupy her time for the next week. She would then work over the weekend to complete the summaries and reports on the findings. The following Monday she would be able to e-mail the documents to Joan, her boss in New York. Then she would have two weeks to relax.

She was planning to go down to Charleston for one of those weeks and pamper herself in a small, nineteenth-century bed-and-breakfast that was frequented by honeymooners. She would take a few novels, a collection of haiku she had bought on a whim at the used bookstore, and spend her days living a life as far from her own world as possible. No one knew about this, not even Leonora. She hoped to keep it that way.

But it would be hard. Leonora wanted to go shopping in Atlanta, and Keisha felt that she owed Leonora at least that for just being around and for letting Keisha use her house in downtown Columbia as a temporary shelter during the first month she had been home. Leonora was the buffer between her and the rest of the family. Keisha saw the family on Sundays but hurried back to Columbia Sunday night. Kingstree, in the lush cotton-rich belly of the state, the small town, the gossip, the rules, the pressure of blood ties, and the memories of all her varied and twisted messes were too much for Keisha. Leonora understood this and helped cover for her.

Even as she weighed her options, her mind slipped back to Kofi. She had dreamt of him last night. As she remembered this she reached into her bag and tacked his card up on the notice board, and she decided that nothing about this feeling, about her connection with Kofi, felt like an ending. There had to be more. Her whole body seemed to be assuming this.

She took a sip of water and keyed the Small Axe web address. Something flickered in her stomach as she skimmed through the pages, till she saw a photograph of Kofi.

He was sitting on the stump of a tree, a rusted zinc fence behind him. In the foreground appeared a carefully arranged assortment of urban debris: a ripped apart old tire, twisted cans, strips of rags, a dented garbage bin, yellowing newspapers, twigs, cigarette packets—all with a strange uniformity of color: brown, sick yellow, and a peculiar beige tone. He looked morose, thoughtful, somewhat bored, holding his head in his hands. His leather jacket was appropriately worn, and his open white shirt revealed the shiny curls on his chest.

It was a sexy pose—a star's pose. But the attraction was in his eyes, their deep sadness; they contained a quality of honesty that salvaged some truth from the posed nature of the portrait. A blue sky interrupted by the occasional coconut tree loomed above him. *Tropical cool,* Keisha thought. He was what she had remembered, except he seemed much younger, less tired. His hair was cut lower—so close you could catch the glare of the sunlight on his scalp. He wore a small golden stud on his right earlobe, another accessory she had not noticed when he sat on her porch. He seemed to be squinting, his eyes intense but half closed. His face was virtually covered with a beard that seemed to have gotten away from itself. She liked his lips—they were full, bold, sensual. His hands were resting on his knees. The nails were clean and the fingers were long, expressive, and tender. She scrolled down to a block of writing etched in reverse yellow on a black background.

*African Traveler: Kofi—progeny of the great highlife master guitarist Fifii Mensah, Kofi is the product of tradition and roots. "I never play serious music with my old man, but when I was born, he planted a seed inside me—seed of the griot musicians. Maybe these things are in the genes, but I never see myself as anything but a player of instruments. I love my old man, still, and he digs my sound, yeah, but him never raise me directly. No, that was Jamaica. Jamaica raise me from the ground. My old man seed me, but Jamdown raise me." Kofi completed his middle passage years later than most of the Africans in the Caribbean, landing on the shores of Kingston at a young age. He would go on to become one of the great songwriters and guitarists in the tradition of roots lyricists Marley, Culture, Toots, Tosh, Spear. Kofi grew up in the studios of Lee Scratch Perry and sucked up every bit of madness and genius from the great maverick himself. Small Axe is on a mission: "If Bob was alive today, what would he be doing musical wise? That is the question we ask ourselves daily. For one thing about Bob is that he never stood still. Listened to nuff style of music and pushed his creativity while maintaining his vision. So we ask that on a daily basis and answer it with the music."*

Keisha scrolled down further. Another shot of Kofi, this time a close-up of his face. A pair of shades dangled on the edge of his nose, and he peered over them into the camera. Lashes—dark irises. *Man, he has nice lips,* she said to herself. On stage he had seemed at the helm of the band, but only barely so—he seemed to take cues and encouragement from the rest of the band, especially the bass player. She imagined they were good friends. His manner when she went backstage had been a relief. She had feared he would assume the "star" manner—expecting praise, expecting a certain pandering. But he had shown none of this. Had she seen the website before going to the show, she probably would not have gone backstage. On the website, he was the star.

*"My woman is the most important thing in my life. When I think of my woman, everything else must fade into irrelevance, you know? 'Cause that is reality. And when I seed some youths, they shall be everything to me. For me, simple as I might seem, and despite that my family life was not no conventional family life, family is crucial to me. Family come first and everything else next . . ."*

*What woman?* He had mentioned no woman. But then, she had not told him about Troy. So they were even. She had asked him though. Had he lied? He did not say there was no woman—he had simply made a joke. It was charming, deft, but an evasion. Maybe there was no woman. But why would he mention his woman? Perhaps he had been thinking about this woman on Saturday night. Yes, he is a good man.

Among the tour dates listed on the site, she saw that they would be performing in New York at Irving Plaza on October 31.

She was due in New York on November 8 to complete interviews with women in a halfway house. After this her schedule would be open—depending on some choices that she had to make. Her contract would expire by Thanksgiving. There was another offer—to set up and direct a community initiative in Canada. The opportunity was attractive; Toronto had a thriving theater scene, and she would be paid in U.S. dollars, which would guarantee a very comfortable existence.

On the other hand, she needed time to complete her degree. She had finished the coursework, but her thesis was outstanding; and from experience she knew that the

Toronto project would turn out to be more work than Joan had said it would be. Without her full degree she would simply be an educated migrant laborer.

She needed to have a talk with Joan. She had collected all her material and she just needed the time to write. She pulled out the case of tapes she had collected during her time in the field in Columbia. Before beginning, she paused to listen as Small Axe kicked into the song Kofi had offered her that night on stage. She thought of the way he had raised his hand, smiled, telling her without words that it was for her. It was now her song even though she knew it was someone else's song—perhaps his woman's song. She sat back, looked out into the green trees and the pale blue autumn sky, letting herself be transported, her thighs relaxing against the seat.

*She was a friend of mine,*
*Selling her soul for a lickle money*
*She was a friend of mine*
*Selling her body for a lickle honey;*
*Then one day she woke up;*
*Sun come shining, shining bright;*
*Oh yes,*
*Crisp as a miracle, it is morning!*
*Crisp as a miracle, it is morning!*

Perhaps she should go to New York a little early.

# Chapter Six

In a golden dress that brushed her ankles at the hem and a dark brown leather jacket that she had stolen from Troy years ago, Keisha came to find Kofi. She caught a cab early in the evening to the Irving Plaza, an old theater just off Union Square in Gramercy Park, a wealthy New York enclave.

He walked forward from the back of the stage, out of the darkness, toward the clean spot at the front. Decked in a shimmering kaftan that undulated in waves as he moved, he looked strong, assured, and sensual.

Small Axe seemed bigger than she had remembered from Columbia. There was something about the way the stage at the Irving Plaza served them up—the space between the audience and the musicians was deeper, and the music, perhaps because she knew it now so well, triggered a disquiet in her joints, a familiar looseness that she relished. When they segued into "Crisp Morning," she understood the way music can put a spell on you. She had the urge to tell all the women standing around her cheering, moving, clearly enjoying this bearded man, that just a few weeks ago he had sung this song for her.

> Crisp as a miracle, it is morning!
> Crisp as a miracle, it is morning!

Small Axe was inspired that night, playing as if they

wanted everyone to know that they understood the back beat and the funk. The show displayed a certain commitment to guitar pyrotechnics, though under the glitter she sensed the reassurance of a brooding calm in the bass and the undertones of the Hammond B-3 organ that suggested the wisdom of elders.

Then Kofi shouted, "Irie!" and his flowing blue kaftan disappeared into the wings, while the band, in a red tint, jammed their way into an extended climax. She found her way out of the theater and pushed her way through the massive red doors that opened to the narrow, rain-slicked street.

Beneath the raised eyebrow of a pediment, Keisha waited for Kofi, not knowing if she would speak to him, just knowing that she needed to. She had considered going backstage, but what would she have said to the bouncer? That she was a fan? A friend? What if he had forgotten her or simply didn't care?

She waited through a veil of silver rain until the crowd had gone. According to the website, Small Axe didn't have another show. This was it. The tour was over. If she missed him now, she thought, she would take it as a sign from God.

She walked a few yards down the street and then crossed to the opposite side and lingered in the shadows. She still had a good view of the front entrance of Irving Plaza; she would see him before he saw her.

Soon, in the crowd on the piazza, she recognized Pedro, tall and wiry in denim and black leather. He lit a cigarette quickly and began to pace—agitated, glaring back up the stairs. Then Kofi trundled down the steps looking at his watch. He was draped in a black cotton shirt with tails that hung down toward his knees. It was unbuttoned at the neck and seemed too thin for the cold.

He looked toward Pedro and then moved a few yards down the sidewalk in the opposite direction.

Pedro flicked the cigarette, and with a cloud of smoke around his head, he strode the few yards between the two and palmed Kofi's shoulder. Kofi's face was warped in a pained expression and she began to wonder why he needed cooling down.

"I not doing it!" Kofi barked when Pedro overtook him.

"Don't run them joke wid me, Kofi," Pedro replied, moving in front of his bandmate, stiffening his open palm into a machete and thrusting it into Kofi's face.

"No joke," Kofi told him calmly. "I really have to go." He patted Pedro's wrist and Pedro dropped his hand.

"Look here, man, unoo cyaan deal with this out hereso," Anthony, the guitarist, chimed in, as he joined the two men on the sidewalk.

"Anthony, just go ahead, man, and leave us. I will call yuh, seen?" Kofi said this sternly but with love. And as Anthony began to protest, he added with a small laugh, "It all right, man. We cool. Me no 'fraid a Pedro . . ."

"Yeah man, gwaan," Pedro said.

The other two band members came outside with four tall, strikingly beautiful black women, and Pedro switched his mood: "Yo, Lucas, buy me a Chinese, nuh. Some veggie fry rice and some veggie noodles, cool. Soon come, but you can leave it in my room, yeah?"

The drummer shouted, "Irie!" and led the troop toward Park Avenue, where the traffic was insistent. Anthony went with them, looking warily at Kofi as he walked away. "Check me when you come in, Kofi."

"Yeah man," Kofi nodded. "Soon reach."

Pedro watched the others disappear, then said to Kofi more gently: "Yuh taking your ting or what? De medication, yuh taking it?"

"That not gwine help me right now," Kofi said, switching his weight from leg to leg. He raised his arms and stretched overhead, arching his back and tipping up on his toes. "I have to go home. I said my aunt is sick."

"She sick long time, Kofi. Why yuh never go from long time? Dat woman gwine outlive de whole a we. You really take me fe a idiot, man?" Pedro's voice began to rise again.

"Yeah, like you woulda 'low me fe leave during the tour," Kofi said, speaking quickly, like a man cornered.

"If is dead she was gwine dead, somebody other than Dorothy woulda write and tell you, Kofi. You and me know dat is a Dorothy business going on here." Pedro lit another cigarette, started smoking deeply, barely exhaling smoke.

"You don't understand what that mean? If I stay out here, I won't be no good to nobody. I am worried about her. My mind . . . My head is . . ." He held his head.

"Jesus, man. I tell them, you know. I tell them I don't want a fucking madman in the band. I don't need this shit, man. Yuh sign a damn contract, Kofi. Yuh cyaan do dis, man. What is wrong wid you?"

"Looking for shelter, man. Sometimes you can be in Babylon too long. The other day, I catch myself in a mirror and I couldn't recognize myself. I come here to win the lost souls, but not a soul give a damn 'bout reggae, Pedro. I gwine to Jamaica. I cyaan tek the cold, I cyaan tek the—"

"Yuh fucking wid me, Kofi."

Kofi grinned. Keisha knit her brows. Who was Dorothy? Was she his woman? Pedro sighed in exasperation and annoyance.

"All right, all right. Listen, I need rest. I need rest. Tiredness eating me. I need rest. My head . . ." Kofi said, his smile fading.

"Kofi."

The singer was still rubbing his forehead. Keisha could see he was ready for the argument to end. It was as if Pedro's voice was an irritant. She herself was growing impatient with Pedro, yet she could not shake the nagging question: Who was Dorothy?

"Yuh is a damn big man, Kofi. Stop go on like a lickle pickney, man."

"Why we can't record the thing in JA? The vibes better there, man. I just need to go home. Why we cyaan record it there?" Kofi asked, his tone altered again—this time pleading, attempting to sound reasonable.

"You know why. The Ethiopian guys are not traveling to JA to lay down the track dem, all right. We cyaan fly down everybody, man. It done arrange already. Why yuh want to mash it up over foolishness? Two weeks, man, that is all."

"No, no, it's because that piece-a-crap white producer bwoy don' want to travel, just say is that an' done," Kofi said. "Look, you don' need me for the tracks, man. I will lay dem down when yuh finish the master dem with Don. It will work out better anyway. The idiot don't like me, so this way it will be better."

"We never plan it dis way, Kofi," Pedro said.

"Well, change the focking plan, man."

A bus rumbled past slowly. Keisha could not hear them for few seconds, then Pedro's voice cut through the air.

"Kofi, if you fuck wid me this time, it done. You hearing me? If you fuck wid me this time, Kofi, we finish."

"Why yuh gwine on like dat, man?"

"You know what? Do whatever the rass you want to do. Jus' don' come back and beg me for a nex' 'bligh, man. Don't. I cyaan work like this, man. I is a damn professional, you understand?" Pedro lifted his black duffle bag from the ground and pulled it over his shoulder. "Session start Wednesday. Do whatever the rass you want to do." He lifted his bass guitar and walked off.

"Pedro, be reasonable, man." Kofi was still holding his forehead. "Pedro . . ."

The bass player did not stop. Kofi dropped his hand and sat down on the step. His body crumbled, closing up.

Keisha's mind was racing. She could walk away and he would not see her. She would go on with her life and he would go on with his. The moment was so full of uncertainty and confusion. She wanted to help him. But she would not know where to begin, or where to go with him. This was what her Aunt Rose would call "a mess," and then there was this woman, Dorothy. Getting involved would not be good. A wise woman would avoid it . . . but he looked so tired. He just needed someone to take him home.

# Chapter Seven

How come Pedro doesn't understand? Kofi thought. *My aunt is sick. My aunt is sick. Of course I should have left earlier, but he really expects me to postpone even more? So she might outlive all of us, but who is to know these things? And anyway, Pedro don't need to know any more than that: I am worried about her, I need to go home. What is wrong with Pedro? What him think everything is Dorothy? Dorothy write and tell me, so of course she must involve. But him a try mek it look like is a Dorothy ting. All dem argument deh 'bout how Dorothy is a politician and know how fe manipulate people is just . . . cho . . . who nuh know that? Me know that. Everybody know that. You can't be in Parliament in Jamaica and don't know how to turn people mind. But she can't turn my mind. I know how her mind work. I know her. How him mean to come tell me what I must do, to tell me that Dorothy is running me?*

Kofi stood and opened his eyes. What to do? Where to go? *Maybe Union Square . . . Virgin suppose to have* Meeting of the Minds *in the window. The big Barnes & Noble by the park might be closed already. Man, I'm hungry.*

As he tossed these thoughts around in his head, Kofi heard his name and looked up to see Keisha. For a minute he couldn't be sure it was her. She was the last person he expected to see. But there she was, a ginkgo tree of gold and yellow, her hair pulled together in a high bun with a sable tail that reached down to her right shoulder. Her arms were wrapped around her body, the wind licking at the hem of her dress around her shins, her feet slightly apart, firmly set in a simple pair of maroon loafers. She was smiling but there was a questioning in her eyes, as if she was not sure he would recognize her.

"What are you doing here?" he asked, smiling.

"It's a free country. I heard a killer band was playing tonight. I came to check them out."

"Well?" he asked, moving toward her.

"They sucked. There was this ugly singer who couldn't hold a tune. I wasted my money." She was laughing. Her hands had fallen from around her, letting the jacket open up to reveal the curve of her chest. Her laughter echoed between the buildings. He walked his loping gait toward her, smiling, his arms outstretched.

Keisha took him in. There was a strange intensity and satisfaction in the act. She came to find him, and it made sense to him that she would.

"You okay?" she asked, looking up at him.

"Yes, man. Thanks for coming, I needed a friendly face, you know?" He let his hands hold hers. "You smell of White Musk," he said, smiling.

"It's the only name you know, isn't it? You are such a fronter," she said, laughing.

"Yuh ketch me, man," he replied, feeling a familiar lightness and ease. "So you wearing something else, even though you know it's my favorite?"

"It's White Musk, fool, but I just want you to know that I don't fall for every line a musician gives me."

"True, true." He suddenly felt tired again, unsure what to do next. He looked out into the street, his mind slipping back into the turmoil he thought had left him when he saw her walk up.

Keisha touched his shoulder. "Come home."

They caught a cab on Broadway. "110th and Fifth," Keisha said, sliding across the seat to make room for Kofi. They traveled in silence, Keisha wondering what Kofi was thinking. Did he expect to make love to her tonight? The prospect both excited and disturbed her. It was the worst position to be in for a woman. She could not accuse him of being presumptuous. Why wouldn't he expect sex? She had traveled far to find him. He did not pursue her, she pursued him. She imagined making love to him. He had to notice how curiosity showed in her eyes, in the way her body opened to him, and he had been around, he could tell. But she worried about the calculated nature of this thing. This would be a premeditated sin, one she would find hard to forgive herself for if things went awry. She stared ahead, trying to avoid his eyes.

Kofi looked at her and smiled until she felt his eyes on her. When she met his gaze, he spoke. "Glad you came to rescue me." He reached out and touched her face.

"I'm glad I came, too." She wanted to ask about the argument with Pedro, about Dorothy, but was afraid of what she would learn. "So where are you staying?" she asked instead.

The flickering lights of the streets flashed across his face. His thighs pressed against hers. She moved her leg away slightly and waited for him to follow. He followed. Now that they were closer, she could see him more clearly—the short hair, tight balls of curls over his scalp. His eyes were in a perpetual squint, constantly laughing, but he looked very tired.

"A hotel with the rest of the band," he said. "But they gwine leave out of there tomorrow. We're on our own now. I'll stay there till I leave."

"Back to Jamaica."

"Yeah, yard."

"You like it there?"

"Yeah. After I come home with you, you want to come home with me?"

"Are you kidding?"

"No, I'm serious." He had been joking. But it quickly occurred to him that maybe he wasn't.

Keisha gathered her coat around her. He leaned back on the seat and closed his eyes.

Her apartment was basic—an L-shaped studio in a new high-rise that overlooked the Harlem Meer in Central Park: cream walls, a row of sealed glass windows. The kitchenette was small, with a fridge that seemed designed to hold leftovers.

The furniture was a bed and a chair, then Kofi looked again and saw a computer screened off in an alcove. Against the walls were stacked big boxes crammed with papers.

"My research," Keisha said as Kofi raised his brows. "Notes. I do a lot of research."

"I see." He waited for something to happen in his head to help him say something interesting. He was blanking. "You don' like the place?"

"Why do you say that?"

"Is like you moving. Like you ready fe pick up any time. How long you living here?"

"Had it for three years," she said. "But I go and come, you know."

"How long you were in Columbia?"

"Six months or so, just got back . . ."

"Three years," he mused, then chuckling lightly he added, "Yeah, you don' like it."

"I like it just fine. But it's an apartment. Can't settle. I grew up in houses all my life." She stood in the kitchenette area and shook her head. "It ain't that bad. Come on, now. You one of those guys who judge a woman by how her place looks?"

"Yeah."

"So you ready to leave then?"

He sat on the bed and began to shuffle through her CD rack: Marley, Tosh, Marvin Gaye, Traci Chapman, Youssou N'Dour, Salif Keita, Lucky Dube, Fela, Joni Mitchell, Bob Dylan, Paul Simon, Reverend James Cleveland, and a set of gospel artists he did not know. He was excited by the mix. On a whim he pressed *play* on her stereo, and his own voice filled the room.

"You know how to make a man feel nice," he said.

She was standing by the little fridge, her back toward him, and he watched her body seize the sound and hold it as she put some snacks together. His mind cast back to the sight of her moving toward him in the club in South Carolina. Water in her waistline—*sexy bowlegs*. She turned.

"Is there anybody sitting alone somewhere now who would be angry or sad or devastated if she could see you here?" she asked, as she poured some chips into a bowl. She brought the bowl and placed it on a small table, then sat beside him.

He reached into the bowl and took out some of the chips. He chewed on them, and then dipped into the bowl again, nibbling at the pointed edge of one.

"What's her name?" Keisha asked as she got up and walked to the fridge.

"Who?"

"Juice?" she said over her shoulder.

"Thanks," he said with a mouthful of chips. "You have nice taste in music."

She turned around with the glass of juice. He was grinning at her—playing a game.

"Your woman, what's her name?"

"You gwine tell me about your man?"

"If you want to know," she said with forced casualness, as she began quickly gathering papers scattered on the ground.

"I don't want to know," he said, scratching his head.

"So I should not want to know, too, right?" She moved across the room and put a pile on her desk, then began to pick up some books on the ground by the television. He was waiting for her to say more. "I have more to lose in this . . ."

Kofi leaned over and started to unlace his shoes. Then he stopped and looked at her. "You don't mind?"

She hesitated for a minute, and then spoke softly. "Are you teasing me or being evasive?"

"You want to know about my . . . about my situation," he said.

"Yes, I do."

His leaned his head back, closing his eyes.

She knelt down in front of him and finished the unlacing of his sensible leather shoes. They came off easily. She looked up at him. The curve of his neck rested on the soft back of the chair. He had a serene face. The light caught his beard. She had the urge to reach and touch its strange silkiness. Instead, she reached under the damp cuff of his trousers for the edge of his socks. Her fingers touched his skin. She rolled one sock down then pulled it off. She dangled it in front of her nose and then fell back dramatically, as if passing out.

"You think yuh funny?" Kofi said, half smiling.

Keisha did not move. She was flat on her back with a sock in her hand.

"Really funny."

She stayed still. He leaned over her and gently patted her stomach. She did not move. He pushed his body forward and covered her with his shadow. "I wonder if she's breathing . . ." he said, as if to himself. He brought his cheek close to her mouth. "Oh my God, I gwine to have to do mouth to mouth." His hand touched her cheek and Keisha yanked her face away, laughed loudly, and snaked her body from under him.

"You are such a freak, such a worthless freak," she laughed.

"You lucky you move so fast, girl," Kofi said, sitting on the bed.

"Take off the other," she demanded, nodding at his feet. He peeled the other sock off with his toe and kicked it forward. She rolled it and placed it in one of his shoes. "Let me put them in the closet," she said, then stood and walked to the closet beside the front door. He watched the slow roll of her hips; their casual, unhurried circling.

"You ever been in love?" he asked as she walked back to sit beside him. "I mean love a man till you turn fool?"

"I don't know. I have felt things deeply for someone. So deep they hurt. Is that it?"

"No. That's not it. I mean stupid in love, break-away-and-turn-into-a-fool in love. Let-go-everything in love." His voice was far away.

"You?" she asked him, perching forward at the other end of the bed, her chest pressed down on her lap, her hands stroking the sides of her calves.

"I don't know," he answered. And then they both smiled. "Sometimes women love me. They tell me that they have fallen for me."

"You like that, huh?"

"Sometimes. Sometimes not."

"You are just a big stud man, aren't you? A mack daddy. Got the girls all crazy for you."

"No, no. It's not like that at all—macking is a cold art, I don't do it well."

"You think I am about to tell you that I have feelings for you?" she asked.

"I didn't say that, I wasn't saying that . . ." he said defensively, sensing that she was getting upset. "I was just asking a question. It just came to me to ask—"

"Are you married, Kofi?" she asked abruptly. "I ain't fooling around now. I mean, I need to know that. You can mess with everything else . . ." Keisha looked at him hard.

"No, no. I am not married. No. But does it matter? I don't think it matters to us right now, you know? We want this. We want to escape into this. But you know what? Let me not speak for you. I want this . . . whatever it is. Me and you, right here, like this. I know you have a man, but I don't know what kind of man. I don't want to know. I want to be in this room as if this is the only place in the world. I want to just be here and live like you and me been living for years like this, with nothing outside."

Keisha nodded. "Baby, I am a woman not a child. I have been through a lot of crap in my life. I brought you up here. I know what time it is. Okay?"

She drew herself closer to him. With her fingers she drew lines on his face. She liked his eyes, their full wetness. But she lingered on his lips. Like fruit, she thought, like wet fruit, they were full, peering out of the wiry moustache, their dark brown into pink into purple texturing, the tidy lining of the upper lip, the fullness of the lower lip, wrinkled but tender. She traced the line of the lips, then let his tongue gather around her finger like a sausage in a roll.

She took his hands. "I like your hands."

She let him kiss her, allowing her body to fall to the bed. He coaxed her gently to lie on her stomach and began to slowly massage her back.

"Nice, nice, baby," she groaned. "I hoped I would feel that massage again. You are good, boy, good . . ."

*What am I doing?* Kofi asked himself. *What am I doing? Here . . . this room . . . with this woman? I should be calling home to see about Aunt Josephine. So much things. So much things. So much things.*

His hands kneaded the soft contours of her back, the giving flesh.

"You called me *baby*," Kofi said.

"Yeah—I call people who look after me nice, *baby*," she said, her voice slightly muffled by the pillow. "You don't like it."

"I like it, sweets . . ."

"You called me *sweets*."

"I call every 'oman *sweets*."

"Fool."

They laughed. His hands reached for her ankle—the right one.

"How that Tae Bo injury doing?" he asked her.

"You know, it's raining. It gets bad on nights like this. You know how far I walked to find you?" she said, turning her head to the side so he could hear her.

"How far?"

"From Columbia, South Carolina—the things I will do for a man."

He massaged her legs, trying to will healing into them, trying to reshape that right ankle which he noticed was slightly deformed. He put pressure on her ankle as if trying to push the sharply protruding ball on the outside back to its original place so that she could have the natural slope of a perfect ankle. He tried to draw the pain out with his fingers. She was grateful.

His hands traveled along her legs, massaging. He undressed her easily, touching her body as he did.

He parted her legs and bent his face down between her thighs. The sensation, a pleasant and comforting one, like falling into a pool of water, gathered around her legs and thighs before she felt the lap of his tongue on her. She groaned and waited for her body to wince, but it did not. He was licking her slowly with brush strokes that made her body move toward him. His breath came out like a cooling balm every time the heat seemed too much. He barely moved. For an instant, she wondered whether he had fallen asleep there. But his tongue was still moving, a snaking that gradually stirred her deep in her womb, making it watery with floods of her juice. She lay there naked with his cheek against her left thigh. Uttering a soft groan, she draped her right leg over his shoulder, maneuvering her clitoris against his mouth.

"I could live here forever," she heard him say.

"That's sweet."

"You have no idea," he chuckled.

He nudged her until she was on her stomach. His hands caressed her softly now, drawing lines across her feet, between the tender soft of her toes, along the taut of her calves, and down the line of wetness on her thighs. His hands worked the muscles loose in her back and unknotted the clutch of her shoulders, until they sank into the mattress, her palms opening. And the shiver gave way to a shudder, which gave way to a trembling, which gave way to frantic breathing that was caught up in her rapid pulse. His hands were waves of cheesecloth sheets, white softness over her body.

"Come inside," she said, turning over. She felt open now. Wide, free, freshly plowed earth. "Come inside."

"It's not safe," he said. "I don't have a rubber—"

"I do. I do."

He, for the first time, felt a twinge of nervousness as

he waited for her. He was about to throw himself into her, and he was afraid.

She knelt before him and touched him. He grew. She slipped the condom on, then rolled him between her palms like kindling. She straddled him, and as he bore in, she gasped, as any man would want a woman to gasp. She held onto his neck, and moved.

"You are warm," he said.

"You are hard," she said.

"Smooth, smooth, move smooth, like that," he commanded her gently.

"Like that?"

"Uhuh."

"Like that?"

"Uhuh."

"Like that, like that, like that, like that."

He was in her, and she was on him, and she was moving, and he felt first the sense of his orgasm crawling around his back, but that is where it stayed. At least at first. It stayed where it always stayed. Something different was happening to him, though. Normally he came with his body, not his head. He could tell what he was doing, always. He could tell. He could tell when he would push everything from his head to his groin, to his back, to his penis. But not there in the room, not in the orange light, not with this woman holding onto him and moving, and talking like she was talking. And when these things started to come into his head, when he began to feel that he was starting to lose himself in this moment, he realized that he had forgotten Keisha's name. He panicked.

"What's your name?" he asked quickly.

"What?" She kept moving.

"Your name, what is your name?"

"Keisha. Keisha." She paused, looked at him. His eyes were filling with tears. "You forgot my name?"

"I am very confused. I am feeling . . ." He could not finish. He was feeling his whole body going into her, feeling everything acutely now. He started to sense that this orgasm was going to break him in two. "Hold me . . ."

She did.

She began to grind hard against him, her hips rotating, moving with an irrevocable sense of purpose. He pushed upwards to meet her. He wanted to pull away, to stop this falling to climb back to the edge, but the sharp stab tensed his bottom and she held him there sternly, controlling him with the hiccups in her flesh, and he gave up on everything, letting himself fall until he felt the drowning in his head. He grasped her hip, to feel her running her slickness along his taut and pained cock, now certain of itself. He felt now that to shout would be his only recourse—to shout now at this whipping of flesh on flesh, this trembling, this sensation of her holding him in a tight clench deep inside her. He could love her now, as he felt so completely fallen and so thankful to her for what she was doing to him. He rested in the hold of her, the rock of her on him, her fingers a vice on his nipples, her tenderness as gentle as nothing he could remember feeling before.

And he came with tears and uncontrollable moaning. He came with all the tears of the brilliant day: the water, the light. Then he latched onto something that seemed to make sense, something that he had to say, again and again and again, as everything poured from him: "Don't leave me. Don't leave me. Don't leave me."

And she calmed him, softly whispering, "Yes, yes, yes, yes . . ." like something being cooled, being wiped away, his body salty and heavy like after tears and rain.

She came too because he cried.

# Chapter Eight

*Baby, you so nice*
*I'd like to do the same thing twice*

Y ou want this to last a little longer?" he asked her. It was almost 1 o'clock in the afternoon the next day. They sat on a bench outside her apartment building. Her stomach was heavy with fresh fruit and the scrambled eggs he had made for her—eggs fluffy and savory with the pungency of garlic and green onions. The fruit he went out to the street to buy—sliced mango, grapes, and bits of juicy purple and gold plum, stuffed into the gutted halves of two cantaloupes. He sprinkled a little brown sugar and lemon juice on the mix. She ate looking at him. She ate it all.

Now they were sitting outside waiting for him to leave. They watched a dead pigeon that lay nested in some leaves on the sidewalk. It was a chilly and gray day.

Kofi's hands dangled between his legs. He asked her the question again.

"You want this to last a little longer?"

"What do you mean?" She did not want him to leave. She would have kept him in her room, in that safe place, for several days. Just being with him.

"I can walk away now. You wouldn' know how to find me. I would jus' be a sweet memory, like a dream . . ."

"That's what you want?"

"I wan' tek yuh back upstairs an' set up camp between yuh leg dem," he said smiling.

"One-track mind," she teased.

"Nice track, though, right?"

She slapped him on the shoulder playfully.

They grew silent. The traffic on the wide avenue was steady. People strolled past. A breeze ruffled the pigeon's feathers.

"So what you saying?" he asked.

"About seeing you?"

"Yeah."

"You're going to Jamaica. This is not an issue."

"Then come with me."

"To Jamaica?"

"Yeah, come with me."

"Oh, please be real, Kofi."

"Serious, serious. Look on me." He stared into her eyes. She could see the sharp intensity of his dark irises. He was serious. "So what is wrong with that?"

"Just get up and head to Jamaica?"

"People do it all the time. Nothing big in that."

"Come on, I have commitments," she laughed.

"Like what?"

"Like my job," she said with a hint of sarcasm.

"Take a holiday. When last you take a holiday, anyway? I know you, you know. You don't tek a holiday yet, right?"

"Look, these things cost money." She was searching for a good excuse, but already her mind was drifting to the thought of sun and beaches.

"Money is not no problem. Yuh covered."

"I don't want you paying for me."

"Why? Is so yuh proud? All right, I lend you the money."

"You would?"

He nodded. She laughed nervously.

"So what, you will do it?"

"You are serious, aren't you?"

"Nothing to it, really. Yuh don' have nutting to lose. Call it a holiday, man. People tek holiday all the while. One month, no more. I have a decent place where we can share the shelter of my single bed." He sang out the last few words, grinning. He looked down and softly sang her name. "Keisha. Keisha, Keisha . . ."

"Yes?"

"I like yuh name. Love call it: Keisha, Keisha, Keisha."

"You're so silly."

"I want to make this go on as long as it can go on. Life too short, you know. That is all. I going home to silence. It woulda nice fe have you there wid me . . ."

"Oh yeah, so that one of those Lady Saw–type tough Jamaican women can come and beat me up for taking her man. You are setting me up." She was trying humor again.

His answer was calm and serious. "Just you and me. Just you and me one."

"I don't think Joan will go for it . . ."

"Joan?"

"My boss. I do research work for her . . . And the money . . ."

"You can get a small temporary work in Jamaica. I know people. If that is the problem . . ."

"I thought it was a holiday . . ."

"I know you like you independence, you know. It free you up when it comes to making love."

"That is your theory . . ."

"Independent woman don't need to prove nutting . . ."

"God, it sounds so tempting."

"Check your boss, then call me. Yeah? We doing this."

He stood and walked over to the pigeon. "You have a shovel?"

She led him to the backyard of the apartment. He walked close behind. She could feel his warmth. She stopped and he drew closer. She leaned back into him. He reached his hand around to her breasts and squeezed. She turned around and faced him. He kissed her fully. Their tongues lapped each other. He slipped his mouth from hers and kissed her cheeks, then gently kissed her forehead, holding her face in his palms.

"You are starting something," she said.

"Long time, baby, this one gone bad already, baby." Then still holding her, he said, "Shovel, shovel, before I cause us to dirty up your nice skirt."

"You can be so rude."

"Yeah."

There was a toolshed at the end of the overgrown narrow backyard. The door to the shed was locked. He found a piece of wood leaning against it. He took it to the front. She followed behind, watching his bopping gait. He used a stick to nudge the bird onto the plank, then carried the thing to the back. He dug a shallow hole with the stick, scooping the soft soil out with his hands. She watched him as he ritualized the burial in deep silence.

She wanted to go with him to Jamaica. Leaving New York would not be terribly difficult. She had been preparing for this ever since she arrived in the city. Her friend Andrea would look after the apartment. Andrea wanted to get out of her parents' place and had often stayed at Keisha's apartment whenever Keisha was out of town on business.

Keisha calculated, while standing there watching Kofi. If Keisha agreed to pay half the rent, Andrea would leap at the chance. Joan might balk, but Joan was unpredictable sometimes. If Keisha pitched it as a time for her to find some inner balance, Joan might well go for it. Empowerment was a big thing for Joan. Anyway, the truth was that she did need a holiday, and just the mention to Joan of a handsome island man would make her agree. Joan wanted Keisha to have a good man. The menstruation project was virtually finished. All the interviews were in the can and she had transcribed eighty percent of them. She had already started completing the charts based on the data. The formula was in place. Anybody could finish the rest. It was just for a month. Kofi was not a future, just an adventure.

By the time he had covered the bird with the dirt, she was decided. She would go and see Joan and ask. Kofi patted the loam down and said, "Rest in peace." Solemnly. Then he stood and began to sing in a deep baritone:

*Abide with me fast falls the evening tide,*
*The darkness deepens, Lord with me abide*

His eyes were closed, his head thrown back. She was afraid that he was seriously in mourning when his hands went toward his face, covering it, as if to hide tears.

"Kofi . . ."

Then his shoulders began to shake and his hands fell away, revealing a face crumpled into an exaggerated grimace of sorrow.

"He was such a beautiful bird. *Fly, robin, fly, up, up to the sky, sky* . . ." And he began to do a '70s vintage hand flip and spin while singing.

They laughed as they walked back to the front of the building.

"It don't have to finish just so, Keisha. You know that."

"I will see."

"You want to do it?"

She smiled slyly, licking her lips.

"Not that, you freaky idiot."

"Yes, if it can happen, it will."

He wrote the hotel number on a slip of paper and gave it to her. She took it and made a big show of putting it in her bra. He leaned down and kissed her, his tongue dancing over her teeth.

"Loveliness," he said.

"I will call." She stepped back.

He walked away and she expected him to turn to look back. But he didn't. He turned the corner at the first intersection and was gone. She pulled the slip of paper from her bra. The number was there. It could have been a fake number. The name on the slip of paper was *Peter Tosh*. A parting joke? Her heart began to pound. She felt slightly nauseated at the thought that he had made a fool of her.

She hurried up to her apartment and punched in the number. It was the hotel. Peter Tosh was booked in the hotel, room 1523. But no one was picking up his line. Did she want to leave a message? She said no and hung up.

Then she called Joan.

Rocking on the subway heading for his hotel in Manhattan, Kofi realized two things. First, he was tired. Very tired. He had not been sleeping well, and he could tell he had been in something of a daze for several days. The stress of his constant arguing with Pedro had been taking a toll on him. He wanted so much to run. And then Keisha had arrived and given him something to run to. The second thing he admitted to himself was that he had been trying not to think about what was happening, trying not to analyze it. The moment he saw Keisha outside the theater, he told himself to stop thinking, stop second guessing, stop asking questions, and just let go and see what would happen. She was beautiful, she had come to look for him, she had been gentle, she liked him, she was a gift, and he was not going to think about it.

But on the subway, everything slowed down. He was thinking. Keisha, he knew, would say yes. She would. While he was with her he did not think she would, but the moment he walked away, he knew she would. She trusted him to make her feel safe in Jamaica. The idea frightened him because he did not trust himself. She allowed herself to buy into his holiday argument. She allowed herself to push back all her fears that she would be walking into a messy situation. He could see her doing this, and yet he did not allow himself to slow down the pressure, to tell her the truth. The truth was that he did not know what she would have to deal with in Jamaica. He did not know how he would handle Dorothy. He did not know how she would handle Kingston and the madness and violence of that city. He did not even know who he would be in Kingston. So why did he ask her to come with him? Why was he doing this to her?

Here he allowed himself to admit his greatest fear— that perhaps he really liked her, that somewhere in him he believed that he could actually fall in love with her. He knew that if there was any moment in his life when he felt that he could take a step that might lead to genuine happiness, this was it. He did not know Keisha at all. He knew virtually nothing about her family, about her life in South Carolina, about her history. He did not know if she had a closet full of skeletons that could make a mess of his life. How was he to know whether she was not just an opportunist pursuing a successful artist? The questions settled on him as he dangled his arms between his legs and his body rocked to the sway and jerk of the train.

But as soon as the doubts came, he would think of her face, of her voice while she moved her body against his—the tenderness of their relationship, the way she looked at him with complete trust. It had to be real. And if it wasn't, what the hell? It was more real and more beautiful than anything he had experienced in a long time and anything that he faced going back to Jamaica. It was not as if he was going to Jamaica to peace of mind, to a beautiful relationship. He was going to Jamaica to try and finally extricate himself from Dorothy. With Dorothy he always felt he was engaged in something perverse, something clandestine—a temporary pathology. He wanted normal. Keisha would be normal. He wanted to wake up beside her every morning like he had this morning, for as long as it could last.

It was selfish to make her come to Jamaica, to make her come to his terrain. But he convinced himself that perhaps she needed to leave America as well. That she needed a new space, a new life, even for a little while.

So he was tired, and yet he was feeling a great exhilaration. It was not just the sex, although he could already feel himself growing aroused as he thought of Keisha and the way she held him close before he walked away.

He wanted to see her. This moment of allowing himself to think had changed something in him. At first he was confident that she would say yes, and he was pleased about that. But now he realized that he *needed* her to say yes. He began to worry about whether she knew he was serious about lending her the money, and about making sure she was comfortable in Jamaica. He wondered whether he should have assured her that his family had some means and that he would be able to support her.

The subway was slowing down. He got up and headed to the doors.

He was still in Brooklyn. He got out of the station and walked into the gray light, finding himself on a part of Flatbush Avenue that was teeming with West Indian shops and pulsing with reggae music. He wanted to go back to her, to see her again, to make sure she was going to come with him to Jamaica. He stopped at a small bookstore filled with paintings, lovely ceramics, and rows of books. He bought gifts, offerings. He found a travel agency called Caribbean Tours beside a Jamaican Golden Crust patty shop. He walked in and bought an open-return ticket to Kingston for Keisha.

He was tired, but he was walking like a man on a mission, the wind biting his face, a package in his arms, and his mind arriving at only one reasonable conclusion: She was going to come with him to Jamaica. She was.

⊙প

It was not that she was a simple person—she just had simple dreams. Kofi and Jamaica and the perfectly shaped sun of the Caribbean formed such a dream, and she was drawn.

She hated leaving Joan in a lurch, but Joan was supportive. She smiled as Keisha nervously explained again what she was doing. This time it was in person. Joan had been cool on the phone, almost disapproving: "This is the kind of news that most decent people would give face to face, Keisha, don't you think?"

So Keisha dressed and made her way downtown. Following a man to Jamaica was the kind of thing that Keisha would regard as stupid, a sign of a woman's weakness. But she felt strong doing this, pushing everything aside and going off with Kofi. Calling Troy on a lonely night—that was weakness, the kind of behavior that she fought hard to resist now that she was in New York. But she knew that if there was a hint of tragic vulnerability in this act, Joan would sniff it out and let her know it at once. Joan was good at that kind of thing.

But for some reason, Joan decided to be supportive, to do what she did best: make the most unusual things seem quite normal.

"Think of it as a holiday is what I say. Hell, I always said you needed to do something crazy. Crazy, maybe, but not lethal . . . There is always work, there's always grants to write, baby. Have fun."

So it was settled. Andrea agreed to move into the apartment. Keisha was going. But she still had her doubts.

If it was a holiday—a trip she was making on her own—that would have been easy. But leaving with Kofi was not as easy. She had to do something with her mind. He was someone fresh. Maybe a chance to start rewriting her life, start telling it in another way.

She left Joan's office ready to pack and travel. If there was any residual hesitation, it went away in a flood of laughter and warmth when she got home and found in the mail a single rose resting on a small volume, the cover of which was a grainy black-and-white photograph of the chest and throat of a woman, all shadow and light. Etched in a delicate mauve color was the curled-up script: *Song of Songs*. A bundle of shimmering red wrapping paper with a pink ribbon tied in a bow rested in the box. She opened the package and found six small brown balls covered with white sugar wrapped in wax paper. They had a tangy scent. She nibbled into one of the sweets and her mouth filled with saliva from the tart and sweet taste that burst in her mouth. There was a gingery, peppery taste, and the meaty bits of it were sticky. She was eating a fruit, she could tell. She read a small note on a card beneath the balls: *These are tamarind balls—one day I will make you my special recipe.* She put a whole one in her mouth and chewed. The rush of sensation caused her skin to pimple. She liked it. She liked it a lot. As she ate, she went back to the box. She found the airline ticket. It startled her. His note on a fuchsia post-it said, *No pressure, just letting you know I am serious. It's a loan, okay, pay me back when you are ready.* Her heart sped up. It was that simple? A ticket. Now she could go. On a holiday. As simple as that. And he was serious.

There was one more item in the package—a green bottle shaped like an obelisk with a thin cork wrapped with bits of straw. The label read, *Almond Oils,* and she found an inscription in the book:

> *Your name, Keisha (if that is really your name), is like perfume poured out, my dark and comely Black Cinderella. Do not arouse or awaken love until it so desires . . .*
>
> —Kofi
>
> *Come away with me. Come away with me.*

On another slip of paper, he asked her to call him at 10:30 in the hotel to tell him the good news. She called immediately and left a message: "Let me hear your voice, for your voice is sweet."

"Tell him," she told the desk clerk, "that it is from Black Cinderella, my real name."

She started to pack.

She was happy and relearning herself, letting go, though all her instincts as a Southern girl raised in a house of secrets, a village of secrets, a state of secrets, told her to hold on tightly to some things. Jamaica was a kind of start. She left with him.

# BOOK II

# Chapter Nine

When they arrived in the sweltering heat of Jamaica, when she saw the stunning mountains that rose over Kingston, when she saw the unruly madness of greens all around her as they drove out of the city, when she saw so many black people, more black people than she had seen even in South Carolina, Keisha's doubts about her decision faded. She liked the sweat on her body, the way the older women seemed to own the world they lived in, the drama and intensity of the crowds of people, the goats in the streets, the madness of the minivan and taxi drivers—the sheer chaos of the place excited her. Kofi was pleased. He seemed to want her to understand the place, to like it, to see what he saw. He talked a lot and he pulled himself against her whenever he had the chance. He fed her food that he loved—stew peas and rice, dip-and-fall-back, a coconut-milk-flavored stew of sweet smoked herring, onions, tomatoes, and a lively orgy of spices. He fed her yams—the firm yellow yams, the soft subtly flavored cocoa yams, and the sweet potatoes that turned a greenish purplish color when boiled. He collected fruits, all kinds of fruits, and blindfolding her, he would feed her strips of every variety of mango he could find, scoops of star apple, the tart-sweet flesh of guineps, mouths full of sweet sop and sour sop, lichen, stinking toe, cherries, June plums, coolie plums. He would name them softly as she tasted them and gave her opinion. It was how she had expected it to happen—his ownership of the country, his laughter, and his excitement about showing her everything. He read to her the towns in Jamaica, naming them with such devotion that it sounded like a prayer—he promised her that she would see all these places with him: "Oracabessa, Clonmel, Heartsease, Soon Come, Moco, Accompong Town, Black River, Exchange, Mile Gully, Browns Town, Alexandria." The names came out of him like a song. He smiled when he spoke the quirky ones, and the ones loaded with meaning he intoned with a reverence.

They stayed in one of his Aunt Josephine's houses, a small duplex that she rented to civil servants and teachers in the suburbs of Spanish Town—an old, well-worn town of narrow streets and dilapidated colonial buildings settled by the Spanish in the middle of the seventeenth century. The town stood on a plain, Villa de la Vega, west of the winding Rio Cobre that twisted its way through undulating and rocky mountain terrain before spilling out into Old Harbour. The Spanish Town that Keisha met was a far cry from the colonial Spanish settlement. When the British invaded the island in 1655, they destroyed almost all of the buildings the Spaniards had built, but they kept the layout of the town—a series of streets arranged like an irregular checkerboard. The surviving eighteenth-century British streets were too narrow for automobiles, and Keisha's first impression driving through the city was of clutter and disorder—a teeming space of heat and dust. Kofi liked Spanish Town. He showed her the market that was situated at the old location of the Negro Market, where slaves had been sold. He pointed out the prison, formerly a military barracks, like virtually all the prisons in Jamaica.

They traveled every day for two weeks, up in the hills, down into lush plains, cottages nestled in rain forests. They made love at each stop, Kofi laughing, teaching, teasing. She wondered why she had hesitated. Her body felt so much like her own for the first time in years; she felt so comfortable in her own skin, in its fullness, in the heft of her thighs, felt herself filling out and she loved it, loved the abandon of it. Sometimes she would catch Kofi watching her from a distance as she bartered with a vendor on the street or chatted with school children. He would be smiling, tenderly nodding.

After a month, she felt settled in their little duplex. She was happy. Kofi grew quieter, but remained gentle with her.

Keisha took to the place at first. She was speaking Jamaican in no time. Aunt Josephine arranged for her to get a job teaching in one of the better high schools in Kingston.

Kofi said he was writing songs, and those songs seemed to consume him, swallowed him into a world of his own. Sometimes Keisha was blocked out. To write, he said, he had to stay at home when most other people were at work. He said he was producing some "wicked lyrics" and that the band in New York would be dying to hear what he had.

Kofi had no discernable source of income, but they never wanted for anything. He always had money. Some evenings he would appear at the house with a taxi full of produce and meat. Keisha assumed that Kofi had done well in the music business and was independently wealthy. But he never flaunted whatever wealth he might have. He dressed in khakis and T-shirts. He preferred sandals and sneakers. He spent hours under the tamarind tree at the end of their street, squatting among a group of men who would occasionally break into a soccer scrimmage or a game of dominoes. She would arrive home and see him laughing with the men, sucking on plastic bags full of crushed ice and sweet syrup. When Kofi saw her walking up, he would excuse himself and join her to walk the rest of the way home.

"You wrote any great songs today, Kofi?" she would ask, with not a little sarcasm.

"You are my inspiration, baby," he liked to say.

Since coming to Jamaica, his accent had thickened. Sometimes she was not sure who she was with. But she liked all of it: his strange manner, his ability to sit for hours and talk about stupid things. She liked to watch his skin grow dark in the Jamaican sun, and she loved to watch him eat her cooking, the way he relished it. It was not that she was a simple person. She just had simple dreams.

She was enjoying the feeling of escape and the feeling that a world was happening outside the one that she had known all her life. She liked the new food, the new faces, and the sun—the brilliant sun and the warm sea breezes.

Kingston came at you like the rapid fire of a deejay's lyrics—gruff, scattering indiscriminately with such intensity that you could only retreat, feeling the blows of words on you. And yet in all of this barrage, there was always the rhythm, suggesting itself gradually until your body was moving with the sound. The traffic had its own maddening logic—cars of all makes and vintages twisting and turning along the narrow streets, making roadways out of sidewalks. People piled in and out of crammed minivans, their voices loud and incoherent to a stranger. Above the swirl of dust and exhaust smoke was a sky of such startling and benign blue that you could forget you were jammed in a city with three-quarters of a million people.

She walked through the city aware of its energy. This was a place that could make beauty out of the most tragic of conditions—the way a reggae song could crawl from the broken-down hut of a ghetto, the way a madman would dance elegantly in the street, his clothes barely concealing his blackened nakedness. She understood what she saw and was seduced by it. She liked the flaming temper of the city, the way that blood would spill without warning and the way that love could suddenly tumble into her lap. She loved the quiet at night and the way it was interrupted by the occasional *pop-pop* of gunshots.

Sometimes, watching Kofi, she felt guilty for romanticizing his country. He seemed to carry the pain and hopelessness of the city deep inside him. She was used to seeing people walking through life with no real sense of hope. She had seen it in South Carolina. Many of the people she knew lived to die. It was not for her, but it was not strange. And she had never developed the sense of pity that others felt for poor people—maybe because she had been poor herself.

One night she found him sitting at the dinning table reading the *Daily Gleaner*. He looked depressed. He held his head in his hands while he stared at the page.

"You see this?" he said. "You see this?"

She looked at the spread. *Riverton City*—a slum area where she caught the bus from Six Miles. The photos showed the poverty. The paper talked about how the images reminded some of the older Jamaicans of the Dungle, where years before people had followed garbage trucks waiting for the chance to paw through the waste, fighting over stale bread and whatever else they found. They were doing the same in Riverton City today.

"My people. My people." Kofi assumed a voice of such lamentation that Keisha had to laugh.

"God, you sound like Jeremiah," she said.

"Is a joke to you, eh? Yuh find it funny." He was angry.

"Oh, give me a break, Kofi. These people are as much your people as they are mine. You know anybody who lives in that place?"

"Yes, baby. Yes. My people."

"Yeah, right." She opened the refrigerator to look for something to eat. "You didn't cook."

"My heart was heavy."

"And the funny thing is that you are serious."

"Dere are things you wouldn't understand."

"I suppose. So what are you going to do?" She was buttering a slice of bread. "You going to go down there and feed the poor?"

"Maybe."

"You know, I am tired. I am going to rest. I hate when you get into this kind of mood. You sit at home all day and lament the suffering of *the people*. Somebody is feeding you well to do it. I think you should tell your aunt to take some of that money that she is giving to you and send it to the Riverton City Rescue Team."

"Everything is a joke to you," he said.

She went to bed.

Late that night, she heard Kofi singing and strumming his guitar. He would stop and start. He was composing. She listened. The lamentation in the voice, in the soft melody, was haunting.

*What a tragic irony*
*And a sad, sad prophecy*
*What a vision brutalize my eyes, yeah*
*Revelations traumatize my soul, now*

Despite the major chords he was using, the song had a terrible sadness to it. She felt some skepticism about all his righteous burden-bearing, yet she was drawn into the song. It was the only way he could talk to her about it and not sound like a hypocrite.

*In this sufferah, sufferah city*
*Man an' woman dem a fight wid the hog, yes,*
*Sufferah, sufferah city*
*Fe one dry up piece a bread*
*Sufferah, sufferah city*
*Man an john crow dem a friend*
*Sufferah city, Oh God*

The guitar cut a sharp light through the night. Kofi's voice was filled with tears and a strange desperation. Then his voice grew softer and softer, slowly fading into a whisper.

*How can we call ourselves a civilized nation?*
*How can we call ourselves a civilized nation?*

His voice fell into silence. The guitar went quiet. She waited for him. He did not come. She got up and walked into the room. He was hunched over the guitar, the sheets of newspaper scattered about him. His eyes were red with sheer fatigue. She walked to him and held him.

"Sometimes, you know . . . Sometimes, I feel such a heaviness. Like a darkness," he said.

It was the sincerity of his words that frightened her most. He seemed to be slipping, coming unhinged, and she could only watch and fear. He held her tightly, and that night they made love—at least *he* made love—with a terrible intensity. She felt like a spectator, her body moving, reacting, but her mind trying to read this man who kept speaking as he moved over her.

"I want to do it like it's the last night on this earth. I want to do it like it's the last time. Like it's the last time."

She came quietly. He came after, but it was not like normal, not as if he was waiting for her. He shouted out as he came. A howl that tore out of him and filled the room. She held his head to her. Then she heard him muttering, "Sorry, baby, sorry." Then he was breathing in that labored way of deep sleep. She stayed awake thinking of what they were doing with each other. Listening to him breathing. Eventually, she too fell asleep.

# Chapter Ten

He was gone the next morning. It was a Saturday and she had planned to stay in the house all day to rest and do laundry. She was not sure where Kofi had gone, but at least he had cleaned the living room and the kitchen before he left.

She was outside hanging clothes on the line at about 11:00 when she heard a car pull into the driveway. She went to the front and saw Kofi climbing out of a silver Ford Escort. She wondered where the car had come from. She stood looking at him as he walked up to her.

"Keisha, come, get ready, we going by my aunty's place. She says she want to see you. I think it is time." He walked into the house.

"What are you talking about?" Keisha asked, following him inside.

"She called this morning, said she want to see you. She even arrange for the car and everything. She is like that. The woman is dying. I think we better see her before she goes. She wants to know who I am with, that kind of thing." He spoke hurriedly. He was changing his shirt and then combing his hair.

"Now?" she said.

"Yeah. Now," he said.

"Just like that."

"What, you busy? Keisha, come, man. Ready, ready." He was laughing, and that made her relax a little.

"I don't know if I want to meet her, you know. I don't

trust this secrecy stuff and then this summons. It is too weird, man." She was already getting herself together as she spoke.

"You think *this* is weird?" he said, laughing.

A storm appeared as soon as they started out of the drive. The thick clouds filled the sky, and just as suddenly, it began to rain.

"The clothes!" Keisha shouted.

"Forget the clothes, man. Rain water is good for the clothes. The best softener."

They drove toward Spanish Town in a surreal atmosphere of darkness and light. The rain was relentless. Huge craters opened up and filled with water. Rain always shocked the landscape, the streets, the light.

Once in Spanish Town, Kofi did not drive along the Mandela Highway toward Kingston. Instead he turned onto a narrow street that Keisha had never been on. The road began to rise slowly, and then Kofi turned northwards up into the looming Red Hills that separated Spanish Town from Kingston.

CASTLEVALE, JAMAICA

They drove through torrential rains. Keisha was worried. Kofi drove frantically, switching into second gear to climb the hills, jamming forcefully on the brakes at the corners, blasting his horn to warn the traffic coming around the hills. It was just as well—trucks and minivans would come hurtling around the corners, leaning precariously to one side, barely missing them as they rode over potholes, swerved around bundles of dirt and rock that had fallen in landslides. The radio played deejay music, rapid dancehall, and it seemed to drive Kofi into a demonic frenzy. At every stretch of straight road, he would accelerate with such breakneck speed that she grabbed onto the dashboard, her right foot jamming on brakes that were not there. Kofi said nothing. The windshield wiper moved with the same maddening speed—everything was animated. Keisha tried to close her eyes, but could not. She grew nauseated when she did.

But as the sun abruptly bloomed ahead, Kofi finally grew calm. There was no sign in the road that it had rained.

"Could it have dried up that quickly?" Keisha asked, staring at the bone-dry road, the dust along the sides, the pale green of the scraggly bushes along the roadside.

"No, no, we lef' the rain behin'," Kofi said. She sensed a hint of pride in his voice.

Keisha looked back. Above the hills that they had just come over, the darkness was thick and purple. The rain was behind. It could follow them the rest of the way.

They drove on listening to the music from the radio. Deejay after deejay sounded to Keisha like the same person—men with thick, gruff voices riding percussive rhythms and speaking of things she could not understand. She was trying to make out a lyric when Kofi slowed the car in what seemed like the middle of nowhere. Just around a bend, the spill of gravel and yellow sand into the road was the only hint of a small dirt turnoff. Kofi turned the car virtually 360 degrees to start the ascent up this narrow strip of road—two dirt grooves flanking a ridge of thick grass in a tunnel of trees and overgrown bushes. Occasionally, a startling vista of open hillside would appear, the car almost reaching over a precipice before Kofi would turn sharply to negotiate the next rise. Keisha stared at the land below her. Open fields and rolling hill country, not evenly mapped out like she would see in South Carolina, but rugged and disorganized—a criss-cross of barbed-wire fences scarring the landscape, small wooden houses tucked into clutches of trees and hedges. To the right of the valley was the glassy smoothness of three ponds, large bodies of water too small to be called lakes but too evenly shaped to be accidental makings of nature.

"Fish farm," Kofi said. "She trying to grow rainbow trout. But the people dem t'ief everything."

They climbed for about twenty-five minutes before the road ended in a cul-de-sac. Kofi parked in the circle and Keisha could see a small path leading into a thickness of blooming hibiscus hedges. Another small path led downward through another hedge.

As soon as she stepped out of the car, she heard music—familiar music—loud enough for anyone on the hill to hear. It was martial music, complete with the tattoo of drums and the blaring horns. The music swung with that sweet orderliness of a marching band, reminding Keisha of high school football games back in Sumter. But that memory was totally out of place now. There was nothing in this lush pastoral place that made sense of the music that leapt and swirled and goose-stepped at her.

Kofi did not seem perturbed. He started to walk toward the small opening in the hedge, along the path that led uphill. Keisha followed.

"Wait," she said. "Look, I think you ought to prepare me a little better for this. I don't like this shit, Kofi. I mean, you don't tell me a thing, you don't tell me what the woman wants, what she is like. Hell, I don't even know what she is to you. She is your aunt, right?"

"Right," he said. "Just chill, baby. Nothing to it. She just want to look at you, see what kind of woman you is. She been feeding us for a few months, she deserve dat. Come."

He walked ahead, following the sound of the brass

band and the drums. The moment they cleared the hedge, the back of the house became visible. It was massive with gray tiled roofs and off-white walls, large windows with black ironwork frames, and a series of balconies and stairways that protruded from all four sides. The arched cellar doorways that surrounded the base of the house were some ten feet tall. The main area rose two stories. Immediately to the right of the house, Keisha could see an elevated slab of uneven and partially blackened paving. This patio was tightly hemmed in by a jungle of tall trees that continued in absolute density toward the hill face rising sharply about half a mile away.

Beyond the house, Keisha could see the main driveway, what must have been the proper way to get to the place. A large lawn stretched out from the house toward a tall gate in a low white wall that looked to her like the walls that lined the roadway as they had climbed the hill toward the house. The lawn was impeccably manicured—from the hill it looked like a carpet jeweled by clusters of blooming plants: reds, pinks, whites, blues.

Kofi started to jog down the gradient and Keisha followed. The music was blaring out of windows that were wide open at the back of the house. To get to the house proper, they had to walk around a large pen filled with farm machinery, oil drums, and two large impressive sedans. They headed to a graveled road that circled the entire front lawn and led up to the house.

At the front entrance, a canopy covered an ornate staircase that rose to meet the grand doorway of the house.

"This place looks old," Keisha said, trying to keep pace with Kofi.

"Yeah," Kofi replied.

The sound of the music had diminished somewhat

now that they were at the front of the house. But as soon as Kofi opened the front door, the noise was deafening. She could hear every instrument, the stumping rhythm of the tuba and the bass drum, the silliness of the fifes and flutes, and the shattering chaos of the trumpets and trombones.

"Jesus Christ, man. What is wrong wid dat woman, man?" Kofi shouted above the music, as they walked along a narrow and dark corridor that opened out into the living room area. The corridor was lined with paintings, rustic landscapes done in a post-modern style. Keisha stared at the artwork as she moved along the corridor. The bodies of the people looked to her like they had been included as last-minute indulgences. The hills were made of blocks of paint, piled onto each other, and in every canvas a fire caused smoke to mix with the almost photographically rendered skies.

Beyond the corridor, the house began to show itself. Keisha peered around the corner and saw the huge living room. Here the light was better. The large window she had noticed outside was before her now, and she could see the path they had taken up the driveway into the house. Keisha was stunned by the room—by the floor, composed of polished wooden panels of rich and varied color, the wooden paneling along the walls, the olive green sofas and chairs, the thick rug that looked like a dead polar bear, and the chandelier, a cascade of crystal dangling from the high wood ceilings.

Because of the glare, Keisha did not immediately see the small head poking above the back of a chair that faced out to the window. But she saw the hand raised, open, and she knew to wait while the music moved toward a finale.

Keisha studied the hand: small, old, draped in white

filmy material. There were two rings—one was a thick band and the other had a stone—both on her marriage finger.

The horns exploded in the final march and then stepped out while the drums, accented by crashing cymbals, completed the march. Keisha could not help picturing a drum major tossing his baton into the sky.

Silence followed. The hand stayed raised for a few more seconds, and then slowly sank.

"TURN IT OFF NOW, MARY!" a shrill voice erupted from behind the chair. The drum roll of another song started and was then sharply aborted. "Thank you, love."

Keisha was afraid of this woman.

"My guests!" the voice said. It was a command. Kofi shook his head and went forward. Keisha followed.

She could have been white. Her skin was a pale, yellowish color with blotches of a tender light brown on her hands, her chest, and her face. Her veins were a dull bluish green and they crawled across her forehead, along the scaffolding of bones in her neck, and in thin streaks along her arms. Her eyes were a pale gray. Small eyes behind gold-rimmed glasses that sat on the broad bridge of her nose. She could have been white, except that apart from skin color, she was black. There was something almost albino about her. Her full pulpy lips seemed to have been stolen from a woman forty years her junior. And her nose flared wide and dramatic like Kofi's. Keisha stared at this woman with more intensity than was polite.

Kofi's aunt was a small thin woman. She sat small, her legs were crossed under her light cotton dress, which was cut low with tassels and a series of pleats where the bosom should have been. She wore a pearl necklace. She looked hard at Keisha—without any self-consciousness, looked her up and down—so that Keisha felt exposed, aware of her naked legs, the hair that had grown there since she last shaved, the sloppiness of her casual leather sandals.

"Sit, sit, sit," Kofi's aunt said, pointing to the sofa in front of her. Kofi faced her, leaned down, and kissed her on the lips. She opened her palm tenderly on Kofi's face, letting it take the contour of his cheek.

"I thought you stop listen to that music. Laro said it making the cow dem milk sour." Kofi was laughing as he sat beside Keisha.

"I told Laro to stop troubling those cows and the milk will be fine," she said. "But you know these country people—old habits die hard. Anyway, his wife left him."

"You are scandalous. Why you have to say that about Laro?" Kofi asked.

"Say what? I am not condemning anyone. There is nothing morally wrong with doing that kind of thing with cows—at least I don't think so. But it must affect the cow's milk production. After all, they are used to larger . . . well, things."

"Can we change the subject? This is Keisha."

"My nephew is a prude, you know. Don't be fooled by all his sweet talk. He is a prude. He was going to be a minister. Said he had a revelation. In the hills. Did he tell you? I suppose he didn't tell you that he used to come here with a Bible to convert me to the Holy Ghost. He was only fifteen then. My husband—the second—he always said that Kofi waited too long to clear his . . . well, his maiden deposit. I like that. Thank God he did not turn to the cows, though. At least I don't think he did. Did you, Kofi?"

"Don't be ridiculous!" Kofi said, too quickly.

Keisha could not help laughing. "No, he did not tell me any of this."

"Ah, secrets. Lovely." The old woman smiled brightly

at Keisha. She had wide-spaced teeth, but those Keisha saw looked yellow enough to be original. "Mary! MARY! Put the record back on, but turn it low, nuh?"

"Aunt Josephine, please," Kofi protested.

"Just be quiet, boy. The music reminds me of Umberto. I like to remember Umberto."

"Keisha?" She raised her eyebrows, questioning.

"Yes, Keisha."

"Very black name. Black American, that is. We don't have many Keishas here. I hear you have many in America. You know where it came from?"

"No, ma'am." Keisha found herself reverting to her Southern politeness. Kofi looked at her oddly.

"No, you wouldn't, you wouldn't," Aunt Josephine spoke almost to herself. "Well, Keisha, my husband Umberto—he was my second husband, really, after I had worked my first one and the father of my late son to death—was a Brazilian. He was a writer. Did Kofi tell you?" She did not wait for a response. "Yes, he wrote poetry and some fiction. He was published and well-known in Brazil. He was such a renaissance man. Painted, wrote, sang. Lovely man. Anyway, I am telling you this for a reason . . . He liked this martial music. He did. Strange, because he could not have been much of a military man. They tortured him, you see—the military, when he was young. He never ever spoke of it, but I think it affected his psyche. I think that is why he loved that music. It made him, well, it made him stand to." She laughed and clapped her hands. And then, as if she was suddenly uncertain whether Keisha understood, she added, "You do know what I mean, right?"

"I think she does," Kofi said impatiently.

"So these songs remind me of him. Are you shocked?" She leaned forward to look at Keisha.

Keisha blushed slightly, for she was sure that the woman could see the image that had formed in her head— a large-bellied Brazilian, with a moustache and bushy eyebrows, standing naked at attention while martial music swirled around him, his penis jutting out in an absurd salute. She spoke quickly as if she had been caught. "Looking at you, I am not shocked. Not really."

"Nice. Anyway, it worked for him. I suppose the secret of life is to know what makes us stand to, yes?"

Keisha nodded. She looked at Kofi. He shrugged. Keisha could not work out this relationship. She wanted to understand it.

"I am Josephine, his aunt," she said.

"Yes," Keisha said, nodding.

"So you can call me Aunt Josephine."

"Yes."

"You blacks in America do that, don't you?"

"What, ma'am?" Keisha was surprised at the way she was lapsing into that Southern language when faced with the authority of this woman. Seeing the house made her understand right away that Aunt Josephine had been her benefactor for the last two months.

"Calling non-relatives aunts and uncles. It is an African thing, you see. You black folks have retained that too, haven't you?"

"Yes, ma'am."

"Stop saying that. It is sweet and polite, but . . ."

"Yes—"

"MARY! Music!" she shouted. "Put on the Sousa. I swear by Sousa. He saved my marriage."

The music started again, this time a lot softer.

"Mary hates this music. Reminds her of Empire Day. Poor black people marching around assuring white Britons that they will never be slaves. Mary is savvy.

Anyway, she prefer this to the boogoyaga music that Kofi brings to the house. At least this one is not full of sinful words. But she knows what Umberto and I used to do to this music." The woman laughed, patting the side of her face with her hand—a strange affectation that she would repeat again and again. Her hands touched her skin as if trying to remove a wayward cobweb.

"So you like teaching in Kingston?" Aunt Josephine asked.

"It is fine."

"I arranged that. I got you the job," the woman said. Keisha was not sure how to respond. There was a hint of power in the statement.

"Thank you, ma'am."

"Stop saying that," Aunt Josephine said again, her fingers on her face. "You are staying at one of my houses."

"I see."

"You could have stayed here, but Kofi did not want to. I suppose he feared shocking me with your sinful living."

"Yes, that is it," Kofi said sarcastically.

"We look after Kofi." The tone was one of ownership, and she looked at Kofi tenderly. "His mother was my dearest friend—my sister. She is the one who did what we all wanted to do. She went to Africa, found herself an African. She went to America, she saw the world. We did not, and soon we were all too old to really live life. Adventures. Oh, that woman had adventures. Has Kofi told you about them?"

"No, not really."

"Yes, he is ashamed of his mother. Angry with her. Kofi can be sexist that way, you see. He does not understand women, really. He thinks he does, but he doesn't at all."

"We came to see how you were," Kofi smiled wryly.

"You came because I told you to come. That's why you came." Her stare was cold. Keisha could see the stark power in this woman. Then Aunt Josephine's voice became cordial again. "He hates his mother and now he has found her."

"I don't understand," Keisha said.

"I knew he would find a Yankee. An African-American. That is what you are, isn't it?"

"Yes," said Keisha.

"I mean, you have no West Indian traces, do you? Where are you from? I mean, in America."

"South Carolina. My family has been there—"

"Oh. Well, that is funny. We may actually be related. We may have shared the same white ancestors. The same black ancestors, too. That stretch of Caribbean waters between Kingston and Charleston was like a highway. History. But you people don't know a thing about history." She stopped talking and stared outside. Keisha was not sure whether a question had been asked. She looked at Kofi, who suddenly appeared quite helpless and sheepish. "Now, this place was built by a French, what they used to call *émigré*, around 1790-something. But you know these British, they took it from him. It fell into the hands of a family called Sturge—they were ancestors of one of your Civil War generals—a Southerner who fought for the North or something complicated like that. Then they sold it to the Castleberrys in the middle of the 1800s. Now, Castleberry liked this place, all that wonderful timber—mahogany, rosewood, ebony, orange, and all kinds of good hardwoods with all those colors—you can see them. Beautiful. He liked it and he looked after it well. Of course, Castleberry knew he couldn't make much money growing sugar in Jamaica after they did away with slavery, so he put his money in South Carolina. You know, the Castleberrys who owned this place also owned a plantation in South Carolina. Rice, I think. Yes, somewhere on the coast. Beaufort? Of all things, rice. Beaufort, right? That's my ancestor. A backhanded way, of course, but in Jamaica, we tend to do things like that."

"The islands on the coast, they cultivated rice there . . ." Keisha said.

"Yes, rice. Fancy that. They used to take the slaves from here and put them to work up there. Just yank them. We could be relatives, you know? Small world. You could be tupping your cousin, Kofi," she said, laughing and patting her face. "The vultures are circling, Kofi," she said, changing the subject abruptly. Her voice came from far away. "They can smell the rotting flesh. Some mornings I wake up and smell it, too. Cancer, you know, has a certain smell. I remember it. My mother had that smell. I used to take deep breaths before going into her room and try not to breathe while I let her hug me into her. But I could not hold my breath forever and the stench would fill my body—my stomach would turn. It was a horrible smell. I can smell it when I wake in the mornings now. I know everyone smells it. They are gathering. Suddenly they all love me."

"Aunt Josephine, dem have a long wait, man," Kofi said, leaning forward to touch her hand.

"They are circling, I am telling you. It come in like even the people in the area know. Them coming up to the fish farm to t'ief. Had to kill one a dem the other day." She stopped for effect.

"What?" Kofi asked.

She turned to look at him. She looked very distraught.

"What you mean?"

"Shot him. The fool come out in broad daylight, and instead of just take the fish, the boy start to shoot off at us."

"Where were you?"

"Right out there inspecting. You know. Me and Mr. Marshal. So Mr. Marshal says, 'Ah gwine shot him.' I say, 'No, Marshal.' Then the boy fired again. So he shot him." She looked out again. "Just a boy. Dead on the spot. Over fish."

"He was shooting at you." Kofi walked to her and touched her shoulder.

"Nice-looking boy. Dead. Over fish." She shook her head. "Blood on the hands . . ."

"The boy's?" Kofi was confused.

"No, me. My hands." She held up her hands, her palms facing out. Her fingers were yellow and spotted brown.

"But Marshal shot him."

"Marshal? Marshal shot him because he knew I wanted it. I wanted the boy dead. I was scared."

"This is not good," Kofi said.

"The mother used to pick coffee for us, you know? She told me he was wutliss. His mother said that to me after I killed her son. She said it like that made it right what I did. I don't understand that."

"Marshal is getting old. You need someone younger, someone who—"

"They are circling. They can smell it. The decay," she said. "Do you smell it, Keisha?" She kept staring out the window.

"No, ma'am. I don't smell it."

"Ah, you are kind. It is a smell you need to learn."

Then the silence again. Keisha could smell nothing. The silence lasted a long time, and then Aunt Josephine spoke.

"It is my duty, Keisha, to ask you, are you born again?" She looked at Keisha with such an intensity that Keisha quickly dismissed the thought that she was joking.

"Can you not do that, Aunt Josephine?" Kofi said.

"Don't tell me to not do that—"

"I didn't come here for this—"

"You came because I told you to come and because you know which side yuh bread butter!"

"I don't ask you for nothing, Aunt Josephine—"

"I will do my duty. I am a dead woman. I can smell it. You not gwine let me die without doing my duty, okay?" Her finger was sticking menacingly out at Kofi. "Okay?"

Kofi stood up and walked toward the window.

"Adam and Eve sinned in the Garden. But the plan was perfection. We would be still here today, living forever, making babies, no labor pains, but they sinned. So Jesus came to clean us up so he could use us. I am being used. Two weakness I have, Keisha. Two. Martial music and my gospel. The latter is a new thing with me. It is a family tradition. When we know we are dying; if we are blessed enough to know this in advance, the balance of our life is devoted to spreading the gospel of Christ. Why Christ? The absolutes of after-life. We are a family that wants the best. I am going to die, but I sure as hell am not going to get to the Promised Land and be some servant to some two-bit uneducated person. It is terrible, isn't it?"

"Ah, how sweet the sound of Jesus name," Kofi half sang.

"You two are living in sin. But that is not my beef. My beef is that you two don't look happy. You fighting, eh? Sex can last only so long. The problem is simple. You need Jesus. I will tell you something, Keisha, but first I need some guava juice. Go into the kitchen and ask them to give you a glass of guava juice for me and a next one for you. Let that Kofi stew in his own juices while we women talk."

Keisha stood and moved in the direction that Aunt

Josephine pointed. As soon as she walked through the massive doorway to the kitchen, an old woman was standing in front of her with two glasses of a light brown liquid in hand. Keisha took the glasses and walked back to the living room. Kofi was still at the window. Aunt Josephine had not moved either. She took the glass from Keisha and sipped her juice quickly. Keisha sipped as well. A tangy, sweet juice with a distinct flavor, and a strange grittiness of crushed seeds stayed like gravel in the mouth after a long sip. Keisha liked the taste, if not the thick and gritty texture.

"I was an avowed atheist. Now I do this. Sometimes to annoy them, but most times it is because I have dreams and I see things that tell me that this is a smart way to go. Now I am a believer. It is lovely. You are a believer, too, I know. You are a Southern woman. You would be."

"I am," Keisha said. "But I have not kept up—"

"No one really does. How can you?" She turned to Kofi. "Hey, boy, stop the sulking. Going on like you don't know how I behave. Tell me, are you going to marry this woman?"

"No," Kofi said.

"Well, well, so clear, eh?"

"Marriage is not—"

"Spare me. Spare me. You just hurt the woman's feelings. You came here to tell me that she is a slut, a whore?" She kept her head turned on Kofi. "That is what you think about her? Is that it?"

"No. I mean that we are not ready—"

"Yes, yes, yes. Yes!" she said, dismissing him. Then to Keisha: "Kofi has had a few bouts of depression. He should be on medication. He has spent time in an insane asylum. I tell you this because he is a liar. He is sweet, but he is a liar. He is into this reggae business because he has always wanted to be poor. But Kofi has never been poor. Never understood it. So he went into this reggae business to be poor. Kofi would not know what to do with himself in Trenchtown. Kofi went to one of the best schools in the country, went to the university, never went hungry unless he wanted to, and liked light-skinned girls. You need to know these things. You do. Doesn't she, Kofi?"

Keisha looked at Kofi and realized with some discomfort that he was no longer amused or exasperated with his aunt and what she was saying. He did not try to give Keisha a look that would say, *Be patient, she is just an old lady.* It was dawning on her that Aunt Josephine was asserting her role and reminding Kofi of something they had agreed to, and he was acquiescing. Keisha stared hard at him, demanding an answer. He spoke in a mechanical manner as if he had prepared this speech for a long time.

"Keisha, I asked my aunt to tell you about me. That is what I did. I know you have a whole heap a questions, but I can't bring myself to explain everything. Now, she can do it. She might tell lies in there, and she might be a bitch about it, but I asked for it. So there we have it. Now trust me, trust her. I will go out now." Kofi finished the speech and started to walk away without looking back at Keisha.

"Kofi, I would prefer to hear these things from you. I don't understand this. This is crazy."

"Oh, calm down, child. Sit down and let's talk. You won't get it straight like this from anybody again, okay? Ye shall know the truth and it shall set you free. Kofi is my favorite, you see, and I find him fascinating. Fascinating— in a pathological kind of way. But fascinating, nonetheless. Anyway, he is just having a tantrum and there is no need for all three of us to fall into a sulking mood just because he is in one." She patted the chair beside her. "Sit. Sit."

# Chapter Eleven

Kofi walked toward the kitchen. He wanted to get away from Aunt Josephine. He knew the story she would tell Keisha and he did not want to be there to hear it. Kofi had called her earlier that week to ask her to meet Keisha and explain about him. He needed someone, he said, to help her understand that he was the way he was for a reason, and that it was something deep down. Aunt Josephine agreed. She wanted to meet Keisha and she wanted the company.

Mary, a tall thin woman with an angular face, stood at the window looking out. A pot boiled on the stove. The comforting smell of stewed oxtail and butter beans filled the room.

Mary had been with Aunt Josephine for years, and Kofi had grown up with her. She knew everything about him, secrets that he kept from everyone else. She would pile his letters in a neater heap in his hiding place, or move his pornographic magazines to a less obvious place in the room, or she would leave his soiled underwear in the room and give a small admonition that, "Ef yuh big enough fe bruk on yuhself, yuh big enough fe wash it yuhself." Mary was always stern and never familiar with Kofi. She was "big woman" to him and she let him know that again and again. But she was always there to listen to him, and she let him listen to the "big people" talk she had with the gardener and the washing woman about men and women in the community, about his Uncle Umberto's

heavy drinking and affairs, about the madness of Aunt
Josephine, about the craziness and riots going on in
Kingston, about Bob Marley. She would let him sit and
listen as long as he did not ask questions and put his
mouth into big people's matters.

"Oxtail," he said, following her gaze toward the
hillside where the car was parked.

"Yuh park up so?" she asked.

"Yes. It easier."

"One day somebody gwine t'ief it, yuh stay deh."

"Not my car."

"Yuh was always too casual for your own good," she
said, still looking out. She was wearing a shift that hung
down to her shins like a dishcloth on a nail. It was almost
pink, but you could tell from the streaks of sharp rich red
just along her ribs that the dress was once a red, close-
fitting thing. Her head was tied in a white cloth.

"True, true," he said. "How she stay, Mary?"

"Who dat, yuh auntie?"

"Yes."

"She ready, me son. She ready. Anytime now."

"But she look fine."

"Sunset is one a de prettiest time a de day, and den,
*boops*, night."

"I mean, she not complaining about pain or nothing."

"Drugs, baby. But lickle more, dem gwine wear off.
Den she gwine start the bawling. Den she gwine want de
wine. You know how she love de wine. Sometimes, I feel
it's dat kill her. Not even the lickle salvation what come
on her will mek her stop drink de wine. That woman is a
trial. Is a sad ting." Mary clucked her teeth and shook her
head. "She gwine want you leave, though—before. Don't
argue. Just gwaan when she ready, all right?"

Mary's understanding of Aunt Josephine was

complete. It was Mary who had sat with her after Umberto's death and told her that it was time for her to think about God. Aunt Josephine had mourned and then started to talk about finding another companion. Mary told her, "Is Jesus time now." There was no reason to think that the seed planted would take—none, except that Mary's brand of faith was a fiery kind that believed in healings, prophecy, discernment, and the perfect timing of a word spoken in season. She was commanding Aunt Josephine to come to Jesus, and that is what happened. Aunt Josephine turned to Jesus, and was soon declaring herself saved to the rest of the family. Most thought she had lost her mind, but Mary spoke to Kofi and explained that it was serious. Kofi should have known, though, when he began to get Aunt Josephine's prophetic letters. They came in reams of paper written with a neat but tiny hand. Mary accepted Aunt Josephine as a fruit of her faithfulness and obedience.

"That woman and her wine-bibbing. I tell you. But it mek her feel good, you know?"

"Yes."

"Dat and de work. You know seh she still a work, eh? Still doing all this chipping and chipping." She pushed her chin toward the back door, which led to a garage area that had been converted into his aunt's studio.

"But she shouldn't be—"

"She a dead, Kofi. Yuh don' understan'?"

Kofi nodded. He had fallen into the illusion that his aunt had created when they first walked in. Her talking, the combativeness. But he had smelled that smell that his aunt had mentioned. It was not a terrible smell, but it had a quality of neglect. Aunt Josephine was not neglected, but the smell was there.

Mary lifted the lid of the pot and turned a long steel

spoon through the stew, her slender arms rippling with those tidy tendons that Kofi knew to be sturdy as steel rods.

"You gwine eat some?" she asked him.

"Yes, man." He moved behind her and touched her on the back. "So what you gwine do when she gone?"

"But what is wrong wid unoo people, anyway? Eh? It come in like unoo feel seh me no 'ave no life but dis one. When she dead, life go on. Me have a few more year. I mighta tek it easy, stay wid my grand pickney dem. Nutting inna it."

Kofi wanted to hear her say that she too would be devastated, but he knew she would not say that. Mary was right about having her own existence. Anyway, Mary had seen too much death in that family to be shocked or shaken by another.

Mary walked into a pantry area on the other side of the large kitchen and brought a large plastic container of rice to the counter. She pried open the cover and began to scoop rice with her hands and toss it into a black pot.

"Ah gone outside lickle bit," Kofi said.

"You like dat woman, Kofi?"

"Who, Keisha?"

"No, de queen a Sheba."

Kofi chuckled. "I like her. But, well, maybe we wasn't ready fe all a dis, you know? Is a spur-of-the-moment ting and now, well, you start think and . . . But she nice."

"Uh-uh." Mary closed up at once. It was the end of the conversation.

Kofi opened the garage door and stepped down, moving his hand along the wall at the side of the door until he found a switch. The light was sudden and dramatic.

* * *

Aunt Josephine walked slowly to an ornately designed cabinet and pulled from it a bottle of wine. As she walked back, Keisha could see how much pain the woman was in. Her body hunched over her stomach, which protruded strangely. The old woman sat down with a large sigh.

"Pain, sometimes, you know. Knock the wind out . . ." She breathed slowly and then poured herself a glass of wine. It must have been quite warm, but she did not seem to mind. "My little indulgence. You know, Paul said it is good for the stomach." She smiled. "I gave up much for the Lord, but the wine. My thorn. You want some? It is kind of warm, but I can't bother with the chilling. I like it like this, you know."

Keisha shook her head. Aunt Josephine took a quick gulp, closed her eyes, and breathed. Then she began to talk. She was not looking at Keisha. Her eyes were focused outside, but Keisha could tell that she was not seeing. She was thinking back.

"Now, Kofi's mother is my sister—my baby sister. We don't have the same mother, but our father got around. He left Jamaica in 1938—left a family, three children and a wife—to go and live in Cuba. We never heard from him. At least, I have no recollection of hearing from him or about him. I did know he was in Cuba. I found out later that he used to send money and that kind of thing and that my mother mailed him pictures of us every year. But she didn't talk about him. She lived her life like he never existed. Then we heard that he was in America. That must have been about three years later. Turns out that he went to New York and found a woman, a Jamaican woman that he knew from his parish. They didn't marry or anything, but they had two children together. Kofi's mother was the first child. They sent her to Jamaica when she was about two or three to stay with our father's mother. But she was old and she couldn't manage that girl, so they brought her to live with us.

"That is how Stella and I met and how we became sisters. I was twelve years older than she, but it was my job to look after her. So I did. Maybe it's because she was my connection to my father, but I took care of that child. And she was something else. She always told people she was American. Told them how her mother was in America, and was going to come and get her soon. But it never happened. My old man got sick in America—just plain old. The cold, the tough streets, and all the drinking he was doing mash him up. So he came home to die. That is when I met him. He was almost white. His hair was white. He was tall, but he had that big nose—that huge nose like all of us have. He liked to talk, but he couldn't make us family. He couldn't do it and he never even tried. Now, my mother, she cared for the man like he had been with her all along. I couldn't understand it, after everything he had done to her. But it was nothing to her. She cleaned up his shit, fed him, sat and talked to him when he couldn't talk back. Then he died.

"Stella took it badly. Which I found funny, because I know that she never know the man at all. She never did. But she cried for days and I couldn't do anything to comfort her. All she kept saying was that she wanted to go back home—to go back to America to her mother. But we knew that her mother was not going to take her. Her mother was what you people call a *junkie*. People will disappear on you sometimes. And this woman disappeared. Like she dropped dead somewhere and that was the end of that. Stella kept in touch with her brother who lived in America. He still lives up there—in Canada, I think. Don't know much about him. Kofi don't know much about him neither. They belong to a different world.

"As for Stella, she got over the death and all she could talk about after that was going to America to be famous. She said that this family was a sick one, that sister and brother must have copulated somewhere not too far back because we all had that look of incest. She used to say things like that. I mean, I was twelve years older than her, but when I was twenty-four, a big woman starting to look at my first husband, this girl, this twelve-year-old girl, was the one I told everything. She was my best friend. She was bigger than her age. It was something. When she hit sixteen she left Jamaica. She took the SAT and got a very high score. Some school in Texas, Rice or something, gave her a scholarship, and she managed to convince my mother to give her spending money to go there and study. She left me then. I missed her. But she was gone and that was the start of her mad travels. The woman used to write me and call me and tell me all the trouble she was getting in. Men? Men? That woman had men like I never knew a woman could have men. She went through them like nothing.

"She ended up in Ghana. What we heard was that she was going to Ghana to work for a British-born American diplomat there. An old man. But a man with a whole heap of money. And it made sense. She was a woman who could smell money, and to be honest, she liked the comforts of life and went after them in ways that embarrassed foolish prudes like me. I really envied her. The thing is that she liked men—but she liked them for their company. She used to write me all the time about the men who wanted her. She said that all they wanted was sex, and the moment they had sex, they stopped thinking, stopped being intelligent and witty. She didn't like sex. She had a lot of it, but she didn't like it. For her it was a ritual, you know. A simple inconvenience that men wanted and she was willing to give. But sometimes she would grow bitter with men who wanted her to do more and who did not understand that she dressed the way she did and she smiled and cooed the way she did as one would in a ritual of behavior. So her running off to Ghana with a white man made sense. He was old, he was rich, she was enjoying him and his nice ways. He liked ritual, she said. He would put rose petals on her bed or fill her bath with champagne—I am serious. He was like that. He understood rituals because he was not able to demand sex all the time.

"But something must have happened in Ghana while they were there. Actually, a lot of things happened then. There was a coup. It was a damnation. It was a bloody, damned coup. Right. So that was one thing. And she got pregnant. That was the other thing."

The more she talked, the quicker she drank. Keisha could tell that she was growing more and more relaxed, but there was a strange weariness in her eyes, which were reddening as she drank. She kept drinking, though, and talking. After a while Keisha wondered whether Aunt Josephine would make it to the end of the story before completely succumbing to the wine. The room felt muggy and the air was thick with the sweet smell of the wine.

The garage was musky. The large blinds covering two windows were drawn tight. Aunt Josephine used to work with the natural light in the studio, and at night she worked with a small lamp, depending, she liked to say, on the language of the moonlight or the blackness.

She would wake Kofi up at 2 or 3 in the morning to come and help her. At least that was the pretext, but mostly she wanted him to look at the work she had done, to say something. She would hand him the large bucket of Vaseline.

"Smear it on smooth," she would say.

Kofi would fill his hands with the Vaseline and smear it on the clay piece. Searching for all the crevices, the spots inside elbows, the smooth underside of a chin, the detail of ears, all along the bodies of these animated black people, almost always looking stoic with the blunt glare of a people learning every day to suffer and to stand it well. He would feel the shape of women's thighs, the round of buttocks, the clefts, the dip of the spine at the back. And while he was doing that, Aunt Josephine would mix the Plaster of Paris in a large plastic bucket that she tucked between her legs like a drum. Her arms would fall deep into the warm fluid and turn and then rise out, coated with the brilliant white of the mixture.

"Ready, ready?" she asked Kofi. "Make sure you get everything, okay?"

When he was finished, he nodded to his aunt. She dragged the bucket to the piece and began to scoop up the wet plaster to cover the clay. Kofi joined her. The plaster was always warm, warmer than he expected.

"The chemicals," Aunt Josephine explained. "Chemicals."

They worked slowly, piling the plaster onto the clay until it vanished into an ugly mountain of white.

"There is one good thing about being an artist, Kofi. One good thing. It is with you all the time. You make things. You make things and that is something that won't go away from you. You know that feeling, that feeling when you make something and it stands there, and it looks like something made, and you know you made it. That is a privilege, honey. I mean, you could be the biggest wutliss man in the world, you could be a useless mother, you could be nothing, but in that moment you have something magic. Like when you make a song, and you hear the song, and the song starts to come into you. Now, if you ask somebody what is the value of a song, they will say nothing. But sing them the song, and they start to cry. They start to cry because it is something so deep inside them that they don't know what it is. You are an artist, Kofi. That is all you have, really. So you can laugh and sometimes feel good in yourself. Sometimes that is all we need."

While they waited for the plaster to harden, Aunt Josephine poured a glass of wine for herself. She would put a little in a cup for Kofi. They sat there not talking while she sipped the wine. The room smelled sweet with the thick fermentation of wine. Aunt Josephine occasionally touched the plaster.

"You feel the heat? Feel it. It is shaping the beauty."

Kofi touched the plaster with his palm and felt the heat. The thing was like a living being.

After a while, the plaster now firm, she pried open the mold at the clay wall that ran over the sculpting. She never allowed him to do this part. She pulled apart the plaster with care until she had two molds in her hands. Then she examined the smooth inside of the molds, stained with the residue of the clay and the streaky Vaseline.

"This will stand you in better stead than any stupid O-levels!" Aunt Josephine said.

When Umberto was sick, she did not bother waking Kofi, and would come out to the studio alone. Umberto seemed to spend his nights awake, coughing. He slept in the daytime. At night, whenever he grew quiet, or when she could not stand being around his pain, she went into the garage. She worked. She drank. She smoked.

One night Kofi saw the glow of a low orange lamp spilling into the kitchen. He had come out for some water. It was about 3:00 in the morning. The house was silent—

as silent as old houses could be. He walked to the door and looked into the garage. Aunt Josephine was silhouetted in this orange glow from a naked lamp—the shade was tossed to one side. She was working furiously. She was not doing clay work, she was chipping aggressively at a cylindrical piece of red wood. The chips burst away from her chisel and hammer. Around her bare feet on the floor was a carpet of red specks of wood. He watched her working at this strange *bas relief*, the body of an angel, skeletal, defined only by the rack of ribs and the hollow cheeks of its face. The body was somehow framed in a box—a casket. Yet the creature was not resigned. It was rising from the box even though its legs—a roughly outlined spread of scratches and gouges—seemed rooted to it. There was flight. She was chipping at the bark, the casket, which was like a barge—a kind of funeral barge. The figure was dead, and yet eerie in its strange aliveness.

He stood there and watched her. He could hear her breathing. She was panting, groaning at each hammer hit. The groans would turn into gentle hums and coaxings, as if she was trying to usher in the shape of the wood. Her whole body—that thin frame covered by a loose silk shift that shimmered its floral indulgence every time she moved—focused on the task. The strap on her shoulder fell, revealing her spotted back, the muscles working in that compact and efficient way. She leaned to one side to look and he saw the way her calf muscles flexed and relaxed, twitching.

She stopped and drank from a coffee mug. She was not drinking coffee. The half-empty wine bottle refracted green light onto the floor by her feet.

Kofi stood watching for as long as he could. Then he walked to his room. He wrote it all down. Then he made a song.

Umberto died the next afternoon.

Kofi played the song for her. She would ask him to sing it every night for a month. Now, when he went to visit, he had to sing for her. It was their simple ritual.

He stood in the garage remembering the image of this woman working at the wood, fighting it, taming it. He loved her. Sometimes he imagined her dead. He could not imagine what would happen when she went.

She was talking to Keisha now, he knew. Telling her everything. He was not sure what he hoped would happen, but it felt like the only thing he could do.

"Kofi was born at midmorning in the Koloboo Hospital in Accra, Ghana, on February 7, 1968. His mother was annoyed that he had come when he did. She already had the tickets to travel to New York to have him, but he had insisted. While she was driving to the airport, the pains started. She said she was all right—that is what she told his father, a Ghanaian. You see, she left that white man in no time at all for a native. 'My Mandingo,' she used to call him. And virile! She was pregnant in no time. But he was a nice man. He was so patient and so cooperative that he was willing to accept that his first child was not going to be born in Ghana. But she started to howl with pain. At each contraction she would order his father to turn the car around and take her to the hospital. He would stop the car on the motorway and turn it around. Then she would stop him again. The man was so confused, so nervous. She did that to people, to men. I have seen it for myself. I think eventually she lost that knack. She ended up with a bit of a fool. A short noisy man who has no charm, no grace. A stiff with a big mouth. But she had her day.

"It is so funny—I want to laugh every time I tell this story, not because it is a funny story, but because of the way Stella told me the story. She told it to me while holding Kofi in her arms, seeming like she might accidentally drop him on the ground. She was never comfortable with him, with holding him, with feeding him. She had just gotten back from America with him. Come to Jamaica for some R&R, she said. But she came to drop him off. 'I am not cut out for this mother thing. He cries a lot.' Can you believe that? So she dropped him off at my parents'. They couldn't manage Kofi. So guess who kept him? She said that she hoped that the child-rearing instincts would grow on her, but they didn't. The best part of having her son, she said, was the adventure and confusion around the delivery. It was all downhill after that. She was too much. You should hear her tell the story. I can see everything now. It is funny.

"In between those contractions, she was screaming that she needed to be put on the plane this blasted minute, because she was going to have her child over the Atlantic rather than in that godforsaken country.

"Of course, things were hard in Ghana at the time. There was a coup working itself out there, for heaven's sake. Stella coped with it her own way. She went on with her drinking and carousing, big-bellied and all, as if nothing had happened.

"So, Keisha, can you imagine this? They are in Ghana, a coup is raging, and what does she want? She wants to go and have her child in America."

She laughed loudly. Keisha smiled. She wanted to hear more.

"But you know contractions. Or maybe you don't. Hot, my dear. Hot like fire. They come closer, they start to rip at every piece of good sense you mighta have, so you just can't tell whether you coming or going. And so, on February 7, twenty-nine years ago, Kofi came howling into the world. He was bundled into the car three days later, put on the plane, and transported with his mother to a brownstone in Brooklyn. That did not last very long. They left soon after to come to Jamaica.

"But that was not the only problem, you see. Story really come to bump when people started to talk about Kofi's pigmentation, my dear. You see, Kofi was proving to be a lot darker than anyone expected him to be, and that never please some of her family. Me, I couldn't care less, but you must understand that this family puts a premium on light skin. All right? That is how we are. So they had high hopes for this boy. High, high hopes. After all, she had told us that she was living with a white man in Accra. But Kofi's father was not white. So when they came to expect a lighter child, and Kofi showed up, they were upset because they now felt that Kofi's mother had been cheating on Kofi's father, the white man, and this was just not acceptable.

"It is hard when you born into that kind of disappointment. It wasn't his fault, but he was a disappointment, no matter. God bless them and rest their souls, but my parents were a backward set of people, you understand. So I kept him. Infected him with my madness, but there are worse things in life. There are."

She stopped and drank deeply. Then she rested her head back and closed her eyes.

"I am tired," she said. Her voice was far away. "Please call Mary."

Keisha got up and hurried to the kitchen. Mary came out slowly and stood over the old woman.

"Miss Josephine? Miss Josephine, you want me to call Kofi?" Mary asked.

"I'll get him," Keisha said quickly. She started toward the kitchen but realized that she did not know where Kofi was.

"Him in the garage. Go through the kitchen," Mary said. As Keisha walked out, she heard Mary's voice, soothing, "You drink too much of this thing. Too much this time. And you talk too much. Hush, hush, Kofi soon come . . ."

He was standing in the middle of the garage when Keisha found him. The room was in darkness. He followed Keisha through the kitchen as if he had been expecting this call. He said nothing. It did not seem to bother him when Keisha said she thought it was serious.

Mary was wiping Josephine's forehead when they walked in.

"The guitar is behind the kitchen door," Josephine said, pointing.

Kofi walked back and returned with the guitar. He sat on a footstool in front of his aunt. Mary stepped back to the kitchen door and watched.

Kofi started to play the guitar. It was out of tune. He fiddled with the knobs.

"I like it slightly off," Aunt Josephine said. "Nothing is ever in perfect tune. Nothing."

He played a plaintive minor key but the progressions were not sudden or unexpected—they built up in a series of rises and sweetly settled into a mellow resolution. He began to sing softly, looking at his aunt as he did so.

*This candle's flame is lifting*
*heavenward, and you have come to work*
*through the night, the tears*
*turning all into a blur,*
*Muting all pain in mist*
*Muting all pain in mist*
*Muting all pain in mist.*

His voice seemed to cup the words and pour them out gently, slowly. He almost spoke the words, and yet there was a distinct melody. The refrain was a tender, surreal articulation of loss.

*You wince, take the pain*
*Like you take your sorrow*
*You wince, take your pain*
*Like you take your sorrow.*

The bridge then lifted him upwards—the words created a space that Keisha could physically imagine. The trees, the sound of knocking, the strange enticement of night.

*In the trees, the ring*
*of metal on metal on wood,*
*carries for miles.*
*Around your feet, the scatterings*
*of a dream being whittled.*

He returned to the chorus that began the song. Aunt Josephine was mouthing the words as she nodded. Kofi smiled at her. She looked at him and smiled back.

The last strum hung in the air and they sat in silence. In that moment, Keisha realized how far away she was from this man. Yet she saw things that she had never really seen. He was crying and smiling.

Aunt Josephine closed her eyes, but raised her hand to him. He came closer to her and she touched his face, the same gesture that she had made when he walked in.

"I will miss you more than you will miss me. Imagine that," she said. "I am such a vain woman, eh? I can't get over a song about me. I am such a vain woman."

Mary walked into the room. "You gwine haffe go now, Kofi. She tiaad."

"Yes, yes," Kofi said. He looked at Keisha, but whatever he was trying to say was unclear. "I will come by and see you soon, Aunt Josephine, okay?"

"Yes, son. Yes," Aunt Josephine said. Mary stood beside her waiting.

Kofi put the guitar down and kissed his aunt, then he nodded to the door.

"It was good meeting you," Keisha said as she backed out.

"Sorry I couldn't finish the story, but Kofi can do that . . ." Josephine said weakly.

"You said much. Thanks."

Mary went inside quickly and came back with two large plastic containers that were misted with heat under their tight lids. "Oxtail," she said, handing the container to Keisha.

They walked out into the backyard, which was growing cool and dark in the sunset.

"She has to take her medication. She don't want nobody there when she taking it. Proud woman," Kofi said. Then he walked ahead at a steady pace. Keisha had to hurry to keep up. She was panting when they got to the car.

Keisha ate as they drove. The thick stew of tender oxtail and butter beans, sweet strips of orange and black plantains, soggy lettuce and tomato slices topped with bits of sweat-pimpled diced avocado, lay on a bed of rice. The food was peppery but also rich with thyme and fresh cilantro. Keisha ate quickly. She offered Kofi a spoonful. He shook his head staring at the road.

For a while the only sound was her chewing and sucking on the bone of the oxtail. Then Kofi spoke.

"She reminds me of what I am. You understand that? She reminds me of the good things I am. She always takes me for what I am. I mean, I can be a worthless person with her. That is what I mean. And when she gone, I won't have that. I will be just a piece. I will be the piece that you see, and the piece that somebody else see. But not the full piece. We don't really get along, you know. No sah. And I don't see her much. Not really. Because she really can get on you nerves. Really. But I just need to know that she deh 'bout, you know? That she around. That if I want I can just call her up and she will hear me out. Straight. Now if she go, I don't know . . ." He stopped talking.

Keisha wanted to comfort or reassure him. In a way she knew what he was saying, but she did not understand it fully. Nothing in the way Kofi and his aunt had dealt with each other meshed with what he was saying now. Nothing, except that song. The way Kofi sang it tenderly, and the way the woman touched him on his face. Beyond that, they seemed like two separate people with a strange shared history.

"I suppose you will survive." The moment she said this she regretted it.

He said nothing in response. He just kept driving.

"Does she have any children?" Keisha asked, trying to shift the conversation.

"Who?"

"Josephine."

"She had three—stillborn. She miscarried also—twice. But the stillbirths nearly drove her mad."

"Oh dear," Keisha said.

The sky was bleeding red and bright orange into the plate of blue above. Everything was crumbling into flame—the stern stability of the afternoon replaced by the dappled disquiet of sunset.

"So you are in touch with your mother at all?"

"My mother is dead," Kofi replied, almost surprised that she did not know this.

"She didn't tell me that," Keisha said with some embarrassment. "I didn't know she died. I thought she was still in the States."

"No, she dead. Years now. Years now."

"And your father?"

"Well, him wasn't really a father, you know. He lives in Ghana. Nothing to it. We met once. When he was working as a diplomat at the U.N. in New York. Nice guy, but a complete stranger. He looked, well, he looked like a Ghanaian, I suppose. Not terribly tall, a bit of a belly, huge muscular arms and shoulders, but other than that, very normal, you know. He asked me if I needed anything . . . I said no. It was enough. He just looked at me, and then he said, 'Sometimes thing are just strange that way, you see.' That was all he said. I am not even sure what he meant. But that was enough. Nice man, but it's a different country and my mother was a short thing for him. You understand. Nothing much there."

"So you don't feel the need to—"

"No," he said sharply.

Keisha stayed quiet a moment, then spoke. "You asked her to tell me all of this?"

"Yeah."

"So why couldn't you tell me yourself?"

"Sometimes it's hard to talk to you."

"Hard?"

"Yeah. Sometimes. Or maybe it's me."

"No, you said it was me." She was getting angry. "So this was supposed to help us? I get to know how screwed up you are, and that way I can deal with the way you behave sometimes? Like that?"

"I wanted you to meet Aunt Josephine. She is important to me."

"That's right. That's right. Okay." She crossed her arms and stared into the road.

"Don't make a big thing out of this."

She nodded. He looked at her a few times. She stared ahead. Then she spoke.

"There is nothing screwed up about your life, Kofi. We all have some mess, you know? Nothing so special about your life, at all."

# Chapter Twelve

He wants to tell someone his secret. He wants to tell someone that he would rather sit in a small room where it is warm and where the light is good and eat simple meals like *fufu* and groundnut soup with fish and beef, or some bread and bits of chicken, or slices of fruit, or chocolate, or drink something common like water or juice—simple juice—or laugh a laugh of nonsense at the sit-coms on television.

He wants to say that when he wants to rest he remembers the times when he would take a bus and travel into the green embrace of St. Mary and walk that slow hot walk along the blindingly white limestone and crystallized pink marl path that cut through the thick groves of cocoa trees, to that bare hill, where a house, a simple house with a leaning coconut tree and a scattering of chickens, stood. And he would go into the house and they would tell him hello and let him sit and stare into the mountain while he smelled the fish frying. They would put a plate of fried fish and bread on the table for him and a glass of milk. And he would feast on this with the reverence of a communion meal. They would let him think that at least here he would not have to worry about the pain in his groin, the woman at his door in the early morning come for her embrace. He would not need to think about the moment he felt to take her and press her against the wall and throw her back on the bed, and lift her skirt and eat hungrily and brutally at her softness—

how he wanted to frighten her so she would understand that the flame of desire she seemed to want could burn into a madness that she would not understand.

He wants to forget how he fought to hold his body back and how he pulled away and how terrible he felt for thinking it and for feeling his sex swell for thinking it.

Here in the hills, at sunset, before the last bus to the city, he can even pray and read the Bible, and wonderful revelations appear to him, ways of seeing the world.

He wants to tell the secret of his simplicity, his normalness, and the fact that sometimes he thinks of his name as Musician and wants to tell them to stop calling him that. Because he is afraid that he is not quite that, that by saying he is, by letting them call him that, he will wake up one day and find it all a lie, and find that he has built a dream on a lie and that he has to start all over again, making himself again.

He wants them to stop calling him a musician before he starts to believe it, because sometimes he believes that he is a musician. No, sometimes he believes that he is a Messiah. He calls himself Joseph in his head sometimes. He calls himself Bob in his head sometimes. Especially when the pressure is on. Then he starts to believe that he can make his body do the things that great musicians do. Then he is a great musician. Then he is reincarnate. Then he is the receptacle for the spirit of the *rhygin* prophet. That is when he panics. So he runs to the hills to stay away from himself and his dream and this strange fantasy. It is so compelling that sometimes he believes he knows what it feels like to die, to die with cancer devouring your body.

He is not a rural man, not a country boy, does not understand the seasons, the harvests. He just knows that he is afraid of the masks he is beginning to believe in.

But here, far from that place, from that memory, he trembles with uncertainty, and he wants to say it in simple words so someone will understand. He wants to say that he is now sorry for his arrogance, for standing before people and play-acting to relish the accolades of the crowds. He knows that it is all play-acting, and that inside he is a simple fool who likes to play with words and likes to make women wet with his voice and is too afraid to even reach and touch them if they are wet.

He wants to tell the secret of his fear, the secret of his normalness, and he is afraid to tell the secret because he is afraid that she will say that she knew it all along and that his acting, and her praise and the way she would come to be with him, travel to this country to be with him, all the time was simply a game, too, an indulgence.

This is the diary of a simpler man than the man he parades around the world. And when they say they love him, he does not believe them.

This is his secret. This is what he wants to talk about, but he is always running.

☙

For reasons Keisha could not understand, Kofi elected to grow silent rather than try to explain himself. He was awake to meet the clean sun at dawn, standing in the wash of pink and orange light. And then at dusk he stood to watch it fade. In between he mostly sat silently, staring out. She only saw the dark of his back and heard the inscrutable silence of his thinking.

He would not listen to the radio or watch television.

"That stuff will depress you, man," he said. "Depress the hell out of you."

She asked about his family.

"Treachery," he said.

But she knew better. She knew that his family was Aunt Josephine and that there was more than treachery there.

She also knew now that Kofi was rich. Not that he had money, but that he had grown up in a house that made him understand the meaning of wealth. He was familiar enough with wealth to be able to live as if he were poor. She was beginning to feel that she and Kofi had very little in common. They came not just from different countries but from different worlds. She wanted to rejoice in this fact—the fact of his wealth—but she did not know how to react to it. She did not know how to understand herself and Kofi now.

She remembered his warning in New York: "After a while they realize they can't be satisfied with me, with what I can give."

A week after the visit to Aunt Josephine, Keisha asked him why he was hardly speaking to her. They were sitting on the concrete porch at the back of the house, looking into a brilliant blue sky. They were shaded by a large lime tree, thick with its small dark leaves.

"Sometimes I think it's the heat, you know. Sucks you up. Thinking too hard makes you tired. So you stop thinking," he said.

"You want me to start asking for more, right?"

"What you mean?"

"You want me to start saying that I am not feeling you, not touching you," she said slowly, trying to get it right. "Then you will tell me that I want too much."

"You think too hard, baby."

"Maybe. But you are fading. You know what I mean?"

"You want to go out and enjoy the place, Keisha. You cyaan expect me to make it enjoyable. You have to do for yourself." He spoke with his eyes closed.

"I came here with you."

"Yeah. You came with me. True. But I come to rest," he said.

"Tell me a story, Kofi. A nice story."

He chuckled softly.

"Tell me about the women you were with here. The Jamaican women. You had a girlfriend here, right? Where is she? What happened with her?"

"I don't have a memory, Keisha. I forget things. They leave my mind. Trauma, you know? All of us living here live in trauma. When you live through all them years with political violence and killing, you live with trauma. Some things are best forgotten."

He was making it all up. She could not tell right away, but it was becoming a pattern. His silences were becoming a way of creating mystery. They were always coupled with strange enigmatic statements, comments about wanting to fly, about his deep fears. The more she asked, the more he closed himself off from her.

Soon she was not sure what she was doing there with him. She was growing angry.

Keisha was not surprised by the fact of his withdrawal. She was used to this. Troy was a perfect example of that pattern of male behavior. He would withdraw into his own world of bitter reserve and grow angry and violent when Keisha tried to break into it. She had seen something of that flare of anger in her father. He had been a tender man, but when he withdrew, it was with a fierce desire not to be pursued. One day he withdrew and never returned. He died withdrawn.

With Troy, withdrawal was part of a regular pattern, part of his way of "handling" her, of keeping her off balance. It was part of his way of thinking, a way that he once explained quite clearly to her: "You women get all soft when you know a man is tender for you, you get so that you want him to get soft, and then when he gets all soft, you the first to call him a fucking bitch. You the first one to say he ain't a man. You know it. You crying now, you getting on like you hate me when I tell you what the fuck is what, but I know inside your head you saying to yourself, *Yeah, he a real man. He a real man.*"

But he had never been tender, never given himself to her. She knew this, and in some part of her she believed that maybe it was good that he didn't, because it kept her straight, made her not fall too deeply into him.

He was a brutish man, a man who would kill given half the chance. Above all, he stayed in control. He was a man of simple and basic emotions. Keisha had learned not to try and dig deeper. Whenever she did, she had encountered such a vicious anger that she withdrew immediately. Soon she had come to appreciate the simplicity of what he gave her—it made her think less of the pathology inherent in her staying with him.

Kofi was different. She knew it from the way she felt him dissolving emotionally when he was inside her. Instead of feeling revulsion, as she had feared she would, she wanted to hold him closer. He had cried that night in New York and she experienced a rare feeling of safety with a man. He had talked about himself, about his life, about his desires, about his confusions. And then he cried. She softened to that. Maybe that was all that it took, but it was enough.

So seeing him now—silent, inscrutable, assuming the posture of a man desperate to hide his feelings, desperate to not seem vulnerable—she was confused. She was also angry with herself for hoping. She wanted to take him back to the room in New York, back to the closed world where everything else was shut out and their bodies were there alone. She wanted to make it happen again. But they were far from there. Kofi was behaving like a man, and she was angry at herself for thinking that perhaps he was something else.

Yet his tenderness was still there. He was becoming not hardened and bitter but pathetic—that same soft man who Troy had spoken about. Was she the one who had changed, who had grown tired of the softness in Kofi, the vulnerability that she knew was there?

She tried.

"Something is bothering you—"

"Life hard."

"I want us to talk."

"Uh-uh."

"Do you regret bringing me here?"

"Uh-uh."

"You don't want to talk."

"It's not that. But . . ."

"But what?"

"Nothing, nothing. Talk, talk—"

"Sometimes—" She stopped. Looked at him. He was somewhere else. He looked back at her but did not seem to see her. She could find nothing else to say. She got up and walked inside, where it was cooler and darker. She heard him starting to sing.

*Every morning I get up*
*I sip my cup*
*My eyes get red*
*No one to help me . . .*

She listened. His voice waned, then he stopped, as if he could not remember the lyrics.

She could not penetrate.

# Chapter Thirteen

She went to the funeral dressed in black.

They drove along the same road through the hills of St. Andrew to Aunt Josephine's house. This time the road was dusty, and the few weeks without rain seemed to turn the leaves pale to an olive muteness. It was already dry in Kingston and everything green had turned the same color. She felt more relaxed out here with the open blue sky and the mountains that closed around them.

This time Kofi passed the sharp bend in the road that led up the dirt track to the back of the house and continued until they came to a large gate. They crossed the cattle guard and drove up the white gravel road through an avenue of trees. They pulled into the circular driveway that led to the house. The lawn was filled with men and women all dressed in white. Keisha could have mistaken this for a strange cricket match, like the ones she had seen at the Prison Oval in Spanish Town. But there were women here, and the people were moving around talking, drinking, in a whirl of activity. The sunlight on white was blinding. They all looked as if they belonged in a story book.

Kofi parked the car and got out at once. Keisha took her time.

"I didn't want to come, you know," she said. "I am dressed wrong."

"I have to give my respects. Think about me for once, nuh?"

"Don't start with me, Kofi."

He walked off, and melted in the mass of bodies. She followed slowly.

They were all the same light shade of brown—a strange muddy kind of brown that she realized was the same shade as Kofi, though he was slightly darker because he stayed in the sun more. They were pale. An insipid kind of pale. And all the men had facial hair so closely trimmed that they appeared to have faces of two shades, dark and ochre, rather than beards and moustaches. They all had wet, red, pouting and obscene lips.

She found something perversely sexual, even incestuous, about the way they laughed. They never opened their mouths wide but simply spread their lips to make small o's with these lips, through which drippings of fatty sounds passed. They all wore straw hats with yellow silk bands. The women's bands ribboned out in the breeze. In fact, everyone there, including Kofi, was dressed in something white or cream-colored.

The women wore long flowing skirts and yellow scarves and pushed their bosoms forward, straining the tightly hugging dresses. They flirted with their open bosoms, and the men with their little small o's watched and laughed. The men wore slacks of white or cream and white long-sleeved shirts buttoned to the wrists and right up to the neck. They all wore yellow or cream cravats that gave the gathering a look from another century.

Four women, older and matronly, directed the waiters and servers. The women wore sharply pressed white blouses and full Victorian skirts—black, stern, and sensible. Keisha watched the waiters move through the white-clad people with such grace that the whole thing seemed choreographed. The tall, severe presence of Mary dominated the proceedings. She stood at the top of the stairs leading to the front door of the house, her arms folded across her chest. She rarely moved.

On the lawn, the family moved around the white coffin as if it, too, were a guest. They talked to the dead woman in the coffin and they drank toasts to her. The world that Keisha saw here was like none she had seen in Jamaica and none that she had ever expected to see.

She felt out of place, angry at Kofi for not telling her to wear white. She felt marked, tawdry, and very much like the alien she was.

It was a grand fête. The food was copious and the drinking astounding. Men and women imbibed with equal gusto, but no one seemed hopelessly drunk. Then they danced. They danced something they called a *quadrille*—spinning and spinning, then prancing and promenading in rigid symmetrical patterns across the lawn. They danced to trilling *Mento* music—a fiddle leading the way.

Keisha stood and watched it all, and then fixed her eyes on one of the more mature-looking women at the serving table. Keisha was struck by her high cheekbones and broad forehead which made her skin stretch smoothly over her face. She did not appear to be wearing makeup, and yet her dark face was beautifully textured. She was gorgeous. Keisha began watching the way the woman looked at these people with a peculiar indulgence. It was clear that the woman was removed from them. She kept pushing her hand into a covered basket of chicken and pulling out pieces. She would push a whole wing into her mouth, work her jaws slowly and then quickly, finally producing thin bones from her lips. She ate with such nonchalance.

The woman suddenly rose and shouted up to Mary, "Miss Mary, soon come!"

"Yes, Miss Dorothy," Mary said, stepping forward to take over.

This was Kofi's Aunt Dorothy. Keisha had not met her yet, but she was a strange presence in Kofi's life—an explanation, Keisha was sure, for many things.

As the woman started to move to the back of the house, Keisha followed, not knowing exactly why.

It was getting late and she could barely follow the dark form of this woman as she moved up a path along a gradient in the backyard and then vanished completely. Keisha followed and found the woman squatting beside a hibiscus bush. She was urinating.

"Oh, sorry," Keisha said, turning away.

"Sorry fe what? Piss, piss, tha's all," the woman said.

"I am sorry." Keisha started to move away.

"Is a set a mad people, eh?" the woman said, getting up with a groan. Keisha noticed the red panties. "Mad rass, them. Every one a dem is like dat. Dem fuck one anada too much. The only one wid any sense is dat man Kofi, but dem nuh say him mad." She laughed. She was laughing at Keisha. Keisha was sure of it. The woman started back down the hill.

"I see," Keisha said, following.

"Yuh want a bag fe tek some a de food in? Is good food, yuh hear?"

"No . . ."

"All right, me will get one fe yuh. Tek the jerk chicken, it season de mos'. Will last long. The shrimp is some dutty cheap shrimp dem get from God knows where. Dat spoil already . . ." She was moving faster than Keisha expected she could.

She brought a bag full of jerk chicken for Keisha, and told her to get out of that mad family before something "do her." Keisha understood.

* * *

After the interment in the family plot at the back of the house, Keisha made her way down the hill, followed by the family and servants.

She saw Dorothy getting into an expensive car. One of the men, tall, athletic and impeccably dressed, shouted to Dorothy, "You coming to the party at my place?"

"Sure, honey, couldn' miss it for the worl'." Then she turned to Keisha and smiled. "You want to come, too? Blow off the bwai. He is going to be a misery tonight. Come with me. Don't tell him a ting. Someone will tell him you came down with me."

Keisha looked back to see Kofi standing alone on the landing of the house staring toward the grave. She shouted, and when they made eye contact, she indicated that she was going in the car with the woman. Kofi nodded and then turned away.

As if she had not seen any of this, Dorothy kept talking, explaining that Kofi called her aunt even though there was no blood between them. There was history, she said, and sometimes that was more complicated and more important. Dorothy seemed to relish the task of explaining this strange relationship to Keisha. But there was something else, Keisha felt, a quality of control which she could not figure out. Dorothy wanted Keisha to know that she knew things about Kofi that Keisha would never know; things that Keisha would want to know. And Keisha did want to know. Instead of wanting to pull back, she felt she had to know more, to neutralize this woman's power.

The servers, she told Keisha, were all dancers with one of the leading dance companies in the country. Dorothy was their friend. "A patron of the arts," she said. One of the men, the one who had asked about the party earlier, was Toby, a doctor and the choreographer of the company. He had gone to the same school as Kofi. He was several years older than Kofi, but they were all like family, Dorothy said.

Keisha kept looking back to the front door for Kofi. She was worried about him. A part of her wanted to go with this woman to a party, to anywhere other than the dark and humid duplex in Spanish Town where she knew Kofi would be brooding, grieving. But she also wanted to feel that he needed her.

"I take it you are not coming," Dorothy said to Keisha.

"I have to check and see what Kofi is doing, okay?"

"I will give you a minute."

She found Kofi in the garage touching one of Josephine's pieces. He looked up when he saw her, puzzlement on his face. The place was gloomy; she moved close to him so that she could watch his expressions.

"I met your Aunt Dorothy."

"Yes, I notice."

"She is beautiful—it makes sense," she said, trying to draw out a reaction. He had told her that he was close to Dorothy, that they had had "a thing," but that it had been years ago, and "people outgrow these things." She had wanted to know more—details. But before arriving in Jamaica, she had promised herself not to try and work out all of Kofi's old relationships. Yet his nervous irritability, as he rubbed the back of his neck, made her wonder how long they had been lovers.

"She says some friends of hers are having a party and she was wondering if I—I mean, we—would like to go . . ."

"A party."

"Well, a get-together. I don't know."

"I just buried my aunt and you want me to go to a party. What kind of foolishness is that?"

Keisha began to backpedal. "She invited us. I am just passing on a message."

"You want to go?"

"If you need to go home, we should go home. She just asked. I didn't know how you were feeling. Look, she is waiting. I will just go and tell her we are not coming, okay?"

"No, no, man. You can go with her man. That is what yuh want to do . . ."

"I said it's all right, okay?"

She left the garage and met Dorothy at her car. She explained that Kofi was not up to it.

"Yeah, yeah. Anyway, I have a nice place on the North Coast. A small resort thing, eh? Been trying to get Kofi to come and stay there with us, free of cost. But that man sometimes get a funny attitude to me. Proud, you know? But the invitation is open to you, okay? Anytime. This Kingston business will make you a sick person. Jamaica is more than this, okay? You don't want that boy to bring you down. So, see my number here," she said, handing Keisha a card embossed with a gold and black trim. "Call me. I like you, you know. Want to get to know you better." She smiled big even teeth.

Keisha nodded and put the card away. She watched as the car lights appeared and disappeared behind the trees and shrubbery, before they finally vanished from sight.

# Chapter Fourteen

Things deteriorated after the funeral. Kofi withdrew further into himself. Keisha tried to talk, tried to get his mind away from the darkness, but he resented her for it. Keisha found him stranger now.

He spent more time out on the cement porch. For days he would eat nothing but oranges. He dragged a huge sack of oranges to the backyard. He would peel the oranges, littering the floor with long spirals like golden snakes. He sucked the oranges and spat seeds out. He did this to one after the other, rarely stopping, while concentrating on the task of peeling the fruit without breaking the peel. He ate little else. He complained about his stomach but did not listen to her when she mentioned his diet.

The summer holidays had arrived and she was no longer needed at the school. There was still food in the house, and Kofi left money on the table for her, making sure that she did not have to ask. After a while she stopped taking the money and started to rely on her savings. The U.S. currency went a long way in Jamaica. She couldn't accept the money, not when she felt that they weren't really together. She stayed in Kingston more. She had made some friends at the school and spent evenings with them going to clubs or to the Carib Cinema in Cross Roads to see a film. They would drive her back to Spanish Town gladly, despite the hour. Kofi said nothing.

Their love-making had changed. At first, when they had come to Jamaica, during those early weeks when things were fresh and they were still discovering each other, she had liked it. She liked the way he would watch her face, waiting for her orgasm to come on her, waiting patiently for her mouth to open. Once she opened her eyes and saw him staring at her from above, moving his body slowly as if he were trying to coax something out of her, trying to make her react to him, to his ministrations. For an instant she felt as if she were being watched by a voyeur, someone who wanted to exert power, a certain control. She couldn't easily complain, because he would never come before her. And he would never come without her coming. If she did not have an orgasm, if it slipped away, leaving her warm but not quite there, he would stop himself from coming, his penis would grow soft in her, and he would slip it out and lie on his back.

"Why didn't you come?" she asked him once.

"Can't come if you don't come."

"But I like to hear you come, to feel you come," she said. She meant it. It was one of the things that had drawn her to him, the complete abandonment of his orgasm, his helplessness, the breaking down of his body when he fell over her.

"I am just that way. My pleasure is in your pleasure," he said, trying to coax her to try again.

At first this was flattering, but she soon recognized it as a problem. It was more than just her orgasm. It was her arousal. It had to be there for him to be aroused himself. He would not touch her unless she showed some interest, some desire to have him. When she was tired, when she was lying down hoping that he would touch her and convince her body to want him, he would reach for her, touch her, wait a few seconds, and if she did not move, did not turn over and open herself to him, he would roll over and sleep. It was not difficult for him to do that. She grew resentful and started to show no response, just to see how long he could go on like that.

He said nothing. He simply did not act. He would wake in the mornings with an erection and a heavy bladder. She could see it. He would go to the bathroom and shower. One morning she walked into the bathroom and saw him masturbating. He dropped his hands and his head. She tried to laugh but he didn't join her. His silence made what would have been funny awkward, embarrassing. She could have been brazen and said something like, *You need some help with that?* But his almost accusing look intimidated her. She left the bathroom realizing that he was making a statement to her.

The two stopped talking about their sexuality after the incident in the bathroom. Soon they stopped having regular sex. When they did make love, it was fast, fierce, and the orgasms were strong, then suddenly over.

They were quiet. They did not talk. They breathed, rested, and then slept.

Maybe his mind was elsewhere. Maybe he preferred the fantasy of their life, the one he constructed in the stories he liked to tell. Maybe this was all that made sense to him, the fantasy and not the reality. Now, faced with the reality, faced with her, he could not construct her, and this was killing something in him. It made him quiet. He could not make up stories for her. And she noticed.

"Tell me a story about us," she said to him one afternoon. "Like the stories you told me when we were in my apartment."

"We not no story, Keisha," Kofi replied. "We is this. Nutting else."

"Then tell me about *this*. Make it sound tender." She was growing angry.

"Keisha, res' it, all right?"

"Tell me a story, Kofi. What is wrong? What is wrong? You know too much now, too much to make it up, to make it look good?"

"I am just tired. That's all. Okay? Tired."

"I know you are dealing with her dying and all that. I know. But why do you have to carry it on your own? I mean, at least talk to me about it. Can't you do that?"

"Baby, I am just tired, you know. Tired." He spoke without feeling.

"Yes, yes. Tired." She walked out of the room.

For a long time she had allowed herself to think of this relationship as something special, as something that was beyond the hard scrutiny that her family had taught her to give her life. When she first moved to Jamaica with Kofi, she would have had no trouble explaining her decision to her relatives. They would disagree—but love, or the thought of love, had a way of making those pragmatic considerations fade. Five months into her visit, she was starting to realize that she would not want to talk to her relatives now. She would have no good answers. Her life with Kofi was becoming habit, and she knew it.

If she told this story to her relatives in Ridgeway, they would laugh at her. Their pragmatism was something that had kept them all safe, even if bitter and a little lonely. Men had to show their worth, not just in love, not just in the bed, but in materialistic ways. A foolish woman allowed a man to sleep with her without having anything to show for it. Only a foolish woman wasted her life on a man if he did not have the goods. The code was clearly understood by these women. It did not stop them from making mistakes, from falling in with a man who was useless. But those were failures, and they understood and sympathized with one another when it happened to one of them. Keisha knew that she had followed Kofi into a world that made no sense. He had money, but she didn't care too much about money—and for all she knew, his family was broke. He was a musician, but there was no glamour in it because he was not into the glamour. She couldn't even claim to be obsessed with him. She liked Kofi—sometimes she thought she loved him—but most of the time these days, she was asking herself what she was doing there.

Leaving, however, seemed like declaring defeat too easily. A part of her was certain that Kofi would snap out of it. She allowed herself to think that he was focused on his songwriting, and trying to work through his aunt's passing. She did not want to abandon him like that. And the more she thought about it, the more she had to admit she was enjoying Jamaica—the friends she was making, the energy of the city, and her growing confidence in being a settled person, a part of the country and not a hapless tourist. The challenge was one she had embraced and now she felt she was winning.

Kofi nonetheless remained in deep silence for weeks. Keisha hovered on the edges of his gloom, uncertain about how and when to step in. She knew it was unfair of her to expect him to get over his loss in a short time, but she wanted him to at least talk to her, allow her to grieve with him.

She could hear her Aunt Rose's voice in her head. *This is just screwing, baby. That ain't worth wrecking your life over. That ain't worth offending the Lord Jesus over, sweetheart. You know that when you let them hot feelings guide you, you gonna end up far from God, far from your dignity, and all messed up. You know that. You got to pray, girl.*

Aunt Rose had said this to Keisha during the years with Troy in Columbia. During the beatings and the affairs he was having that everybody knew about. Leonora once said, "That man must have the biggest dick in the world to make you keep going back." The logic had to be reduced to humor. She did keep going back. She would go back and then run to the church and pray for her soul. But she kept going back. Hoping. Aunt Rose called it sin and foolish. The rest of her relatives—the women—commiserated, but they called it sorry, real sorry. That is what they would say about her and Kofi now. Keisha knew that. She also knew that she would find it hard to argue with them.

She resisted calling Leonora or Aunt Rose because she knew what the conversation would be like. But she needed to talk, and since she had made a rule that she would not talk to her teaching friends about the details of her life, Dorothy's calls seemed like the open door that she was looking for.

At first Dorothy asked to speak to Kofi. Those conversations ended quickly. Kofi grunted through the calls. Then Kofi stopped taking any calls. Dorothy, unfazed, said she would talk to Keisha, then, instead of that miserable madman.

"I know he must be madding you with the silence. Hush. We will talk." Dorothy laughed.

Dorothy seemed determined to befriend Keisha, to create a space in which she, Dorothy, could talk freely about Kofi and his family. Keisha enjoyed having someone to talk to. She did recognize that Dorothy's pattern was always to be in control. But Keisha felt no strong attachment to Kofi's family, so she listened. She defended Kofi when things got out of hand, but she listened and enjoyed the distraction. Dorothy painted a picture of a lively and hip party scene in Ocho Rios. It was the world that Keisha had thought she was entering when she decided to go to Jamaica.

Dorothy always repeated her offer to Keisha. After a while it became absurd to say no. Kofi was not speaking. Keisha was bored. She reminded herself that she had decided to come for a holiday. She was going to have a holiday.

"I told you, that woman is a vampire. You don' know that?" Kofi shouted at her when she mentioned that she was thinking of going. He was stretched out on the sofa, staring at the ceiling. Around him, on scattered newspapers, were the guts of several oranges, the large kitchen knife, still slick with the wetness of the oranges, a scattering of orange seeds, and the entwining of orange rinds. The room smelled tart with acid.

"Well, it's not about her, okay? I could use a break. You are too busy with yourself to . . ." She paused, trying to control herself. "Look, can we not argue about this? I want to go. I would love for you to come. But if you can't come, I am still going. I need a break. I really do. It might help us."

"It's a free country," he said, and closed his eyes.

If he had asked her to stay, she probably would have. She wanted him to say that he needed her around. It occurred to her that she had convinced herself that despite his coldness and distance, he really, deep down, wanted her around. But now he said nothing.

Keisha made sure to call Dorothy in front of Kofi. Dorothy said she would pick her up the next day. Kofi said nothing to her from that moment until she left with Dorothy the next afternoon. When Keisha said goodbye to him, he nodded and grunted. That was the most he would offer.

# Chapter Fifteen

OCHO RIOS, JAMAICA

The sensation of passing from one world to another hit her when she traveled across the mountains and into the valley and densely forrested foothills that opened out onto the North Coast.

From the dry brilliance of Mount Diablo, the entry into the soft belly of Fern Gully was a revelation. The dense vegetation darkened everything around them, and the breeze that filled the van was cool, almost cold. The road was slippery with the moisture of this patch of rain forest. She could see the spray of ferns catching the strangled light all along the roadsides. The earth was dark. The floor of the thick forest was mossy, a rich almost otherworldly green. Keisha felt she had left one country and entered another unexpected place. Her excitement about leaving Kofi in Spanish Town and coming to see the rest of the island was total now. The van swerved around the hairpin turns, a meandering coil of road with the shimmering white line, thick and uncompromising, running through the center. This was Fern Gully. The road was narrow and other vehicles passed so closely that you could see the gawking faces of the people riding by. Where the road widened periodically, vendors had set up shop selling fruit, juices, and trinkets.

Keisha kept looking around, feeling the moisture in the air, enjoying the sudden sense of pleasure in the way the temperature had changed. But she did not expect the vision that would open up to her at the end of this deep valley. The incline toward light was gradual. The gully grew darkest just before the sudden light of the coast. The brilliant shimmer of the blue Caribbean Sea winked through the almond and sea grape trees. The sea was impossible to Keisha—the light, the blue, the way the bias of the horizon sat steady and almost painted before her. She could smell that salt taste that she was familiar with in Myrtle Beach and in Charleston. But she was not prepared for the postcard aqua glaze of the sea. The island was a new place to her.

They drove through Ocho Rios, its streets choked with tourist vans and tour buses, hustling trades people, and children in uniforms. She realized then that this was the Jamaica she had secretly wanted to find. This was the Jamaica that she had dreamt of when Kofi said she should come home with him. Now it was here before her and she was breathing it all in, sighing, amazed.

The rhythms of resort life appealed to her immediately. Dorothy wanted her to enjoy this kind of existence, and Keisha was unable to resist it. She accepted the gift, relished it. The horror stories of murder and car accidents in the newspapers, the women standing on the corners in Spanish Town lamenting some dead relative or son in jail, the long line of people standing in the sun outside the hospital prepared to spend the whole day waiting to see a doctor, all those things vanished for her. She was flying from it all.

The room was airy and Dorothy sat facing the sea, her large full arms on the table, open. Keisha had forgotten how striking her face was, with its wonderfully expressive nostrils, wide but languid eyes, and full lips. Dorothy had her head tied in a blue and gold bandana, and she wore gold all over—gold necklaces, a clanging disturbance of gold bracelets, and a golden nose stud. She liked her makeup forceful—a thick layering of silver and gold eye shadow, a brilliant red smear of lipstick, and a somewhat untidily applied stroke of rouge on both cheeks. There was something assured and calming about her though—the matronly manner of an old family friend who was more liberal than your parents, who talked candidly about everything—the aunt who supplied condoms and arranged abortions. Her gestures were always unhurried so she seemed to float around in her wide flowing dresses.

Keisha was enjoying the large bowl of pea soup that had been set before her, but her attention was focused on Dorothy, who scooped spoons full of thick broth, chunks of yam, and strips of tender beef into her large spoon and delicately put the food between her lips, chewing with grace and pleasure. The soup was peppery, but you would never know looking at Dorothy—she did not sweat like Keisha was sweating, and she did not drink from the long glass of water that sat before her.

"Pepper is good for the spleen, child. Eat it. You will get used to it," she said between chews. "Unoo black Americans like to be Africans until the heat come, eh?" She laughed softly. She kept eating and then talking. She talked slowly. Keisha realized that this woman had brought her here to impress her. Dorothy had established a power dynamic in the room, and her loaded silences and calculated slow manner reminded Keisha of Kofi.

And she was worried about what Dorothy thought of her.

At first she was confident that Dorothy was concerned for her safety and happiness. The woman did not seem terribly fond of Kofi, and her warnings were clear—get away from the man, he is mad. That was her refrain when Keisha first called her to talk about coming to the resort. By the time they had been around each other for a day, she had stopped giving advice and begun to ask questions. Now she was starting to make speeches. Keisha had initially felt comfortable in Dorothy's company, but increasingly she felt on edge. Dorothy's tone changed—she was teasing more, laughing more at Keisha's complaints about heat and mosquitoes and the power outages. Then she was growing more aggressive, more impatient with Keisha.

"You have psychological problems," Dorothy said one afternoon three days after she arrived at the resort. "Yes, big problems, and you and that madman cyaan live. That is the simple trut'. Sometime I have to tell myself dat you don' belong here. That is true, too. Yes, you might be black, but you is American first . . ."

"I feel at home here," Keisha said feebly.

"Stop chat foolishness, girl. How you gwine feel at home here? How? You mighta dead hereso, you know? You ready for that? You ready fe buried hereso?" She looked across at Keisha. What Keisha heard was anger, but when she looked into Dorothy's face, she saw something like mischief—a twisted smile on the woman's face. "You think you gwine meet anybody weh know yuh when you go under? Deat' is a lonely ting, Keisha, and a body must have somebody a wait fe dem on the nex' side."

"I am not planning to die here," Keisha said. She was suddenly annoyed with this woman. She wanted to get back to the apartment.

"You read the paper today?" Dorothy asked. "A man. A simple man, a regular working man, walking down Hope

Road in Kingston, minding his own business. Then two boy come up to him. One look on him, right in front of the world, right in broad daylight—2 o'clock, I am telling you. The boy pull out a gun, put it against the man head, and shout: 'Say feh!' The man start to bawl. The boy fire. The man dead. Good man. The man was walking to get his car to take him back to work with some patties for his co-workers. The man sells air tickets at Air Jamaica. Now the man is dead. Somebody said it was because he was politically connected. How? Because him study in America. Then shoot tourist, too, you know?" She stopped talking. She left that hanging in the air like a threat.

Dorothy started to talk again, this time with less drama, but still with the intent of provoking Keisha.

"I like you, Keisha, but whenever I look at you, I have to think that you Americans here to exploit us, you know? It is as simple as that. Now, I come from a successful family, and to be honest, we into the business of exploiting people, but I gave that up. I gave that up long time now. I have turned to a better way. That is why I can't take the kind of talk you like to bring sometimes. I find it naïve and foolish." She stopped talking and drank several spoonfuls of soup.

"There is nothing I can say around you, Dorothy. I was born in the wrong place," Keisha replied.

"Well, I have felt that way, too. In Washington, D.C., I was there and I was looking at the size of those monuments, and all I could think was, what is my significance to all of that. None. None at all. So I come back here." Dorothy seemed to have calmed down. "If I felt that way, you can imagine what your president felt when he come and invade Grenada . . ."

"I am not into politics," Keisha said.

"A sweet luxury, child. But politics write all over you.

Look at the man you come here with. Look at you and him. That is politics. You think it was love?"

"I never said it was love," Keisha said. She had merely hoped for love.

"Yes, but you wanted love though. You was dreaming love. Now you tired of it. Just like that," Dorothy said.

"He is not talking to me. If you ask me, he is the one who is tired of me. That is the truth of it," Keisha said, determined not to let Dorothy bully her again.

"He is a madman. You know that. Anyway, you deserve a little vacation. A lickle tourist life," Dorothy said with a laugh.

The shift in her manner disturbed Keisha, but she was tired of the arguing and relieved at the new direction of the conversation.

"We are going to have a good time, me and you. And when I am tired, you and the boys will have a good time. Now, don't get no ideas about the boys, eh? These fellows not into women—not in that way, anyway. But they are sweet and they will give you a good time. Toby is the chief instigator. You met him at the funeral, remember?"

She did not remember. But she liked the sound of Dorothy's plan.

At night, she slept with the French doors at the back of the bungalow wide open, the sea sounds filling her ears. She slept with the sweet fatigue of a woman drunk on sun, food, a sense of separation from reality. She was in Jamaica at last. She avoided radios, televisions, and newspapers. When Dorothy wanted to talk politics, Keisha avoided her. She stayed with the white tourists as much as she could and told them she was from California. They saw only the beauty of the island and talked only of the sun, food, water, sports. It was a way of coping, and she liked it.

She planned not to speak to Kofi once during that time. If he called she would avoid the call. She would bask in the sun, which seemed so different on the coast than it did in Spanish Town, where it was dull and oppressive. But she did want him to call. Deep down, she wanted him to miss her, to realize that he needed her around. So she would ask Toby if he had seen Kofi while he was in town. Toby smiled that indulgent smile of his, stroking his slick moustache and shaking his head. Keisha tried to hide her disappointment, but Toby seemed to read through it and to mock it gently.

She chose then to focus on where she was. She ate food cooked by Dorothy's servants. Spicy, thick food that filled her and slowed her to a sweet calmness. At first Keisha wondered about not having to pay, about Dorothy's insistence that she not pay.

"If you pay, you would be a tourist like everybody else. You is my guest. The boys will take care of you. They taking care of you, aren't they?" Dorothy said to her one afternoon. "Anyway, why you going on like you could pay for this at all? You don't have the money. Just enjoy yourself and stop being American. Why you feel that you can't take a gift, too?"

The men collected her in the evenings and took her to clubs. She liked dancing with them. It was as if they had found a new existence in the night. It made sense, for in Jamaica their gayness had to be a secret, a nighttime affair. And in the clubs on the coast, among the tourists and under the wonderful canopy of bacchanal, they would turn loose. Keisha watched the bodies, fluent, fit, dancing to sweet reggae through the night. Just watching them move was intoxicating.

# Chapter Sixteen

Kofi was on his back, sweating. The sheet under him was wet. He could smell the musk of his body—a salty scent. He had on nothing but a pair of white briefs. Heat radiated through the room. The windows were open, but there was no breeze. The darkness did not help. Kofi concentrated on keeping still. He did not want to think.

He had been having terrible stomach cramps and diarrhea. He knew it was the oranges, but he felt like eating nothing else. The pain came in waves.

Keisha was far from him. This is what he wanted. He wanted her to go away and leave him to write, to think, to feel for a moment that things were not getting away from him. The salt of his weeping had dried on his face. That morning he had cried for Aunt Josephine. And the emptiness that he had not felt at the time of the funeral was now consuming him. He did not need Keisha around for this.

Still, he lay there and thought about her. He had already forgotten her face. He knew that this should make him panic, and in a way he did panic. But it was calculated—a well-considered reaction. Another part of him was unable to panic, only able to watch the way things changed around him. It was now quite dark.

OCHO RIOS, JAMAICA

A couple of weeks into her stay in Ocho Rios, Keisha cut her hair. She cut it to an almost bald sheen. She sat under the shade of an almond tree in the courtyard of a woman who did braids for a living. The woman wanted to braid her hair, but Keisha insisted that she cut it off. She could feel the cooling of the wind on her scalp as the hair fell away.

The face Keisha saw in the mirror was a revelation to her. Her head looked smaller, but her face seemed to come at her with greater force, a certain boldness that she hardly recognized in herself. Without the framing of hair, her eyes were sharper and wider, her lips fuller, sturdier, suggesting their blackness more. Her ears fanned out of her head. She felt naked and vulnerable, and yet she liked looking different. She liked that people she knew would look at her and wonder why she had done it.

When Dorothy saw her, she was shocked. "New look, eh? You were drunk."

Keisha shook her head.

"I suppose some of us can afford this kind of thing, eh?" There was a terrible condescension in Dorothy's tone.

"I just felt like a change," Keisha replied, trying to seem blasé. But she felt hopeless.

She cried that night. A deep, sad wailing for her loss. And yet, the next morning, seeing her face again, seeing the emptiness above her, she felt somehow complete. She felt a cleanness about herself that she could not explain.

She walked to the market and bought a pair of earrings made from black coral and silver. She bought a delicate matching silver chain with a small black coral dolphin pendant. She felt new.

# Chapter Seventeen

It was not just the nausea that assured her of what had happened. She knew she was pregnant because of the way her skin felt—softer, yet strangely sensitive to touch. She knew she was pregnant even before she saw Toby.

Toby ran a clinic and it made sense that Keisha would go to him. Dorothy had arranged for him to get most of the tourist trade if he would devote a half-day to local patients who did not have a lot of money. It was Wednesday, the day for the local patients, when Dorothy sent Keisha to see him. Toby examined her with all the professionalism that he could muster. He kept raising his eyebrows as he looked at her body.

"Tell Kofi congrats."

"Oh shit, shit! Shit! Fucking shit, shit!"

Toby stepped back instinctively.

"That fucking bastard knew this would happen. Shit. Why did I do this?"

As she left, she could hear Toby whispering to one of the nurses who had come into the room to look at Keisha while she was walking angrily around cursing. She felt weak, stupid, and ashamed. She caught a bus along the coastal road to the guest house. That night she went to the bar on the beach to drink, to get drunk.

The club was empty. It was the middle of the week and the tourist season had not quite started. She picked a spot in a dark corner of the room where she could look out on the water until Dorothy joined her. She was drinking beer. Her head was slowly finding that numbness that she wanted.

Reggae music thumped through the club and Keisha liked that she was consumed by the noise. It created a wall around her. As the club became more and more crowded with Jamaicans, she realized that there was to be a real dance that night—a local dance. The music had changed from easy roots reggae to the staccato and rapid-fire aggression of dancehall.

Keisha was beginning to feel giddy. She was looking around at the bodies of these people, moving to the music, posturing, turning, arms going in all directions. The women were dressed in revealing clothes, tight shorts that marked out the contours of their vaginas, frills around their open tops, flamboyant hats covering braided hairdos and hard-hatted headdresses. The women moved with sweet daring, their bodies opening and closing to the music. And the men in their white suits, their jackets covering close-fitting netted vests that made their thin, firm bodies ripple in the low light, drew Keisha's eyes. In a real sense she felt as if she was home in a club in Columbia—people sizing each other up, the ritual of mating, the juice, the coke in the backroom, the good times.

The air was thick with the sweet aroma of marijuana, although it was hard to tell at first who was smoking. The spliffs were held discreetly by the men, the tough guys who were not dancing but who stood against the walls, with their women pouting at their sides sipping bottles of stout and behaving as if they could not hear the music and were impervious to its rhythms.

Keisha watched it all as she drank. Her mind was feeling as it should—dead to what was happening yet sweetly engulfed in the way these bodies were moving. The men and women held each other and dubbed the life out of each other, not with smiles and giddiness, but with an earnestness, a defiant look that made it all normal, so amazingly normal. Keisha could tell that these were not money people—these folks made their living working for the tourists, as cleaning women, tennis coaches, drivers, cooks in restaurants. They were the backbone of the industry of this coast.

Just as Keisha saw Dorothy enter the club, she noticed a man wearing a glossy running suit and a pair of Nikes, the laces undone, taking the stage, mike in hand, pulled close to his mouth. His hair was cut low with a sharp, angled mark across the front of his head. He wore chains, lots of chains. For a moment, she thought he might be an American, but there was something too subdued about him. He did not smile, except to Dorothy, but mostly scowled. He was about twenty, lanky, and still not yet over that peculiar discomfort that teenage boys seem to have with their bodies—as if their bodies are growing faster than they can manage. Keisha watched his interaction with Dorothy while the other men embraced each other. Keisha knew the others to be gay, but she was not sure of this man. He was not completely strange to her, though. She remembered him or someone like him talking to Dorothy on the beach sometime before. He worked on the garden and the pool in the resort. But he was close to Dorothy; not just a staff member. She had seen him a few times and he was always polite. Now he was a man, moving with such machismo. He was not a dancer like the others. He was a deejay—hard core, tough, confident.

She watched as he strutted, touched peoples' outstretched hands, raised his body upright, and sang with his eyes closed. He slapped his chest, made pistol gestures with his fingers, carried out the carefully defined antics of the dancehall master. She took it all in, feeling herself drawn into his gestures, the way he opened his jacket to expose his chest and the ripple of his stomach. But she liked the strange vulnerability in his eyes, in the way he caught sight of someone and held it in place. She did not understand much of what he was saying, but she found herself taking cues from the crowd, cheering him.

She stayed in the shadows, stayed where she thought he could not see her while she enjoyed his performance. She envied the three women in short shorts and skin-fitting tops who enacted the choreographed simulations of sex around him. They would fall to the floor and begin to hump an imaginary lover, and then they would sit on their bottoms and open and close their outstretched legs, showing a startling flexibility. They would turn profile and curve their bodies into pistons, hips moving in rapid action. The young man moved around them as if they were not there, only occasionally touching one on the ass or doing a quick grind with another. But he was busy with his lyrics, with his chanting. Keisha took it all in. Her breasts tingled.

Occasionally he would stand facing the audience with his legs apart, his face looking upwards, entering his own world of revelations. And then he would look down, focus on his feet, open his legs wide, and start a crablike prancing, knees going up and down, hips jerking back and forth, carrying his groin as if there were a huge penis and scrotum there. Keisha imagined a giant penis protruding from this man's body, dangling, swinging back and forth, while he tried not to fall over on it by leaning his torso back while he moved and jerked around. Her indulgence frightened her, but there was a certain sense of daring and fearlessness. It was the drinking, she knew, but she did not think too much about it. She kept conjuring up the penis on this boy's body.

But she was pregnant. Here she was lusting after this man while she was pregnant and her whole life was in a serious mess. She had come to the club to forget how angry she was with herself for coming to Jamaica with Kofi, for sleeping with him without any protection, for tying her life to his with this baby in her. She was angry with the way her body was responding to the dancer's performance.

Or maybe this is what she needed. She needed to, at least for a night, think of herself as still free, still able to have a life. She was drinking quickly, trying to cloud some things from her mind.

His set was over. He waved to the crowd and disappeared. He was gone.

Much of what happened after was a blur. The deejay stopped her near her room and she thought he was helping her. He was grinning—a sheen of sweat on his forehead. He had changed into a breezy white cotton shirt, the sleeves dangling loosely at the wrist. She was not sure what he was doing there, but she felt a sudden joy at seeing him.

"Hey!" she said too loudly.

"Yes, baby." He kept smiling.

She lurched forward, stumbling on herself. He held her up, preventing her from falling. She felt his body—she would remember that—his body and his smell, a sweetness that made her think of a woman, not a man.

"Yuh fuck up bad, baby. Come."

She remembered, looking at him so close, how much she had liked his look, his cool on the stage, his dark-edged face, his rare smile. The tooth missing in the middle. She handed him her bag to let him find the key. She felt she was laughing.

"You look cute with the bag. It becomes you." He looked down at the bag over his shoulder, touched it, and smiled at her.

She spoke, leaning on the wall by the door: "Careful, I have things in there that could bite you." She was laughing louder than she wanted to, and his smile was indulgent but piercing—as if he was trying to read her. Her laugh again. Her hand on his shoulder for support.

But then she stopped laughing. She could sense that he was thinking about something else, that somehow he was deciding about something else at that moment.

"You don't like Yankees?" she asked him. He said nothing, opened the door, and pulled her in gently. She leaned on him and stumbled to her bed. She fell on it and turned on her side. "Thanks, honey. Pull it shut on your way out. Thanks."

She heard the door close. Then she felt the weight of him on the bed. He was firm, his body pressing on her, his face looming, his teeth. He tried to kiss her. She did not understand what was going on but she knew it was familiar. Familiar as a thing from far back. Something about the smell of everything, and the way she was feeling—the sense of danger and sickness. She felt him on her.

"Come, baby. Hold still. Mek me just tek off the something, all right. Hold still. Yeah. Come, man." He was over her, undoing her blouse buttons which for some reason were done up to the top. He was struggling with the one nearest her throat. She felt she was choking. His elbow pressed against her breasts.

"No, no, no! Don't do that. Don't!" She was shouting. He kept pulling at the button. The first one gave.

"Tek time, tek time . . ." His voice was heavy, alien.

She felt the looping in her stomach and then the sudden rush of everything she had eaten for days coming up to her throat. She forced her face to the side and vomited. He pulled from her in a sudden leap and stood and watched her retching onto the bed. The smell came back to her and made her sick again. She was still retching when she heard the door shut once more. He was gone.

She must have slept for hours on the floor that night. Then she woke suddenly, sweating. She sat with her back against the wall, looking around as if expecting him to be there. Her stomach felt hollow. Her face hurt on one side. She could remember enough.

She was like that for a long time. Then she got up slowly. She peered into the bathroom, then calmly looked around the apartment. He was gone.

She started to cry.

She cried as she changed clothes.

Dorothy knew him. He was Dorothy's friend. Dorothy would comfort her, do something.

"I was wondering when you was going come," Dorothy said. She was standing by a small counter in her room that looked out to the sea. She wore a grand green kimono that was many years old. Her hair was wrapped in a yellow bandana. Her face was free of makeup and looked pale and blotchy—no eyebrows, and more freckles than Keisha had seen on the woman. She was tired. "Toby called me."

He would have told her about the pregnancy then. Keisha did not want to talk about it.

"Do you know the guy who does the yard at the guest house?" Keisha had decided to treat this as a simple matter. She would let Dorothy know what had happened and ask her to have the boy beaten up or killed. She did not care.

"Which one? Whole heap a boys work there, Keisha."

"The one who does the yard. He is tall. Big gap in his teeth. He was singing on stage last night. You know who I mean . . ." Keisha saw his face looming over her, his hands grabbing at her breasts, and she remembered the way that her chest had become a ball of muscle. Her eyes started to smart with a familiar sickening pain.

"He tried to rape me," she said.

"Who?"

"The boy. The one in the yard. The singer guy."

"Oh, so I should know who you are talking about, Keisha?"

"The guy who does the yard. You know who I am talking about, so why the hell are you behaving like this? He tried to rape me yesterday."

"You can remember anything from yesterday, baby? After you was drunk like that?"

"How do you know I was drunk?"

"Who gwine clean up your mess in that room, child? Listen, nuh, if you want to come to this place and make a rass fool of yourself, do it. But don't start call people rapist. People weh trying to help you. Anyway, the people at the club tell me how you was going on. No point in going on like you never like Clive. The boy is helpful. That is why I keep him around here. Why I would harbor a rapist?"

"He said he tried to help me? That is what he said? He tried to rape me."

"Then call the police. Dem must deal wid it. Or call you man. Call Kofi, mek him come deal wid it."

"What the fuck is wrong with you people?" She was pointing viciously at Dorothy.

"You people? You people?" Dorothy turned and looked at Keisha. When she spoke it was cold. Cold and cutting. "Don't you ever point your fucking finger in my face, bitch."

Keisha's arm dropped. She held herself and tried not to cry.

"Don't even start with the bawling," said Dorothy with a dismissive wave of her hand. "I tired of your foolishness. You don't want to be here, right? Den go home. Is not like we not trying. I find a nice place for you. You tell me that you don't want spend time with Kofi because Kofi a go mad. I say fine. Kofi is a strange man and the two a yuh not married so you don' have no reason fe stay wid him. Is a fuck-up family. So I set you up. I introduce you to people. You pay me anything yet for the room? Eh?"

"I said I would pay . . . You insisted."

"Yes, I insist, and all I ask for in return is a lickle respect. You in the habit of going around calling boys rapist? Is a habit you have?" Dorothy sat down. "Jesus Christ, Keisha, look on you. You look bad. You still drunk. You smell awful. Yuh pregnant and start go on like yuh mad. What is wrong wid you?"

"I am fine. I . . . He tried to rape me. But it's all right. I am getting out of this shithole. Really. You all hate me anyway."

"I told you to go back home. You better off." Dorothy got up painfully and walked to the doorway that looked out to the sea. "Freddy! Freddy! Come, come give this woman a drive back to Kingston. Drive quick, you hear? We gwine down to the district tonight for a rally. Mek haste, Freddy . . ."

"I don't need a lift," Keisha said.

"Freddy is seventy years old, Keisha. Freddy could be

yuh great-grandfather. Freddy don't want pussy, all right?"

"You know what?" Keisha said deliberately. "You can keep your damned island and your resort, and you can go fuck Kofi all you want now. That is what this has been about, isn't it? You vindictive cow."

As she spoke the last words, Freddy appeared at the door. He was in full khaki. Keisha liked Freddy, and she would have found comfort in driving to town with him. But trusting people around here was impossible now. He might be laughing at her, too, saying she deserved it. She had made her decision. She was pulling away from everything. She was going.

"Thank you, Freddy, but I will take the bus," she said.

"Suit yourself."

"And here is a hundred dollars for the room. I will send the rest—"

"Keep yuh money, Keisha. It was a gift. Stop that foolishness. Anyway, you need de money."

"I will pay you." Keisha was almost shrill.

"So you can feel better than me again? Keep de money, all right. Buy some diapers for the pickney."

"I will pay it back." Keisha's voice was small, unconvincing. She stepped back, and then turned and walked from the room.

When she got back to her apartment, the place had been cleaned. Her slightly damp dress was hanging on the line outside with her underwear and the sheets she had soiled. Inside, the bed had been made, and the room smelled like a mixture of lemon and antiseptic. Her other clothes had been folded neatly on the chair. She packed her bag, then went outside for the dress and the underwear. She looked toward the pool. The pool boy was dragging it. He waved and smiled. She felt watched, as if everyone knew what had happened.

She started walking in the direction of town. Freddy had the van on the road. He was waiting for her.

"I said it's okay, Freddy."

"It hot, Keisha. Mek me drive you to the bus stop, all right?"

She climbed into the van reluctantly.

"Keisha, that woman is a bitch, everybody know dat. All right?" He turned to look at her. Freddy was a kind man. "Don' mek her mash you down, yuh understan'? She not a nice person."

"He was all over me. You know. He wanted to . . ." She stopped.

"Yes," he said. He did not commit.

He dropped her in the town square where the minivans milled around looking for passengers. Through the car window, he said, "Jamaica is a rough place, baby, but sometime, when your heart is right, it can be a good place. But you have to ready for it, dawta. Yuh hear? Walk good, nuh."

He drove ahead a bit, parked, and she watched as he stepped out and approached one of the minivan drivers. He pointed to her. A boy ran toward her and grabbed her bag. She followed. Freddy was smiling and nodding, encouraging her. He watched her climb into the front of the van, then waved and returned to his own without turning back, his thin body moving slowly on unsteady legs.

# Chapter Eighteen

Keisha sat in the front of the van. The driver would let no one else get into the front, even though two passengers normally sat there. The music was too loud. Everything was a weight on her. The heat, the music, the aggression of the conductor, the shouting of the people in the van. The heat. The heat, thick and overbearing.

She felt filthy. Despite her shower this morning, she still felt uncomfortable and she could smell her body. In the van it was not just her own body that she was smelling, but the exhaust, the dust, the vegetables in a basket that crushed against her legs, the scent of other people around her, and when the van stopped, strong country smells. She felt so tired. But when the van started again, with the window open, she allowed the wind to wash her face, to deafen her, to numb her. She was leaving, she knew, but she was not trying to keep memories, not trying to keep snapshots of her visit. She was leaving and that was enough.

When she got out of the van in Spanish Town, the streets were growing vague in the mute orange twilight—shadows everywhere. She walked all the way to their duplex because she had been sitting too long. It took her forty minutes. She still felt that choking feeling. A world coming in on her. People, voices, faces—all strange to her. She had never experienced the city's squalor the way she did that day walking to the house. The dust, the garbage, the children sprinting around, the chickens in the streets, the lazy dogs sniffing at garbage, the posturing of the men, grabbing crotches, laughing open big-toothed laughs, and the women speaking so fast she could not understand, their hands going, their heads going. Keisha felt like a tourist again. It frightened her.

The house was dark. The acid smell of rotting oranges filled the muggy air. The windows were all closed. She could barely breathe. The back door was ajar. The light from the falling sun cut a sharp-edged wedge across the floor. She shifted and faced the glare, sudden and blinding. Then her eyes adjusted. She could see the scraggly cherry tree in the background and then the silhouette of Kofi sitting on a chair, facing the sun. He was not moving. For a moment she thought he was dead. Then his cat came into the frame, moved around his hand dangling down his side. His fingers touched the cat.

"Kofi," she said quietly. She still had her bag on her shoulder. "We have to talk."

His fingers moved again. She moved closer to the door, and then shifted her body to the right to look into his face. His eyes were open.

"Kofi."

He did not respond.

"I am leaving. I am going back to the States."

He did not move. She stood there waiting for him to respond. He had to respond. He had been silent for too long now.

"Kofi." Nothing. "Somebody tried to rape me last night."

She was not sure why she had said it. She was no longer sure she even believed it. Ocho Rios now seemed like a different world. But she was testing him. If he cared about her he would respond, ask about this. If he was angry with her, that was fine. She had taken off for three weeks, left him alone. But he should care that someone tried to rape her.

When he spoke, she was startled. She had not expected him to.

"That is what she told me you would say."

"What the fuck is that supposed to mean?" she exploded.

He went silent again.

She was facing him now. His beard was overgrown and untidy, his hair was completely disheveled, his eyes were red with deep fatigue, yet they had a strange glow of alertness in them. He was not wearing a shirt and his body was an ashy color. And he had lost weight, a lot of weight. His face was gaunt and his trousers were loose on him. The veins in his arms stood out now, where before they had been blunted by flesh. His eyes were set deeper in his face. He could be ill. Around him were rotting and fresh orange peels and two large empty sacks.

"What the fuck is that supposed to mean, Kofi? I tell you that someone tried to rape me and you say—"

"That is what she told me you would say," he interrupted in the same noncommittal tone.

"And I suppose she told you that I was making it up, right?"

"That is what she said."

"And who the fuck is she to know? Who is she to know?"

"I am saying that she told me you would be upset . . ."

"So you believe her then? You think she is right, that I am making it up?"

"I didn't say that."

"The whole stinking lot of you make me sick!" she shouted, and walked inside.

"Keisha . . ." His call was so weak, so far away, that she did not turn to it.

"Don't say a fucking word to me. Don't. I am sick of it. I really am. I think I'll go mad if I stay here. I tell you that a man tried to rape me, and you don't even get angry, don't even ask me how I am doing!" She was shouting from the room. Pulling down her suitcase and other bags. "I leave you for three weeks, you don't call. You just sit here, sit here and do nothing. You don't care what happens to me. You don't."

"I was making music, baby," he said in that same tone. "You have to be in the shitstem to write against the shitstem."

And in that moment she knew that he was too far away. Her anger subsided and was replaced by a profound sadness. A sadness for herself.

"You've stopped taking the medication?" she asked, walking slowly into the kitchen.

"I needed to think. Those things slow me down. I am fine." He was lucid again. "Did he hurt you?"

"I don't want to talk about it. It is not your problem." She watched him. The sun was lower. His hands dangled. "I am leaving, Kofi."

"Yeah. I know you was going leave. They all leave me. It is a pattern. They all leave me," he said quietly. Then he stood and walked to the edge of the concrete porch, facing away from her.

She looked at his back, the way it curved smoothly into the valley of his spine. She liked that back. Wanted to touch that back like she had before. It was a tender feeling that bothered her. "You should ask yourself why they all leave, Kofi."

She returned to the bedroom and continued packing her things.

On the ride from Ocho Rios, she had worked out her next movements. She would return to Spanish Town, get her things, and go and stay with a woman she had met from the university. She would stay there while she tried to schedule her return flight to New York. She would collect some of her papers from the storage place in New York and then take the Greyhound to Columbia. She would stay there for a while until she figured out what to do next. She needed to go to someplace familiar, to people who knew her, a language she understood, food she was used to. She needed to be away from the madness that consumed her here.

She heard Kofi behind her as she packed. She did not turn.

"I missed you," he said.

She said nothing.

"I really missed you," he said.

"You didn't call."

"I called, but you didn't want to speak to me. I thought you didn't want to talk," he said.

"I was not so far away. Maybe I wanted you to follow me. Maybe I wanted you to come and find me. You knew where I was." She still did not want to look at him, she did not want to look desperate.

"I thought you wanted space. You said you wanted space."

"I said that so that you could get *your* space," she said sharply.

There was a long silence between them.

"Kofi, what do you want with us, anyway? I mean, you think you're in love with me? You think that?" she asked, knowing that whatever he said would make little difference.

"I don't know what being in love means. But I feel like I am falling into something," he said, trying to find words. He was being honest. As honest as he knew how.

"What the hell does that mean? Falling into what? You make it sound like a trap."

He walked into the room and sat on the bed. He wanted her to look at him.

"It's not a trap. I am just saying that I feel like something is happening. I depend on you. I am frightened by it. There is too much stuff going on in my head. I want to sleep most of the time. I want to be with you, but I don't even know if you want to be with me." The words tumbled out quickly. He knew he was not making sense. He did not know how to say that her moods, her anger, her silence, were controlling him. He did not know how to say that right now he just wanted to make love to her. It was not a feeling, just a drive. But he did not know whether she would let him.

"You know what I know? I know that we are in different places. I want stuff that you can't give me. I wanted you to come to me. I wanted that. But if I had told you that, what the fuck would that make me? What is the point of that? You can't think for yourself. I am here now, and I feel filthy and ashamed for wanting that. I feel like a fool. You know . . ."

Kofi sat down and stared at his hands. He could not think.

"It is not perfect, but I like where we are," he said softly.

"I don't," she shot back. "You're not listening to me, Kofi. This thing is messed up and you can't see it."

Suddenly, he felt like leaving. This was too much for him. He could see a coolness in her, a calm that frightened him. What she would say now would hurt him, he could tell. And she was not going to stop. If it was anger she felt, it would be better—then he would know that at some level she was trying to cope with deep feelings for him, something salvageable. But she was calm.

"You should have called me or something, Kofi."

"I tried."

"Well, you didn't try hard enough, okay? It wasn't up to me, man. You was the one not talking, you was the one into yourself. You didn't try hard enough, okay?" She stopped talking and sat down on the bed.

Kofi felt a terrible sense of failure—like he was one of many men who had screwed with her life, and he could do nothing about it. Nothing at all. "I don't know what to say."

"What *can* you say? You know what I am saying is true," she said.

He was still stunned by her coldness, her calm, and the sharpness of her accusing tone.

"If I wasn't me," she continued, "I would laugh at myself. So I am going to get my shit together and get out of this messed up place. I mean, I feel like a real idiot."

"We had something, Keisha," he said. And he believed this.

"*Had*, that's right."

"I mean *have*. I mean we have something," he said quickly.

"Well, it's not worth it to me right now. I can't see it. I can't."

"It's just a bad stretch, you know."

"There ain't nothing here, Kofi. You know that. I am not happy. This whole thing was crazy from the get-go, you know that."

He left the room quietly.

About an hour later, he returned. She was lying on her back, her eyes closed.

"I have a story for you," he said. "About me and you. I dreamt it when you were gone. I woke up and felt . . . felt for you. Felt like I wanted you . . ."

"I don't want to hear it, Kofi."

He looked down and began to move away, then paused. "Dorothy said you have something to tell me."

Keisha knew that Dorothy had not told Kofi she was pregnant. And she did not need that argument now. She wanted to be gone before he knew.

"I told you: Somebody tried to rape me."

"That was it?"

"Like that is not important?"

"No, no. It sounded like something else. Anyway, we can do something 'bout the guy, if . . ." he started.

"No. No. No point," she said.

Kofi walked from the room.

She left later that night. She took a taxi. Kofi stood at the door. He looked the same as when she had said goodbye to him three weeks before. Pathetic, sad, and lost. It was not her problem. It just did not work out. The taxi raced out of the area. She looked back at Kofi. She wondered what the story was—the dream he'd had.

The morning she left Jamaica, the *Gleaner* reported five murders in one night. The national score of killings for the year had already surpassed the previous year, which had peaked at 1,400 deaths.

The university friend she'd stayed with drove her to the airport. They left at 5:00 in the morning, when the roads were still dark and empty, and the city seemed like a peaceful village. It was hard to think what it would be like in a few hours—the sun, the noise, the volatile tempers, the loud music, the energy, and the sense that everything was a hustle. In Kingston, she had the feeling she was in a city of millions, a city with so many bodies, so many complications, and such a callous exterior that it was easy to have a sharply refined nonchalance about the brute forces that seemed to control the city. As she felt the city falling behind her, she realized how tense she had been.

The week she had spent in Kingston after leaving Kofi was a week of siege, and by the time it was over, she was sure she had been raped, that she had been violated, that something horrible had happened to her in Ocho Rios. She had nightmares about Dorothy, nightmares in which the woman was brutally supervising her whipping, calling the dark-faced man to swing that whip with force, calling the numbers. And Kofi was standing at the side looking on helplessly.

Her friend, a secretary at the university, pulled a few strings at the Air Jamaica office to get her on the flight she wanted. She played nurse. She cooed over Keisha, listened to her stories of woe, and she cursed with force and generous indulgence Kofi and his "white" family.

She looked back after boarding the plane. Kingston was still glowing—the lights shimmering like jewels. The warm air was something she wanted to remember. She tried to make out her friend in the waving gallery, but she had already left. Keisha waved anyway. It was a necessary gesture of parting. Despite it all, she was carrying something out of that country. The baby, the memory of making the baby, and a dream that wasn't going to leave her anytime soon.

# Chapter Nineteen

Kofi waited, expecting Keisha to call to see if things could be worked out. She did call, finally, but the conversation was simple.

"I fly out this morning, Kofi. I left a few things at your place. Send them to my New York address, please," she said in a controlled tone.

"Keisha, we need to talk."

"I have to go, Kofi. I am already late. Bye, Kofi, take care."

She hung up. There was nothing in her voice that suggested she was in pain. He would have taken a taxi to the airport if he had sensed pain, if he had sensed even a hint of emotion in her. At least this is what he said to himself. He heard nothing. She was leaving. It was as simple as that.

He waited several days to hear from her—to hear that she had not actually left. But Keisha was gone.

He borrowed the car from Castlevale and drove to the North Coast to see Dorothy.

"The pressure going to kill me, you know? It going to kill me," she said, washing down several pills with long gulps of ice water from a glass the helper had brought from the kitchen. She sat on the bed and motioned to Kofi to sit on a chair in front of her.

"You come to look for me, eh? Family, Kofi. That is family. You remember that. To be honest, I thought you would malice me, Kofi. Because some people would say that is me make that woman of yours, that Yankee bitch, go back to America. You know she is a Southerner, eh? A Southerner. Those people was slaves for thirty years after we get freedom, Kofi. You know that. And now them putting on airs. That bitch coming here to tell me what I must do about my country. Like I don't know. Like she would know." The more she talked, the less drowsy she seemed. "But you know that. Tha's why you and she wasn't talking. You know that. That is why she couldn' stay in the house with you. You know is over here she was, eh? All the time she staying down here trying to fool with every man what come into this place."

Kofi felt his heart thicken with anxiety. He did not want to hear this. It was obvious on his face.

"Oh, you never know? Don't worry, honey. Is only the most refined of homosexuals I keep around me. Them never have nothing to do with her, but I swear she try, and I can't vouch for what she do when she went out walking late at night. You can't vouch for nobody, you hear? All I know is she was looking for trouble. These black woman from that place come over here like them name Stella, coming to look a island man. I hate the word. I hate 'the island's this' and 'the island's that.' This is a country. This is a damn country. She wasn't no different." Dorothy stared at Kofi, who had pulled away to the window. "Oh, sweet boy, I hurt you? I hurt you? I never mean to hurt you. You love her, eh? Yes. I know. Bitch! Anyway, my advice is you better find her, you hear? That is my advice. That woman carrying your seed, and trust me, she gwine want to make that child a Yankee. You hear what I am saying? She pregnant."

"You sure?" Kofi's thighs felt watery, his stomach sank. He sat down.

"Sure as day. Toby looked at her. He told her she was

pregnant. She pregnant," Dorothy said casually. "But the way how that woman was bawling and going on bad when he told her, you would think is some disease she have. You better mind sharp she don't do away with that thing. I tell you, find her and bring court injunction on her rass. Honey, I am too tired for all of this shit."

Kofi stood up. "Did any of your boys fuck with her, Aunt Dorothy?" he asked in as steady a voice as he could muster.

"She say Clive try rape her. But Kofi, Keisha was drunk. If anything happen with Clive and she, she did want it."

"I see."

"Kofi, eat dinner with me later, yuh hear?"

She stood up and moved her hand over his face tenderly. Her own face softened with a smile full of desire that Kofi knew well. But he was revolted by everything about her in that instance and moved his face away.

"Baby, don't . . ." she said.

"Dorothy, I have to go."

He walked out.

Freddy was in the yard. He approached Kofi and nodded him toward the large almond tree at the side of the house.

"Mister Kofi, sorry 'bout your Aunt Josephine. She was good woman," Freddy said. Kofi knew that the man had something to tell him.

"What happen with Keisha, Freddy?"

"Bwai, Mister Kofi, I don't rightly know, sah, but I ask Clivey, you know—the tall yout' who work here? Is him she say nearly rape har. Clivey say she drunk and nearly fall down. Couldn' even go into her place. So him help her out. Him say the way she a go on, him feel that she did want somet'ing, you know. So 'im try. 'Im say 'im feel her up lickle bit, but same time she throw up and so 'im leave the place. Now Clivey is not a yout' fe tell lie. 'Im mighta read her wrong, but Clivey never fuck her, Mister Kofi. But she never tek it too good. Mi drive her to the St. Ann Bay and put her on a van. How she stay, Mister Kofi? She an' Miss D never get on too right. You know how dat woman stay with Yankee, and worse, you never come look for her. You know how she bawl when you leave, and the night she hear dat you bring back a woman, well, she never tek it so well, Mister Kofi. So how Keisha doing?"

"She gone, Freddy."

"Gone back a 'Merica?"

"Yes. Freddy, thanks. Thanks." He shook Freddy's hand.

"Sorry 'bout your Aunt Josephine, Mister Kofi. Is a good woman dat."

"Life."

"Yeah, life."

Kofi called Toby to be certain about the pregnancy. He thought of going over to the clinic but decided that he didn't want to deal with a face-to-face meeting. He phoned from the lobby of one of the hotels in St. Ann's Bay.

"Yes, man. A month or two. That is the good thing. She was pregnant, but I can tell you she never take it too well, you know. It happen like that to some people. You know, panic and that kind of thing. It can be traumatic when you don't expect these things. Nope, she was not happy. I hope you work it out though. I hear she's left. She was having some problems, man. Maybe it was better."

"What kind of problems?"

"Bwai, you gwine have to ask her. Whatever I know is confidential and Dorothy will kill me, you see. Ask Lady D, man. She will tell you."

"Yeah. She probably told me already."

"So how you keeping, Kofi?" Toby paused. He waited. He wanted an answer. "You still on the medication?"

"No . . . Not necessary again. I am fine," Kofi said.

"So you done with the band business? I thought them was doing good, man."

"No, I gwine back to join up with them. Just took a break to come get some writing done and fe check out the new sounds, you know?" Kofi tried to appear confident and bright. He did not have to prove anything to Toby, but Toby was the success and Kofi was the failure. They had both attended the same high school and were in the same year. Kofi had been the prodigy and Toby had resented it. Kofi had also known about Toby's homosexuality during those years, and it was an unspoken threat that Kofi held over Toby. The exposure would have killed him. Kofi was popular, played sports, played music; Toby stayed to himself. Now, Toby was the one who had cared for Kofi when he was admitted to the hospital. Toby had arranged for the best psychiatrist in the university hospital to see Kofi. Toby was on top now. And Kofi heard condescension in every word Toby spoke to him.

"Nice, man. Nice. So you write some nice tings, eh? Cyaan wait to hear dem, Bob." He laughed cruelly. Toby called Kofi *Bob* when he wanted to remind him of his madness. "Every generation need a new Bob Marley, man. Yeah."

"Yeah, yuh right," Kofi said quietly.

"So how you meet up with Keisha then, eh?"

Kofi remained silent for a moment, then he spoke. "Listen, nuh, have to run, man."

"Hey, Kofi." Toby now had his doctor's voice again. "You must stay on the medication. You go America and tell people you name Bob Marley and they will lock up your rass. Stay on the medication. This woman will mad you. She don't care. She have her own baggage and she don't give a rass about you. Take your medication, you hear me?"

"Yes, man," Kofi said, but in his head he said, *Fuck you.*

# BOOK III

# Chapter Twenty

A part of her wanted him back. It was a hard thing for her to admit to herself, but she did want the original Kofi back. Maybe she felt a sense of failure, or simply loss for what she had hoped to have with him, but back in South Carolina, away from Jamaica and the strangeness of the place, away from the heaviness of Kofi's presence, she imagined him as something else. She did not resist the fantasy. It helped convince her that going with him had not been a complete mistake. When asked, she would say that her man was in Jamaica. That lie lasted for a short time. But at first it was a good lie.

She even imagined him coming back to America with her. Keisha wanted him here. She wanted to watch this man with a smile so profound, so aware, that it melted her every time she saw it.

When she had landed in New York, she was startled by how much she suddenly felt she was home. Several months back, before she left for Jamaica, she would never have seen New York as home. But the months in Jamaica made her long for the familiarity of America, and New York felt strangely comfortable, like a place where she knew how things worked. The smooth dart-and-swerve of cars in the traffic as she rode into Manhattan in the taxi, and the shelter of the glimmering buildings, their grand presence making the sky an afterthought, were familiar. It was easy to fool herself that she had never left, that her body was not now trying to understanding the meaning of its swelling, its unease with this child inside her.

Andrea had made the apartment her own. The boxes were in storage and the room was decorated like a teenager's bedroom somewhere in an American suburb—in pinks, a wild array of throw pillows all over the carpet, fuchsia curtains with flowers, a white dresser festooned with stuffed toys, and a wide variety of shoes stretched across one wall of the apartment. It was hard to recognize the room. Keisha promised to stay there for only a few days while she checked her mail, made arrangements with Joan, and cleared up some old bills that she had promised to handle. Andrea went home to her parents' place to give her space.

Keisha slept for two days. She stayed inside, watched television, and tried to clear her head.

She had been out for most of the third day when she came home to find Kofi's message on the answering machine.

*This is for Keisha. I hope you are there. Look, Toby told me about the baby. You can't jus' take off, Keisha. We have to talk, man. We have to talk. You can't jus' do dat, all right? Give me a call or something, Keisha. You hearing me?*

He left his number. She deleted the message. A rush of anger came over her—anger at the way he had left a message about her pregnancy on a machine that he knew someone else would be checking. She let the anger consume her, making it even more certain that she would not be talking to Kofi. She knew that it was better to have that anger than the strange sense of satisfaction that had crept into her when she first heard his voice on the machine.

He called later that night. She listened to the message. *Keisha. Keisha. Listen, Kofi again. I need to talk to you, man.*

*Have to talk to you. Keisha, call me, all right?* There was a long pause, and then he spoke slowly. *I am going to find you, do you hear me? I have to find you. You can tell me to my face to go to hell.* He stopped after that, as if he had lost the will to continue. At least that is how she read the tapering off of his voice.

She left for South Carolina two days later. She told Andrea to change the phone number. They made plans to have Andrea take over the lease for the apartment. Keisha was leaving New York.

Back in South Carolina, in the familiar landscape, she could feel herself slipping into old patterns. She had to fight the urge to call Troy. This is why she needed Kofi— to help her to see herself as strong, as the one who had walked away from Troy.

She wanted him with her, she wanted the way he would tell her that she was beautiful, that she was the reason he flew at night. She wanted these things, though it was hard for her to tell this to her family.

They had agreed that Kofi was not worth anything, that she was foolish to have anything to do with a man who seemed to be going nowhere in life. When she came back from Jamaica, she went straight to her people in South Carolina. They welcomed her, and did so with a certain degree of self-righteousness.

"Them island guys sound sexy and all that, with their accent and shit, but they think they better than us. You have to understand that. You know that now, right?" her cousin, Leonora, asked her after they had eaten and were resting their bodies around the table.

Keisha nodded.

"Yeah, I would love to get me some nice Jamaican beach and stuff, but you know how it is. That is a poor country, you know. Poor people over there, and I don't need to go and live in no ghetto. I got me enough ghetto right here," said Leonora.

Keisha had told her family about Kofi's strange behavior. She had to tell them. She was no longer in love with the madness. So she told them and she asked them to promise not to tell him anything if he came looking for her. She did not know if he would. But she told them that she had spoken to him some weeks before and he had said he was going to come find her.

She was not frightened by Kofi. In fact, she found herself fantasizing about traveling the country, running from him, keeping far from him until the baby came or until she decided to have an abortion. She had thought hard about an abortion. She did not want to have this child that connected her to Kofi, his madness, and the terrible time she'd had in Jamaica. Having the child would make her experience there a permanent part of her life. She knew where she could go. She knew the clinic in the strip mall on the west side of Columbia. She had taken Leonora there once. It was like a hairdressing salon. The women sat in blue chairs attached permanently to the wall by black cast-iron frames. There were magazines all over the place. The women watched talk shows on the television framed securely to a corner of the ceiling. After a long wait, Leonora was asked to go into the inside waiting room. Keisha went in with her.

"You have an appointment, right?" a nurse asked.

"Yes," Leonora said.

The nurse, a white girl with a bundle of golden hair piled up high on her head, wearing no makeup and a bored expression that was actually comforting, asked her some more questions.

"How many weeks?"

"Four, I think."

"You spoke to the counselor?"

"No, I spoke to my doctor. He—"

"What's your name?"

"Meredith Leonora Tyson."

"Dr. Gideon, right?"

"Yes."

"Okay. Did they explain to you what you could expect?"

"No. Not really."

"You will feel some discomfort for several days and you will have some bleeding and a little spotting, but if that goes on for more than a few days, you must call. You can take some painkillers for a while if the discomfort is too much. Okay. You have pads and a change of underwear?"

"Yes," Leonora said.

"Okay, just wait over there. It won't be long. The doctor will explain exactly what they are going to do, if you would like to know. You have any questions?"

"What happens to it? What you all do with it?" Leonora asked.

"With what?" The woman looked puzzled.

"The fetus," Keisha said.

"Oh, we dispose of it," the nurse said.

"Where?" Leonora asked. For the first time, Keisha could sense a strangeness in Leonora. Her voice had that strained quality, as if everything depended on the answer to this question.

"It is better this way. It is better that we deal with it. It helps with the separation. It's just tissue. We will treat it with respect, but you need to put it behind you, honey. It is better that way."

"It is better that way," Leonora repeated.

They asked her into the room and she went there

alone. Keisha waited outside. In an hour, Leonora was back. She was quiet. She did not walk awkwardly or anything. She held her bag tightly. She went to the nurse and signed some papers. The nurse repeated the instructions about the bleeding and the painkillers. She gave Leonora a sheet of paper that told her what to watch for. Leonora nodded through it all. She said nothing. They got into the car and Keisha drove out onto the highway. Leonora was not speaking. She looked ahead.

"You okay?"

Leonora nodded.

"You know you couldn't have this child, Leonora. You did the right thing. It was a mistake, okay?" But Keisha did not believe it completely. She was now trying to remember the panic and deep sense of fear she had first felt when Leonora said she was pregnant by a guy she had met at a club and slept with one time. One time. Leonora had not gotten in touch with the man again because she felt so silly. At the time, the abortion made sense. But driving from the clinic when it was over, Keisha felt as if something terrible had happened.

Leonora had started crying and she did not stop for three days. She did not eat unless Keisha cooked for her. She did not shower unless Keisha came in and told her she should shower. She did not go to work for three days. She was in mourning. Her apartment was in darkness. And she said nothing. Keisha worried that Leonora had had a breakdown. But she could understand the need for this darkness. On the fourth day, Keisha came by to see how Leonora was doing before she drove to work. Leonora was not there. Keisha rushed to work, worried. She called Leonora's office. Leonora answered. She was back at work. Her voice seemed normal.

"Thanks, baby, for looking after me," Leonora said.

"You okay?" Keisha asked.

"Yeah. Yeah."

They never spoke about it, but Keisha knew now that if she was going to have the abortion, Leonora would be there for her. She also knew that she, like Leonora, would carry that pain for the rest of her life. Both propositions were equally life-transforming. At least with the abortion she could deceive herself that life was hers again, that she had control again. She was going to have to decide.

# Chapter Twenty-One

Sometimes running is not quite what it seems. Sometimes running is leading. At first it did not seem this way to Keisha, but that changed. Her family could tell that what she imagined to be wavering and indecision on Kofi's part was in fact quiet conviction. Kofi was coming after her. And she was leading him through her life. She wanted him to trace her life. She did not want him to find her, to catch up. That she knew. But she wanted him to follow her across the landscape, across the country, make him fall deeper and deeper into her, into what she meant. She could no longer think constructively about their relationship, about why she had left him. She had tried to think about it, she had spoken about it, and all she could conclude was fear and boredom. She had left him out of fear and boredom. That was one answer. But Aunt Rose had another answer, and because of where they were when the answer was offered, Keisha knew that the answer had to be right.

They were in a clearing in the middle of the swamps that separated Sumter from Columbia. It was a day in March when the swampland seemed surreal, everything now transparent because of the nakedness of the trees. As Keisha drove along the highway, she could see across the broad meridian, the slick surface of the other side of the road—flashes of color as the cars moved past on the other side. It was a strange day. There was sunlight, brilliant and steady, yet there were mountains of clouds, a heaviness of gray scattered across the sky. And it was raining. Spitting rain that would spray a mess of water on the windscreen, just enough to mist everything, but not quite enough to justify the wiper. The road was slippery—in the car everything had a soft swishing sound, a muting of the world. Keisha drove for twenty miles until she crossed into the last stretch of highway before Sumter—that stretch of smooth road that was simply a massive bridge across the heavy swamp. She drove for a few miles and then turned onto a dirt track that led down to the edge of the swamp. She stood in the chill and listened. The cars swishing past beyond the trees, birds, and the deadly weight of the swamp. It was cold. She saw Aunt Rose's red pickup tucked into a grotto of pines.

In this transparent vegetation it is hard to think of getting lost. You walk, you walk, and then you find what it is you are looking for. Keisha walked, breathing heavily. She crushed through leaves and then bramble, and began to see the brown glow of the swamp through the branches. Aunt Rose was in red. She was fishing. Her homemade pole appeared to grow out of her like a limb. She did not turn when Keisha came close, she simply chuckled. Aunt Rose was like that. She carried Keisha's stories. Sometimes, in New York, when Keisha was afraid of herself, afraid of what was happening to her, she would call Aunt Rose and ask the old woman to tell her about Keisha, to tell her stories about Keisha. Many of these were stories Keisha had told Aunt Rose herself. Aunt Rose was her diary, her journal—the place where she stored things. Where some people worried about the void that the death of a parent or a spouse would leave, Keisha always feared the death of Aunt Rose.

Aunt Rose knew about Kofi, and she had little to say

about him. A woman made choices about how much of a man she could take. Keisha had dealt with Troy for so many years that Rose figured anyone else would be an improvement. Men would always hurt Keisha, Aunt Rose thought. Because she would let them. Keisha was not a very strong woman. But Aunt Rose believed that all men were flawed, and if Keisha wanted to try with a man it was not her business to say yes or no.

"I don't know what is wrong with me and this thing, Aunt Rose," Keisha said to her, holding her chest. "Heartburn all the time, and this thing kicking. Like it scared of something . . ."

"That thing can't be kickin' yet, child. Please." Rose stood still. Waiting for fish.

"I know what I feel. What about the heartburn then?" Keisha asked.

"Yep. Heartburn is normal. Might be a girl though. Lots of hair means heartburn, and lots of hair means a girl, or a sissy boy. Your man ain't that way, is he?" She turned to Keisha. Her skin was pale, a beige color broken up by spots of brown—"age spots," Rose would say. Rose had race problems, race issues. She didn't think she was white, but she thought she was beautiful for being what she was, light, with that thin auburn hair that was now a dirty grayish brown. This woman understood her blackness not as a color, but as a condition. She had worked for enough white people to understand that. But she liked her skin. Loved it. It took her places, she said. That was Rose—she talked like that. In another time, with something more of an education, Rose would have been an eloquent Republican ready to straighten out *silly black folks who liked to forget that there is a difference between a negro and a nigger.* Rose understood these distinctions.

Yet the man she married was a black man—a tall,

gangly black man. A man so black that they liked to call him Last Night.

Keisha had grown silent in the swamp. They stood there, both women—Rose patiently waiting for the fish to bite, Keisha waiting for an answer. Keisha had come to say goodbye to Aunt Rose because she was leaving. She had to go somewhere else before Kofi arrived. Keisha came also hoping for Aunt Rose's blessing. And there they were in the clearing.

"You love him?"

"No, ma'am."

"But you carryin' his child."

"Yes, ma'am."

"And you followed him clear to Jamaica."

"Yes, ma'am."

"And you never loved him then?"

"No, ma'am. I just wanted to be with someone. It felt comfortable."

"Then you get tired of the comfort and leave."

"He was getting crazy. It was getting strange. I didn't feel comfortable there. Lots of killing and stuff in Jamaica . . ."

"I thought all they had was beaches and that. But it's black people, huh?"

"Yes, ma'am."

"Then there is bound to be killing. Blood."

There was silence. Keisha had nodded. The conversation was fading to nothing. No fish. It was raining again. Spitting rain. Keisha was feeling cold. She would have to go soon. She wanted to be in North Carolina before dark.

"You know it's the Lenten season?" Rose said. Keisha knew not to answer. "Blood season." She paused. "Night died during the Lent season. Hog killing season."

The fish were not biting. She stood there dangling the

string over the river. Keisha stayed still, aware that something important was going on in this moment. This woman had seen so much and Keisha's simple life seemed trivial in the face of it. Gallivanting off to Jamaica in search of a myth or something less complicated—the pleasure of escape.

Rose dragged in her line and hook and pulled things together without talking. Keisha waited for instructions about what to do. Rose said nothing. She opened an old blue tool box and placed a bottle of bait into it. She then looked around for a piece of twig and began to roll the string on it. When the bundle was neatly wrapped on the twig, she tossed it into the box. Then she stood and walked slowly to the truck. She returned with a flask of coffee, poured some into a Styrofoam cup, and handed it to Keisha. Then she poured a little into the top of the thermos and started to sip slowly. Keisha could feel the cold.

"Night died during hog-killing season. You know that, Keisha? Men will die on you. You only have them for a time, and then they go. They leave you.

"I've gone through nine of my brothers' and sisters' deaths, Keisha. Mama had twelve children. I seen death, lots of death. You get to start thinking that life is something you must enjoy while you have it, and people, people, as bad as they might be sometimes, well, they only come by once, you know? And you figure that sometimes everybody, even the worst of folks, have a little sweetness in them that you can miss when it's gone, and you start to think that maybe, maybe you should just enjoy some of that sweetness while you can."

It was getting very cold. The mist had descended over the swamp and the sky was thick in its grayness. The trees were now skeletons, grotesque and gnarled figures barely showing themselves through the mist. Keisha felt the cold

on her body, and her shoulders trembled. She wanted to
go back to the car. To get into the car and drive as far from
this place as possible. She wanted to get on the road. But
she understood this timelessness that Aunt Rose was
talking about—the way that everything became unimpor-
tant in the face of time. Would Kofi be such a pain in fifty
years? Would she give this child life? How would she
negotiate the fatherhood of Kofi, and her own
motherhood? Thinking about Kofi and his madness, his
strange manner, his distance, his peculiar empty way
while they sat together in that house in Jamaica, made her
feel as if things were beyond her control. She wanted to
be far from him.

Rose sighed deeply, then gathered her things. "Cold,"
she said. "She said little else until she had started the
engine of the truck. Keisha sat beside her. "You gonna go
back up North now, eh?"

"Yes," Keisha said.

"Running from him . . ."

"I need the space."

"You love him?"

"No."

"Never loved him?"

"Maybe. I don't know."

"You liked making love with him though? Sweet,
yeah?"

"I suppose."

"Well, sometimes that is all you get." She smiled as if
remembering something.

She parked beside Keisha's car.

"A child must have a father. Tha's the truth."

Keisha climbed out and walked to her car. She opened
the door, looked over the slick roof, and waved to Rose.
Rose waved back.

"He's not gonna stop following you, girl. I can tell."
She laughed and started the engine. Then she shouted
over the drone of the truck. "Would be nice to close his
eyes, eh? Nothing like closing a man eyes what you been
with for a long time. Nothing like that at all. You feel
kinda free. Strange. I love you, baby. Drive careful now.
It's gonna come down hard. Call me."

Keisha watched the truck slip into the mist. She
started her engine and poined the car toward Ridgeway,
where Leonora lived. As she drove she saw the purple
banners clutching desperately to the crucifixes in the
middle of the church yards. An emptiness consumed her.
She felt lonely. She watched the purple cloths of Lent
flutter in the wind.

It began to rain heavily as she crawled along I-20
heading toward Ridgeway. Keisha turned the radio loud
and tried not to listen to herself. She kept thinking of
Aunt Rose, who did not, not for a moment, consider that
Keisha might have an abortion. Keisha had wanted to ask,
but as they talked she realized that she couldn't. Not of
Aunt Rose. For her aunt, there was going to be a child.
There were worse things than having a child by a man
who screwed up your life. Much worse things.

Leonora cooked soup—thick beef soup with corn and
sweet peas, carrots and chunks of potato. She placed a
loaf of fresh bread on the table beside a tub of butter.
Keisha ate the food slowly while the rain pelted outside.
Leonora was aware that Keisha did not want to talk. She
went into her room to watch television. Then, as if
knowing by instinct when Keisha would finish, Leonora
appeared again and took the bowl.

"I can get it, Leonora."

"It's all right. You need anything else? I got some nice

chocolate here. I know you could eat something sweet now. Or ice cream? Butterscotch. Or both." She served out a bowl of ice cream and placed a chunk of the chocolate on the table. Keisha ate. Leonora disappeared again and did not come back.

Keisha fell asleep in front of the television, but she heard Leonora come in to turn it off, and then the lights, and then cover her with a warm quilt. She kept her eyes closed.

"Sleep tight, baby," Leonora whispered.

Keisha slept peacefully that night. It was the first time in many months.

# Chapter Twenty-Three

"You gonna have to decide soon about the baby," Leonora reminded Keisha two mornings later while they were sipping coffee in the kitchen.

"I will. I will go and see Troy and then decide."

"What that son of a bitch have to do with this?" Leonora shouted.

"You know I have to see him."

"I don't know a damned thing, Keisha. You are a big woman, you not a child no more. You got to decide."

"I don't want no mess this morning, Leonora. I came to stay with you because you are cool and you know me, you know my history with that guy. I have to see him, and then I will know."

"Like magic."

"Maybe, but I will know."

"Baby, why you doing this to yourself?"

"Please leave the keys for the truck, all right?"

"They behind the fridge," said Leonora, gathering her things. At the door she turned and looked at Keisha. "Don't make him fuck you, Keisha. You don't need that trouble."

"Then what would be the point?" Keisha smiled at Leonora. It was a sad smile.

Leonora smiled back. "You could do what some of us do, Keisha."

"I don't share tools." They were both laughing now.

"Girl, you crazy. God gave you not one, but two hands."

"I need girth. Girth, honey. Pregnancy must do that to you, huh?"

Leonora went silent. A sadness covered her face.

"I'll be all right, okay?" Keisha said.

Her need to see Troy and the strange logic of it got more and more intense as the days went on. She had expected it to happen the moment she made her way back to South Carolina. But she had fought it hard for two weeks. Now she was feeling the urge. She was growing impatient with her relatives, with all the talk about Kofi and what a mess he was. She wanted to see Troy. To find out what was happening with that woman he was with, to find out if he still had feelings for her.

Leonora could tell, too: the way Keisha sat around the house, not bothering to get herself together, watching television, seeming lost in her own world. It was just a matter of time before she would start talking about Troy, about wanting to get together just for old time's sake. Leonora had seen it before.

Two weeks after Keisha moved into Leonora's house, Rose called to tell Leonora that their cousin Blossom in Philadelphia was dying of cancer. That side of the family was plagued by tragedies. The last three years had been terrible.

"It's like Satan wants to sift them like wheat," Rose said on the telephone. Keisha was watching a morning news program while Leonora tried to talk on the phone, eat some toast, and get her papers together for work. "First Bobo done died off like that."

"Bobo had it coming, Aunt Rose," Leonora said. "The doctor told him about his liver and the drinking. He made his choice."

"Don't matter whether it's his fault or not, he dead, and poor Martha, poor Martha, a soul wasn't made to take that much death so fast."

Rose went over the litany. Bobo first from cirrhosis of the liver. Then a son was shot in New York—shot and killed. He was a bystander, but he shouldn't have been there. That was two months after they buried Bobo. Then a granddaughter, a girl who was twenty-two, started to faint, have headaches. She died after six weeks. A tumor. Inoperable. The funerals followed each other, and Miss Martha took each death with her inimitable grandeur. That woman had seen things. Philadelphia was her promised land when she moved there in 1946 with Bobo. He had been good with his hands and he worked for some very decent people who sold him a massive fourteen-bedroom dump in a dilapidated part of town. But Bobo fixed that place, made it beautiful, and didn't sell when contractors came to rediscover the nineteenth-century grace of those homes. That house on Bleak Street in Philly was a holiday stop for the family from South Carolina. It was a rest stop during the migration north, a halfway house. Everybody went there, and when they arrived, Martha looked after them. Now Martha was suffering.

"She want us to come up. Blossom ain't gonna make it. The child is bleeding in her stomach and nobody can't tell why she keep bleeding. You ask me, I think the cancer done rotted her out. She dying. We all know. But we got to be with her. We got to be with her," Rose said.

"You plan to go up when?" Leonora asked. She was not sure she wanted to make a fourteen-hour trip to Philadelphia.

"Thursday. We come back Sunday. You can get some time off?"

"Just me and you?"

"No, we got to get one of the boys to drive up."

"Drive what? None of them got a car that could take us up there. Rufus car can't make it there and I really don't want to travel with that fool. You know how he is."

"It got to be Rufus, Leonora. And it got to be your truck. He said he could do it. Jason going to be out of town. Rufus say he want to go, say he want to see Blossom."

"Now, Aunt Rose, Rufus ain't got no business seeing that girl. You know that. It's not right . . ."

"We need somebody to drive with us. I ain't driving and you can't do all the driving, not after work, you can't."

"Okay, okay."

"So Thursday then?" Rose asked.

"Yes, yes."

"Ask Keisha if she want to come."

"You know she not going to want to come. You know that."

"Just ask her, that's all. You never know."

"Okay, okay. I'm going now."

"Ask her, now, okay?"

"Sure. I'll ask her."

"I mean now "

Leonora sighed and turned to the living room.

"Keisha. Blossom really sick in Philly and Aunt Rose say she going up to see her Thursday. I might be going up with her. She wanted to know if you want to drive up and see Blossom."

"Who's going?"

"Well, me and Aunt Rose, and Rufus might be driving . . ."

Keisha turned her head toward Leonora and gave a look of impatience.

"That's what I told her," Leonora said.

"I'll go look for Blossom when I am going up by myself," Keisha said, and turned back to the television.

"You heard her," Leonora said to Rose.

"That girl will carry a grudge to her grave."

"Some grudges are for keeping, is what I say. You know what that boy did to her."

"Just make you get old faster, is what I say."

"Anyway, I got to go."

"All right then. So call me later."

"For what?"

"You got to have a reason to call me?" The line went dead. Rose's phone etiquette was crude. Leonora could never get used to it.

She put down the phone and went into the living room.

"Look, I got to go. I will see you later then, okay?"

"Yeah. No problem."

Leonora left. She knew Keisha was going to see Troy.

# Chapter Twenty-Four

At about ten thirty, Keisha climbed into Leonora's truck and drove to Columbia. She rode on Highway 77, heading south. She exited on Two Notch Road, an extended street that cut right across the northeast of the city. She drove deeper and deeper into the city, pretending to herself that she was simply drifting, that she was not going anywhere in particular. But it was not long before she was in the black area of town. Deep into Two Notch Road, the houses grew a little less elegant, the stores were in roughly painted buildings, and black people moved around with that slow aimless calm that was so familiar to her. Near Allen University and Benedict College, the density of blacks on the road increased. People crossed Taylor Street with cool disregard for the traffic. Women carrying babies and men in baggy trousers lingered around the sidewalks, laughing, pointing, living. She drove through Gonzalez Gardens, the complex of redbrick apartments that was called a project by the South Carolinian blacks who felt that a project is an almost necessary feature of any self-respecting black community. The neat lawns and well-maintained buildings did not suggest drug use, gangs, violence, or anything other than a modest city district. In Jamaica, this would be a middle-class area. The only evidence that this was some kind of harbor for the underclass was the presence of police patrol cars and a community center called the Koban that was run by police officers. The latter was new to Keisha. She saw the large sign on one of the buildings. There were children crowding around the building, laughing and playing, and policemen in gray T-shirts and their typically tight trousers stood there grinning and chatting with the children. Keisha knew that this moment of serenity could explode quickly into something ugly.

Troy lived on one of the streets that spindled southward from Gonzalez Gardens. The houses were large, solidly built edifices that once held whites who eventually continued south, across Gervais Street into the leafy security of Forest Gardens. Now, middle-class blacks lived on these streets. Troy's house was on Shop Street, a narrow lane with speed bumps and a large Baptist Church manning the Gervais end of the street. On the Gonzalez Gardens end stood an abandoned house. As Keisha drove past it she noticed men and women gathered in the yard, looking out from the thick hedges and the shadow caused by the trees, watching for police. The crack house, just down the street from the church—it made sense.

At first Leonora did not want to call Rose. Rose had a temper and suffered from high blood pressure. And she had taken the relationship with Troy very badly. When Keisha ran from Troy, she would go and stay with Rose. Rose would care for her, try to convince her not to go back. But Keisha always did. One day it was too much for Rose. When Keisha called, Rose told her that if she came this time, she had to swear she was not going back to the guy. Keisha went to Leonora's instead and Rose stopped talking to Keisha for more than a year. Rose said she would kill that boy. She would do it.

But Leonora was worried enough about Keisha to call Rose.

"I'll meet you there," Rose said.

"Now, we don't have to—"

"I'll meet you there or I'll be there on my own. He living at the same place?"

"I think so, I don't know . . . But Aunt Rose, ain't no need for us to go—"

"Leonora, there ain't nothing to it, all right? I should have got that child to stay with me, tha's what I should have done."

Leonora smarted at the insult. "What's that suppose to mean, now?"

"You know what I am saying. Look, I got to go. I'm gonna fix that man once and for all." She hung up. Leonora had to go, too. She knew. Aunt Rose was liable to do anything.

The heat had settled into an oppressive weight when she stepped out of her office.

Keisha parked in front of his house. She was no longer nervous—she was excited. She knew he would be there when she saw his red Lexus parked in his driveway. It was 2:00. Troy worked nights as a security guard. After leaving the army as a drill sergeant, he had taken a job as a security director for a few businesses in Columbia. He was in the office for three days during the week, but on weekends he moonlighted as a security guard himself. He moved from business to business. He saved his money and invested it himself, spending hours on the computer trading and at first taking big risks. But he had done well with it. This tough manner, this hard-edged cool about decisions, was something she liked about him but also feared in him. He was cold and he carried that coldness into everything he did.

She knew so much about his business not because he

told her but because she spied on him. He kept everything to himself. But when she suspected that he was sleeping with other women, she followed him around with a desperate and obsessive intensity. When he found out, he started to beat her for it. But by then she didn't care. The anguish of that time, the anger she felt, the fear that he would leave her, the pain she experienced when she imagined him—and then saw him—fucking another woman, washed over her as she sat there in front of his house working out her first line.

She walked along the driveway. For the first time she admitted to herself that she had dressed for Troy. She was dressed as if she were off to work in some professional organization. The black skirt stopped three inches above her knee and fit much closer because she was with child. Her white blouse was spacious and light, and her black bra showed the shape of her breasts. Her hair was still short, and she knew he would have something cruel to say about what she had done to herself, but she applied her makeup with care. She looked exactly the way he liked: clean, professional, and stunning. She hoped he would not notice the slight protrusion of her belly, the suggestion of a world beyond him. They had tried to make babies and couldn't. He had always blamed her, said she was not able to. At least now she confirmed what she had always suspected, that he was the problem.

"Troy," she called softly through the door, which was slightly ajar. "Troy?"

She pushed open the door. The living room was the same as she remembered—off-white carpeting, black furniture, a leather sofa set, lamps with long thin stands and gray shades, a glass coffee table framed in black supports, an elaborate stereo and entertainment set, and three waist-high sculptures of church icons: a preacher preaching, a matriarch singing, and an organist playing. Nothing had changed. Troy's place was always clean. He always had someone to do the housework, even when Keisha was with him.

Keisha stood in the middle of the room and began to feel that strange sense of helplessness that she remembered from her years with him.

"Troy?" she said again.

"Who's that?" His voice was booming. Strong.

"It's me, Keisha."

"Oh fuck!" She could hear his smile. "Bitch, what the fuck you doing here?"

He appeared shirtless, a tall man, his chest matted with thick black hair that darkened his light skin. He was well built, but she noticed that he had thickened somewhat around his waist. He wore a pair of white cotton sweat pants and was barefoot.

"Hi," Keisha said.

"Damn, now here is a surprise." He opened his arms. "Come give me a hug then, baby. I know you want it."

She turned from him.

"Oh, it's like that then," he said, laughing. "Yeah, it would look kind of fucked up and desperate if you came and started to rub up against me two minutes after seeing me, eh? A woman has her pride. You getting holy in your old age, Keisha." He stopped talking. She turned to look at him. He was still smiling. "Your ass is getting big."

"Fuck you."

"Nope, you not saved. Big, but nice. You not getting it firm and hard and regular, you know—that's why. That Jamaican dude wasn't up to it, eh? Too much of that weed . . ."

"Who told you I was in Jamaica?"

"Baby, I know where you are even when you don't

know where it is yourself," he said. "You want something to drink?"

"Water."

"Ahh. Water, then." He moved to the kitchen. "So what the hell you gone and done to your hair, girl?"

"I cut it."

"I thought next time I see you, you would be sporting some fat locks and shit. You go to Jamaica and cut off your hair. That is some fucked up shit."

She was already starting to wonder what she was doing there. She knew, seeing him, that nothing had changed. He was the same. He made her feel as if she had to justify herself in his presence. He was in control. As far as he was concerned, she was there to have sex with him and he was going to treat the meeting as such. She would have to change it if she wanted it changed.

"I came to tell you that—" She stopped. He stared at her, challenging her. She was trying to make up a reason, a reason other than what she was feeling. He was right. She came to see if it would happen, if she would simply fall into the pattern. They would make love, he would insult her, and she would leave feeling that she still had some part of him in her.

She took the glass and started to drink. She looked at him. He sat with his legs apart, his right hand dangling lewdly between his legs. He stared at her with confidence, waiting for her to make the move.

"Give me a sip, baby," he said.

She walked toward him and stretched her hand out with the glass. She put the glass to his lips and gently turned it up and watched as the water filled his mouth. He gulped. Drops spilled from the side. The trickle fell down his jaw and onto his shoulders. She poured more quickly, letting the water spill onto his chest.

"Uh-uh, uh-uh," he groaned between gulps. He rubbed the water on his chest. The spill left a dark stain on his sweat bottoms. She could see that he was aroused. She could feel the warmth of her own arousal. She pulled the glass away and walked to the other side of the room.

"You are living with this woman?" Keisha asked.

"That's because you left me, honey. You know that."

"She lives here. I mean, she is on the answering machine."

"She is my woman now. Yeah. So what is that to you?"

"Nothing. I just wanted to know."

"You want me to leave her? You gonna come back and stay with me? Is that what you want? I can do that. You know I am the best thing for you, baby. I can make you holler like no one else can. You know that."

"Yeah, you right," Keisha said.

He got up and came toward her. He pulled her to him. She felt herself falling into him. He lifted her face and kissed her. His tongue was a snake in her mouth, moving with force. It was all familiar. Her body was responding but her head was drifting. She remembered the child inside her, the body that was not hers.

"You love me, Troy?"

"Yeah, yeah, baby." He ground his erection into her.

"I am not talking about that."

"So what the fuck are you talking about? I am going to fuck you and make you forget love. That's what I am going to do because that is what you want me to do. You need this, baby. You was always like that, baby. You don't want nobody to love you, baby. You want a man to hold you like this, make you feel like you got something for them. Well, you got something for me right in there, and I want that. Yeah. So don't start about love. Love is soft. What I got here is hard. You know you want that." His hands were reaching under her skirt. She was waiting for her body to decide, to give it all up and fall into this. Her legs opened. He knew instinctively that she was parting for him and he reached upwards, touching the frill of her g-string.

Yet she felt a familiar tension, panic even, in her chest. She wanted to run, though her body seemed to need to be there. With Troy she never knew whether what she felt was arousal or fear, love or a deep and terrible anxiety. It was impossible for her to be with this man and feel clean, feel sure of herself. Her mind raced toward a way out, while her body pressed into him.

"I am pregnant," she said.

"What?" His hand grew still.

"I am pregnant."

His hand dropped to his side.

"That Jamaican guy did that to me, you know. Fucked me and made me pregnant. I could feel it when the sperm hit my egg. I could feel it. I got a baby in me. That's what I came to tell you."

He pulled away from her. "You come to fuck with my head, eh?"

For the first time in years she felt powerful. It was strange. She knew it would bother him, but she did not expect him to pull away like that. It may have been the fact that someone else had left such a mark on her. It may have been that he wanted her to be desperate, weak, and helpless, and for this brief moment she was standing strong. She pressed it home.

"You screwed me every night for how many years, Troy? And nothing. Nothing. And you made me feel like it was me. It wasn't me. So, yeah, I came here so you could fuck me. No, so I could fuck *you*. Just a freebie—a little diversion, you know, 'cause you can't give me a whole lot now. I got all I want, really. It's just sometimes I get horny, like today, and I decided Troy would make a nice fuck and I could get off and go home. That's all."

"Fuck you, Keisha," he said. He was sitting down. "You've gone and screwed up your life. That's all. Where is the guy? Eh? You came here to fuck with me, didn't you?" He was angry, yet she was not intimidated. She felt in control.

"When she is born, I will bring her to see you. Show you it is all good," she said, smiling now and meaning it.

"Uh-uh."

"So you not going to walk me out?"

He got up reluctantly. Keisha headed through the living room and into the sunlight. She turned to look at Troy. He was good looking, strong, but there was something pathetic about him. And yet she still felt a thick jealousy when she thought of that woman he was with. She wanted him to be in love with her—she still felt that she needed his approval. Her only solace was that she now had something deep in her that he did not have. It was a small thing, but maybe it was enough for her now. She walked to the car and stepped in. He had followed halfway down the driveway. She started the engine.

She slipped the truck into gear, looked through the side window, and saw Rose's red truck coming up the avenue. For an instant she panicked. She felt caught. Her heart thumped. Troy stared at the driver as she drove past. He recognized her.

"Ain't that your crazy aunt?"

"What the fuck she doing here?" Keisha said, finding her voice.

Rose's beaten-down truck crashed into a hedge a few yards up the road. She climbed out and began to walk toward Keisha. Her hand was in her bag, which was clutched to her stomach.

"She got a gun, Troy, I know she got a gun. You best go inside."

Troy started to back away as Keisha pushed open her door and began to walk toward Aunt Rose. The old woman moved with slow purposefulness. She was not looking at Keisha, she was staring at the retreating Troy. She must have stepped out of the house without any concern for what she had on. She was wearing a faded housedress—a shift that fell loosely around her body. She had on house slippers and her head was tied with a scarf, the curlers underneath making her head seem larger than it was.

"You okay, Keisha? You okay?" Her eyes were on Troy.

"It's okay, Aunt Rose. I'm fine."

"I will shoot that son of a bitch, I tell you. Why you had to come here. Hey, I told you to leave the girl alone. Ain't I told you to leave her alone?" she shouted loudly to Troy, who was now close to his front door and feeling cocky, safe.

"Hey, old bitch, now she came to see *me*, okay? I didn't call her—"

"I'm gonna shoot your fucking head off, you hear me!" The gun was out and she started toward Troy, who vanished into the house.

"Crazy bitch!" he shouted from inside. "I'll call the police on your ass!"

"Aunt Rose, don't be crazy now. I said I'm all right. Ain't nothing happened."

Leonora's car sped around the corner, the wheels screeching modestly. She stopped behind the black truck and hurried out. As soon as she saw Leonora, Rose put the gun back into the bag. Leonora saw it.

"Why you have to be so crazy, Rose? Why you got to be that way?" She turned to Keisha. "She shot him? Is that what happened here?"

"No, no. Ain't nothing happened here, but that fool will call the police. We got to go," Keisha said.

"Fuck the police," Rose said. "I hate that son of a bitch."

"Get in the truck, Rose. That boy is crazy and he liable to have a gun in there. Come on." She pushed Rose to the truck.

Rose complained about being shoved, being treated like a child. "He liable to have a gun? Like that's supposed to scare me. Like he can fire that gun before I plug him with this."

"Just get in the car and shut up. And give me that gun."

"Now that's my gun, Leonora."

"Give it to me. Where you got this?"

"This is Night's old gun. Gave it to me to protect myself, okay?"

Leonora put the weapon in her bag and slammed the door shut.

"We will meet you at your place. Go on, now."

Rose started her truck reluctantly.

Leonora waited for Keisha to drive off. Keisha looked back at Troy. He stayed there in his window watching the two vehicles. He looked so pathetic, and the whole thing suddenly seemed funny. Rose with the gun, this madness over nothing. Keisha started to laugh. Troy looked puzzled by her reaction, but he just stood there watching. She drove off.

"Bye, Troy."

Keisha knew that despite the excitement and mess, something had happened there that day. She also knew that she would have to travel, to leave Columbia, to leave South Carolina and make sense of her life away from all of this.

Keisha drove down to Five Points, where a new restaurant had opened outside the main square. It was a Caribbean place run by some Louisiana folks. Keisha ordered the buffet. She was not hungry though she felt she needed to at least order something. The jerk chicken was fiery. She ate it, punishing herself, knowing that she would feel ill afterwards, but she wanted to be consumed with Jamaica. The music kept coming at her, track after track, and she remembered Kofi, Dorothy, Clive, Toby, as if they were all a part of her childhood. She was crying and eating, secure in the darkness of the place, in the protection of the music.

She did not want to go to see Aunt Rose and Leonora. She wanted to be alone. She left the restaurant and drove toward Finley Park, parked the truck, and walked down the twisting steps until she came to an artificial waterfall area. She found a cool spot there and sat staring at the cascading water, feeling the tiny droplets touching her skin, cooling her. She felt her body trembling as if she had just made love. It was not a feeling of satisfaction, just the feeling that she had been somewhere sexual.

She thought of Kofi. She was still angry with him. He had promised so much. Or maybe she had been dreaming it all. But he shouldn't have allowed her to think that maybe there would be something. There was nothing. And now she was running from everything.

She sat there and watched as the sky began to pink with sunset. It was growing dark when she started back up the stairs to the truck. She had cried enough for one day. Now she felt that fullness of the land after a storm— anticipating with the darkening sky and dark clouds something more, yet strangely fresh and clean after the deluge before. The clouds still heavy, the tears not too far away.

* * *

She left the park and drove to Aunt Rose's home forty miles away in Sumter. Leonora and Rose were waiting on the porch for her to come. Leonora was especially annoyed.

"I told you to come right away. You know I had to call in to work."

"I needed to think."

"You went back to the son of a bitch, didn't you?" Rose said.

"I needed time to think, okay?" Keisha sat on one of the wooden benches that Night had made with wood from a live oak tree that had been tossed to the ground by Hurricane Hugo in 1989. "I told you it was okay with him."

"You know what? You gonna come with us to Philly," Rose said, getting up. Before Keisha could answer, she continued: "I got some fried chicken in there with some fresh grits the way you like 'em, so you sit here and talk to Leonora and I will fix you something nice. You need to eat."

Rose walked into the house. It was an old house, built around 1940. They had been living there since 1956 when Rose and Night came from Manning to settle in Sumter. It was on the north side of Liberty Street. South of Liberty was where the black folks lived in Sumter—the South Side. But those people who worked for the white folks lived in old sturdy houses on the last two avenues of the predominantly white historical district. Rose called them the slave quarters. She used to walk across the street, along the tree-filled avenues, through the whites-only park, to the home of her employers. She had done this for most of her life, cleaned for them. The houses on this end were smaller, but now it was hard to tell any difference between the buildings.

Most of the houses that had been owned by blacks had been bought up by the wealthier white people in Sumter over the years, and now the line of segregation had moved quite clearly to Liberty Street. Rose was one of the remaining black owners. She and Night had carefully tended the quaint house with its wrap-around porch and ivy-thick walls and the dense surrounding garden. People kept offering to buy the place, but they would not sell. With Night now dead, some things were being neglected. She had been pleading with her son Rufus, the social worker, to come and paint the trim of the roof and the windows as they were peeling from the heat. He had promised but had not yet done it. But she wasn't going to sell the house. She would leave it for her family. She wanted Keisha to have the house because she knew that Keisha loved it. It had been Keisha's refuge from the madness of her father's house, which was constantly filled with men—uncles—who would come like shadows into her dreams, making it hard for her to sleep. She slept well at Rose's, and Leonora was always there. Rufus and his cousins—her uncles—were hardly ever there, and when they were, they stayed away from her.

Keisha looked out into the garden, the evenly cut grass, the jumble of flowering plants that came alive with color in the spring but were simply green and calm now. It was warm and the smell of freshly mown grass drew her back to comfortable times.

"You know you got to come with us to Philly, now," Leonora said.

"I know. I just don't want to go up there. I don't know if I could deal with seeing Blossom," Keisha said.

Blossom had lived for years at Aunt Rose's place with Keisha. They were almost like sisters, both abandoned by parents who wanted to find themselves or to find something good. Blossom had stayed there for six years, until things got really bad with Rufus.

"She dying, Keisha," Leonora said.

"Just like that. She is my age. They don't know what it is?"

"She just been bleeding and can't stop. They keep sucking blood from her stomach, but they can't find where it's all coming from. She—" Leonora thought of what she had suspected all along. She had stopped herself from even entertaining the thought, for fear of slipping and saying something to Rose. But she knew what was killing Blossom. "You know she got AIDS, right?"

"No she ain't," Keisha said, leaning toward Leonora. Leonora simply nodded and then rolled her eyes in the direction of the kitchen. "She don't know?"

"Her mama don't even know."

"What you mean Martha don't know, Leonora?"

"It would kill that woman. Blossom don't want her knowing. But she ain't going to make it past next week, I am sure."

Keisha grew silent. The weight of the truth was on her. Leonora rocked her body back and forth and made moaning sounds.

"Come and get something to eat, now, girl," Rose called from inside the house. "You want sweet tea?"

"Yes, ma'am," Keisha said.

"No, ma'am—just some water," Leonora called back.

The two women stood. Keisha turned to go in. Leonora reached her hand and tugged on Keisha's shoulder.

"She don't know nothing and she don't need to know nothing, okay?"

Rose made her speech while they were eating. She did not

eat—she would eat later, when they were finished. This is the way she did it. She ate after everyone else in the kitchen. It took Keisha awhile to realize that Rose did this so she could be alone for once in the day. Her meal, in the orange low light of the kitchen, was her private time. Everyone knew not to talk to her then—even Night had known this. But if anyone asked, she would have some holy comment to make about the last being the first in the Kingdom.

She sat at the head of the table. "Now, I know you going through all kind of stuff, and I know that life wasn't always good to you, but that ain't your fault, right? That ain't your fault. You got to play with what you have. I don't know why you went down to see that beast, and I don't want to know, Keisha, but I want to tell you that I see that as a mistake, and this time, this time I ain't going to let you make no more mistakes with that one. I know things done got messed up with you and that Jamaican man. Maybe that was just your little pleasure, but you got you a child out of it, and that stuff will make you do crazy things. I know that. It's hormones and that kind of thing. But I have to tell you, Keisha, that when Leonora called me to tell me that you was going to see Troy, you know how that hurt my heart. You know what I said? I said, *That's your fault, Rose. That's your fault.* 'Cause Night didn't want you moving out the house with that boy, but you know how we women is sometimes, we hardest on each other, and I just felt that you was betraying me, you was throwing everything back in my face, back in *our* face. You know how it hurt me when you looked me in the face and told me that you was fucking that boy—that is what you said, now. I looked on you and saw a rebellious child, and the good book say . . . Keisha, I treated you like my own daughter 'cause I know you got a hard lot, but when you said that to me, I said that we was now two women and two women can't stay in the same house. That was my mistake. Night said it, you know. He always said it. He always said, *Now with that Keisha, that was your mistake.* I didn't want to know what happened with you and that fool 'cause deep inside I knew it was me who caused you to go with him. And I know you ain't never got over that son of a bitch. So today I was going to just stop it once and for all. 'Cause I believe that you and the Jamaican boy might . . . well, I want to find a way to get that Troy out of your system so that maybe you might have a chance with somebody, you know? So I was going to put him down, Keisha. That is the truth. I ain't got much to lose, you know. They will give me the death sentence and I'll be with Night at last. I was going to put him down. But Leonora come along. So I didn't. But you got to stand in the gap for me and that gun. You got to make it that I don't have to use it, Keisha. You got to stay away from that fool. That is all. 'Cause I love you, and I want what is good for you. You hurting now, you feeling like you alone, but you too close to that man to be feeling that way. I want you here with us, but you can't stay here, Keisha, or somebody gonna die. You need to come with us up to Martha in Philly. Stay with her some. She got space and she need the company. Have the child up there. We will come up and help you out. Then when you done, we work out the rest. But we going on Thursday. You need to come."

Keisha did not leave with them on Thursday. Philadelphia would have been good, an escape. She was looking for escapes. But Rufus was going to be there and Rufus was the last person Keisha needed to be around. He would sit in the van with his head high, his arrogant stupid self acting as if he had not wrecked the lives of both Keisha and Blossom those years when the closet became a terrible nightmare—the hands, the whispered warnings, the smell of smoke, the horror of uncles. It was Rufus who had reversed Night's car into Keisha, knocking her to the ground and then running over her foot with the back wheel, crushing the bones of her tiny leg. It was Rufus who came through the closet door a week later sometime after midnight, to drag her into the bundle of coats and fallen clothes, plaster cast and all, to hoarsely whisper that he would break the other leg if she told anybody. Rufus, Mr. Big Social Worker now. Rufus, who got drunk one night when Keisha was fifteen, and came to her while she sat on the porch looking at the dance of moths around the garage light. He came to mess with her and she pushed him hard. He fell on his bottom, and she kicked him in the head. Kicked him hard in the head and liked the feel of his bone on her foot—the pain of the blow, the sick sound of his nose snapping. And she didn't care. "Fucking shit!" she had yelled, spitting on him and going inside. Rufus had said nothing to her, never messed with her again. But she hated him anyway. Hated him for the way that things he did stayed with her, things he did stayed with Blossom. That son of a bitch, he drove Blossom to drink. Twelve years old and drinking. They all drank. Keisha drank. It was a girl's game, and it became a way for them to laugh a little despite it all. But not for Blossom. She drank so her mother would know that she was dying in South Carolina, that she needed to be back in Philadelphia. Blossom was drunk and weeping when Rose drove her to Philadelphia and left her, fourteen years old, alcoholic and pregnant at her mother's door.

"I told you to come for her, Martha," Aunt Rose had said. "I told you she need a mother. I can't do this no more. That girl need to get out of there. She pregnant,

Martha. She need a mother and I can't be that for her no more."

Keisha learned later that the baby had died in Blossom's womb. Blossom never stopped having problems with her womb after that. And she kept on drinking. That sweet, black-skinned girl with eyes so deep and tender and black, with thick plaits of hair, with a body of such full sweetness. She couldn't stop. Blossom drank herself down as if she was trying to purge herself. It was like the womb was her burden. She never had normal cycles, never had a time without pain. And now it was killing her. AIDS was not killing Blossom, it was Rufus. Keisha believed this fully. And that son of a bitch was going to drive up there, and he was going to go to her bedside and say how sorry he was about how she was feeling, about how she was dying, how she was bleeding to death. Keisha could not tell Aunt Rose why; she did not know how to do that. But she told Leonora that she should not let that happen. That she should not let Rufus be up there with Blossom. That they should let Blossom die in peace.

They were saying goodbye. It was Wednesday and Keisha was packed and her rental car was in the road at the end of the driveway. Leonora held her tightly and told her to take care.

"I'll be all right," Keisha said. "I just need to get my head together, you know. I will call you, okay? When you get in from Philly, I will call you, yeah?"

"You do that."

"Tell Blossom I say I love her and that there'll be no closets up in heaven."

"I'll tell her just like you asked me to."

"And if Kofi calls, you don't know. Yeah?"

"It ain't right, Keisha."

"You don't know."

Leonora nodded. Keisha walked to the car, waved again, and then drove off. She left Ridgeway, headed to I-77, and pointed north toward Charlotte. It was 5:30 in the morning. The sun was starting to lighten the sky. By the time she hit the hills between Tennessee and North Carolina, the light was fresh in the cabin of the car—a clean light. She rolled down the glass and breathed. She felt a little better.

# BOOK IV

# Chapter Twenty-Five

Now, in his room in Spanish Town, Kofi felt no release. He was in a bad state. He wanted to run outside, he wanted to breathe. He felt a familiar tightness in his chest. He would normally take medication at this point. He could feel that something heavy was upon him and he was going to start to see things. He was going to start to fly.

He was not sure why he decided to climb up to Blue Mountain's Peak that next day, but he felt he had to do it. He remembered once getting a revelation, a word, while climbing up that mountain. The word had come in the wind, and below him he could see the blackened remnant of a bush fire. In the wide-open silence of the hillsides he heard the voice of God speaking to him, making sense of his history, of his past, of the distance that he felt from his family. God spoke to him then. Maybe he hoped to find the same voice speaking to him this time.

But this time there was no sun. It rained. The rain was vicious and constant. He took a bus as far as he could and then walked until pain rushed through his legs. He could hardly breathe. He could not see beyond the thick green of the bushes on the path. The path was a muddy stretch of stone and sucking wetness. He was shivering as he panted up the mountain, certain that he would never make it to the top again and uncertain of why he was going there. His thighs flamed with a terrible chafing from the wet khaki on his skin. He began to smell himself, a sickening smell that seemed to seep from his pores.

Soon he could tell that he would not make it to the top of the mountain that afternoon. He could feel that his body was going to have to rest. He remembered through a vague mist of thought that somewhere beyond was a path leading to a small clearing with a stand-pipe. Not far from that clearing was a hut. He had rested in that hut with an old girlfriend once.

The darkness was consuming now even though it was not yet 4 o'clock. He finally saw the path, and his heart leaped.

He dragged himself up, further into the cold of the mountains, along a densely overgrown path, and then deep into a cluster of trees in a valley. He knew that this was not the same place. As he entered what seemed like a grotto, a riot of birds flew into the sky screaming.

He saw the hut at last. He walked in and shut the door. He was in pitch black. He could hear the rain beating hard on the roof.

It was cold and airless, and he felt what seemed like bones all over the floor. Something crawled over his leg. He kicked. It was not heavy like a rat. Lizard, he thought. He sat there and felt the chemicals changing in his head.

After five hours, he started to talk to the lizard. That is when he started to sing. Soon he was taking short runs around the room. He was not sure why. He opened the door and looked outside. Total darkness. He would have to stay there until there was light. He was imprisoned. He walked and trotted around some more until he was sweating. Then when he was tired, he sat down and pulled off his trousers. He used the tip of his fingers to touch the tender and lumpy inside of his thighs. The fire in the chafing was fierce. The skin had blistered. He sniffed the fingers—they smelled like burning hair.

He decided to think. He could hear the thinking going on in his brain. He could hear his mind working. He sat there and felt the way his body was doing the thinking as well. Soon he knew that he could fly. That if he thought hard enough he could fly.

He tried. He sat there and waited for the flight to come. When it did eventually, it must have been about 3 in the morning. He had been locked up for more than ten hours—he could not tell where he was. He was talking to the lizard and crying.

He walked to the door. He waited at the door for a few minutes. Then he opened it and flew out.

He flew out and was soon somewhere far beyond the hut. He was far beyond the thick grotto, the path, now dryer, far beyond his plans to climb to the peak. He was going back into the belly of the city. It was still quite dark and he could see nothing of a path. But he was walking down the hill. He was going home and the chemicals in his brain were speaking to him, telling him how to make his way down. Sometimes he would walk, and then he would fly a few hundred yards and alight on an open area.

It took him most of the day to come off the hill and make it to a main road that twisted down the incline of the mountain to a place called August Town—a hill town where some wealthier people from the city built houses and ascended their steep driveways with Land Rovers and jeeps. The town also housed an older community of farmers and poor people who worked for the wealthy coffee growers producing the famous Blue Mountain coffee. Poor people had lived there for years.

The village was closed down for the night, except for a rum shop on a corner called the World End Café. He walked into the rum shop and asked if they had any food. A man said they had some nice shrimp, and if he had the money to pay for it they would give it to him in a stew with yams and rice.

He put money on the table and the man brought the food. He mentioned that he was a genius. The man in the bar smiled knowingly—he was an old man with skin like the inside of a tangerine peel and eyes brown and transparent with the truth of mixed ancestry staring back for all to see. Kofi talked and ate, and soon he was promising the man that he would reveal the secret of flying to him. The man, curiously, was not interested.

"I don't want to fly," he said, pouring more water for Kofi.

"How come?" Kofi asked.

"That woulda spoil it. No good reason, really. You fly. I watch. Hell, I don't even have to watch. You fly and talk it. I feel good."

"Like that," Kofi said. He was enjoying the sweet fleshiness of the shrimp—it satisfied that need for some sweet with his savory.

"Like that," the man said.

When the meal was almost finished, as he was skillfully scraping the last grains of rice onto his fork, Kofi began to feel a terrible heat at the back of his neck. It was a strange prickly heat that made him slap his neck-back with some force. Then he started to rub it. He felt dizzy. The heat was spreading down, across his back, and it was spreading into his scalp as well. He began to scratch his scalp and neck. The burning sensation was becoming an immense itch, a terrible itch that suddenly consumed his groin. His body was on fire long before the terrible pain of stomach cramps knocked him from the chair against the wall. He bent over and stared at the man.

"What you put in the food, man?" He suddenly began to strip. Kofi was quickly down to his underwear. Soon that was discarded. He knew that his face had swollen and the man was worried.

"Water, water," Kofi said. The man gave him water. Kofi poured it into a cupped hand and began to wash his neck. It was helping the heat on his body but not helping at all the contraction in his throat and the pain in his stomach. He sat down, and then he stood up. He started to walk around the room. He could feel things spinning now. This was definite. He was spinning and he could tell that this thing could kill him.

Kofi looked down and saw massive welts pop up all over his body. He got the jug and began to pour water on his body, on all the welts, and he began to talk himself down. He began to jog on the spot, assuming that the sweating would force the toxins from his body. And he was already sweating. His nose, he could tell, was twice its size. It suddenly felt terribly heavy on his face, and just below his sight-line he could see the protrusion of this thing.

He did not notice the old man returning with a woman, much younger.

Iscilda helped Kofi pour water on his body, trying to calm the heat. He was trying to get himself together so he could fly. "The chemicals," he kept saying. The chemicals. The chemicals. They were causing him much trouble.

"Jesus, have mercy," she breathed as she stood behind him. She was looking at islands of huge welts across his back. "You allergic," she said.

"Him need a purge. The man full a toxins," the old man said. He disappeared behind his counter and then reappeared with a glass of dark fluid.

Kofi saw the fluid coming toward him and suddenly

felt like opening his arms and flying again. Leaving this place.

"Come, bredda. Drink this. Stout, and a lickle senna pod. Come."

Kofi did not want to drink, but when Iscilda took the glass from the old man and offered it to him, he grasped it staring into her eyes. His mind was scattering across the hills. He listened to her cooing. She looked like Keisha. It was a truth he had resisted from the moment he saw Iscilda step out there, but he could no longer fight it. She looked like her.

"Keisha," he said.

"Drink it."

So he drank it. It made him grow weak, a drunken kind of weakness. And then he felt the heaving of his stomach, the pressure in his bowels. Iscilda seemed to know when to help him to the latrine at the back. She sat him down and held his face as he released his insides into the dark hole.

Afterwards he slept.

He dreamt of Keisha lying on a table bleeding from her womb. He dreamt of Keisha making love to him. He dreamt of Keisha with her head bandanaed, preaching a mouthful of revelations into the sky. But in all the dreams Keisha was alone. He was merely watching her.

In the morning, he woke to see that he was lying on a burlap bag at the doorway of the store. He stood up and realized he was naked. His clothes were neatly folded beside him and dry. He put them on. On the counter was an enamel plate decorated with lively colored plums and leaves. On the plate was a sandwich of thickly sliced bread seeping with oil. The spillage of ackee and saltfish assured him of what he saw. He ate the meal quickly, chewing on the soft egglike texture of the fruit flavored with sweet coconut milk. Then he walked outside into the cool morning. His eyes hurt. His body hurt. His stomach muscles hurt.

There was no one around. The dog was pissing against a post at the far end of the street. Kofi wanted to call to someone but thought better of it. He began to walk down the hill. After five minutes, Iscilda appeared, climbing up the hill with a covered basket.

"How yuh feeling?" she asked.

"Fine."

"You look better."

"Yes. Thanks."

"That woman dead?" she asked.

"Who?"

"Keisha . . . All yuh deh 'pon is *Keisha, Keisha,* whole night? She dead?"

"No."

"She lef' yuh." This was a statement of knowing.

"Yes."

"Den yuh mus' run her down," Iscilda said, laughing. "Yuh love her bad. She turn yuh fool."

Kofi was not sure whether the woman was laughing with sympathy or mockery. "Yes. Anyway, I gone. Tell your old man t'anks . . ."

"My old man?" she laughed. "You mean my MAN."

"Yes, yes." Kofi smiled with her.

"Walk good. I like you. You big." She smiled slyly and started to climb past him up the hill.

Below, hidden in spots by the dense trees, Kofi could see the two rivers of the Blue Mountains, Hope and Mammee, meeting in a V. He closed his eyes to avoid the image of blood in the river. He opened them and the air was exploding with a rush of colors.

He walked down the hill, slowly, planting his feet

carefully as if the road might give way if he pressed too hard on the ground.

At the bottom of the hill, instead of heading home, he turned down a road that led to the university hospital where he had been admitted in the past and where he knew Toby worked for part of the week. He found Toby and explained to him as calmly as he could that he needed to rest, needed some medication. Toby took him into his office and called Dorothy. Kofi drooped. Toby woke him and helped him across the hospital to the psychiatric ward, Ward 21.

What happened after that remains unclear to Kofi. He called it a long sleep because he could not remember any of it except as one remembers dreams.

But one midmorning—another brilliant Jamaican morning—he found himself standing on the concrete ramp outside of Ward 21, staring at the future. They were letting him go. Not that they thought he was fine, that he was ready to go home.

Toby had signed the release forms the night before. The two had argued about how he was to get back to his house. Toby wanted him to go to Dorothy's in Ocho Rios. He promised to arrange transportation for Kofi. But Kofi insisted he would take the bus to Spanish Town alone.

So early the next morning he found himself standing in the blazing sun staring at his future.

He found walking difficult. It may have been the sun, which was relentless, oppressive. By the time he was on the bus, Kofi was drenched with sweat and was panting, trying to get a good breath in. He was tired. He was nauseated and he did not think he could make it to where he was going.

He realized that no one had asked him to shower or to

change his clothes for a while. He only realized it then because of the intense smell rising from his crotch, like the stench of a dead thing. He quickly closed his legs, but he could tell that the scent had escaped. It had escaped and was spinning through the van, overpowering every other scent in the sweaty vehicle. Yet no one asked him to get off the bus. No one. In his heart he repented of every cruel word he had spoken about Jamaicans. They forgave him this stench of death that came off his body.

He made it home, into his room. He made it just as the postman was riding away from his gate. The helper Miss Dorothy had sent was staring at him and kept asking Kofi if he was supposed to be there. Kofi said nothing. He knew that he had arrived home and all would be well.

A week later he called the bass player in New York. He said he was ready to return to America to work. He needed money for his airfare.

"You get anything good down there?" the bass player asked.

"Yes, man," Kofi said. Before Keisha had left, he had managed to get three deejays to lay some lyrics on a track that he thought needed a yard feel, some authentic quality. He had overseen the recording, his mind focused on the decision forming in his head. He had also put down his own vocals on the other tracks and arranged for a bunch of studio musicians to do some backup vocals. He was not entirely pleased with the arrangements for the backups, but was sure that he could find other good singers to handle that in New York if necessary.

"Well, we still have the work on the Ethiopian stuff to do. I set up a thing wid a nice group in Addis Ababa. You gwine go there for us?" The bass player knew that he had to get Kofi to commit before investing in bringing him to New York.

"When I come up, I will tell you," Kofi said. "Look, you gwine set me up on the ticket?"

"Not a problem, man."

"Cool. Soon. Next week or so, yeah?"

"Kofi, yuh all right? I mean, all that shit you going t'rough . . ."

"Yeah, yeah. Set things up, and when I come up we can talk. Yuh gwine love the tracks."

"Cool, cool."

In a week Kofi was on an airplane to New York. He was going to find Keisha, and he would begin his search there. He had a number for Joan, her old boss. She would know. He also had numbers for her family in South Carolina. He would find her. They had to work it out. He needed this more than he had needed anything else in his life.

Kofi called Pedro, knowing that he would have a lot of apologies to make. But he was prepared for the ritual. Two days before, he had FedExed a demo of several new songs he'd written; songs he knew would impress Pedro, who, despite his complaints, recognized that any successful recording started with Kofi's songwriting. Kofi had written the songs with the Ethiopian band in mind—hints of North African riffs in the vocals and a lilting guitar-heavy quality. It did not take much for him to convince Pedro that he was ready to begin recording. Pedro was guarded about showing enthusiasm, but he had to tell Kofi how much he liked the tunes.

Kofi spent several days in the studio immediately upon his arrival in New York. He worked quickly, knowing that he intended to take off again, in search of Keisha. He rationalized that he had come to New York to work—he needed to prevent himself from feeling like a desperate man. He was a man on a mission.

# Chapter Twenty-Six

Joan told him where Keisha was.

"Oh, so you are the crazy son of a bitch who stole my best researcher. You must have a big dick." Joan's voice was shrill and familiar on the phone.

"I really need to find her," Kofi said. He found himself smiling. He liked her.

"Hey, if she's taken off without telling you how to find her, maybe she wants you out of her life. I'm just saying . . . You are not some crazy stalking fool, are you?"

He quickly explained what had happened in Jamaica: the strain on Keisha, his own selfishness, and his movement to an understanding that he needed her. He tried not to sound unhinged; he made jokes, kept it light but sincere, and took the brunt of the blame for everything. Joan warmed to him, told him he had fucked up and deserved to lose Keisha. But it was clear that Kofi's honesty and sincerity, along with his charm, were working . . .

"Joan, I can tell that you are a driven woman," he said as charmingly as he could. "Now, if you liked a guy and he screwed up for some reason, and then you decided to take off, wouldn't you want him to try to contact you, to make an effort? I admit I made some mistakes, you know, but I care about that woman and I can't settle until I give this a shot. You wouldn't be the barrier to a sweet love story, would you?"

"Now I know why she followed you down there. You

are a tongue, a tongue, man." She paused for a moment. "Listen, I am into stars, and I am into my gut, and I will tell you how to link with her, but if you fuck with her again, if you hurt her, I promise I will search you out and fuck you up. You may think I am some white girl with no clout, but I can fuck you up. I like Keisha. You understand what I am saying?"

"I understand. I promise I won't do anything to hurt her."

"You are just damned lucky you called me *after* my period." She let out a full, almost insane laugh. "You scared of me? You ought to be. I am a crazy woman. Tell Keisha that I want her to work for me still. I am heading to Switzerland for a while. She has a job with me anytime. Tell her, you hear me? She is down in South Carolina. That is where she said she was going. I will give you the number for her Aunt Rose. They will know where she is at. And one more thing: If she is fucking that ex-boyfriend of hers, you do anything to get her from him."

He called the number in South Carolina as soon as he hung up with Joan. First he spoke to Aunt Rose, then Leonora, then Aunt Grace, then another cousin, a sister, an aunt. They all wanted to speak to him—they wanted to make sure that he was not planning to hurt her.

For two weeks he carried out a ritual of speaking every night with someone from her family. They liked him. They liked the way he listened to them and tried to find out more about Keisha and her life. They liked the way they could come down hard on him and yet he would still persist. They liked the way he asked about their lives and remembered details.

Kofi found Rose outrageous and funny and named her "Tornado Woman." She liked that. They thought he was crazy, but they seemed to trust him. Soon he was talking mainly to Leonora, Keisha's cousin. He began looking forward to the nightly talks, to the laughter. He was drawn to the way her voice sounded like Keisha's.

They were all careful not to say where Keisha was. Sometimes Keisha was in South Carolina, sometimes not. When he asked about the ex-boyfriend, they would talk at length about how terrible he was for Keisha, about how somebody must have tied them together with roots, about how that man's family was from Louisiana where people had weird practices. Every time he heard about Keisha's almost pathological attachment to this man, Kofi would feel a sharp pain of anger, a deep jealousy. He listened, talked, exposed himself, let them know that he was safe. He called night after night until they began asking him to travel down to South Carolina to see them. It was a strange thing. Kofi wanted Keisha to know that he was growing close to her through these people. But he knew that Leonora was also toying with him. He could tell that Leonora in particular wanted to see him.

He made arrangements to fly to Columbia. Without really believing, he still hoped that Keisha had been there all along. That she was orchestrating all this, testing him, trying to see how serious he was. Sometimes he imagined her listening on another line, waiting for him to slip up. And when he did falter with Leonora, he would worry. When he flirted with her, when he told her about how soothing her voice was and how he had a picture of her in his mind when he talked to her, he worried that Keisha would know and pronounce him a failure. But he heard nothing of Keisha. Nothing about her. They kept him dangling.

Then two days before he was to leave, Leonora did something odd.

"You want to talk to her?" she asked.

"I do. You have a number for her?" Kofi's heart was racing.

"No, no. But I asked her about e-mail. She gave me her address," Leonora said. "So I've got what you want, sweets. I can give you that."

"Why you doing this? I mean, she asked you to?"

"No, no. *You* asked me to," Leonora said. Softly.

"Yes, I did. But she gave it to you . . ."

"I haven't told her or nothing. About me and you talking. Well, I told her that you was calling and talking with us. But I just told her that maybe it would be good if she let you write to her like that. No harm in that. I told her that Grace was looking to jump you, and that fixed her right away." Leonora laughed. Kofi laughed with her. "I just know that you are coming down here and all, and I want to make sure . . . I just don't want you coming down here and still wondering what's going on between you and her—" Leonora stopped. She was finding it hard to explain. "I just think that y'all need to work things out. I want y'all to work it out so that you can know what is going on, and maybe I could know, too."

"You feel you need to know?" he asked. He could hear her voice growing tender with its vulnerability. He could tell that she was trying to say more about what she wanted than she was actually able to articulate. He was afraid of her saying it, admitting it. For her to do so would be to force him to commit, to make some decision, to admit that he had been flirting with her.

"Yes, it's good to know these things," he said.

"So, you want it?"

He paused for a long moment. "Yeah."

"Okay." There was disappointment in her voice. "You got a pen?"

Leonora said she had to go immediately after giving

him the address. It was not like her. Some nights she would fall asleep on the phone with him. But she had to leave, she said. Kofi felt a thick sense of guilt.

He wrote Keisha that night.

# Chapter Twenty-Seven

It was snowing as she drove into Bloomington. It was the fine snow that spun around madly in the wind and filled your eyes. It was the seemingly harmless kind of snow that slowly consumed everything around it, first leaving a thin veneer of white, and then, in time, filling every space with this unending and relentless white. To Keisha, this snow signified dogged persistence.

She was looking for the glow of motels. She was tired. Her body was beaten up by the driving. She had been thinking, listening to Lauryn Hill waxing philosophical about the vicissitudes of love, and she found herself nodding. The tape kept playing over and over, the thump of the hip-hop beat provoking images in Keisha's head. Did she love this man who was haunting her in this way? Did she care about the child in her? Was this child to be her Zion? Would she one day speak of the child as worth it all? Did she want to have the child of a madman?

The other day on the plane, Aunt Rose had told her, "Girl, he been calling every day." Her high-pitched voice carried sharply across the lines. Keisha was standing in D.C.'s Union Station; the cavernous hall was busy at 6:30 in the evening.

"Every day?" Keisha asked.

"Sweetheart, your cousins been talking to him like

they got designs on the guy." Aunt Rose laughed. "That's why I figured that it was only fair that I tell you. Them carryin' on as if they doing you a favor. Now I don't mean to tell you your business, Keisha, but this man serious about you. He serious. He following you around like he some kind of stalker. But there is something sweet in that, you know. The way he talk about you is not crazy like you say. And he seem sweet, like he got a good education. And he and the band doing good now, not like the piece-a-crap fool I nearly shot . . ."

"He said that?" Keisha was surprised that she was not angry, not even bothered. For the first time she seemed genuinely pleased to hear something about Kofi. She wanted to hear more about the band. Rose was still talking though.

"I didn't give him no information, Keisha. But he wants to talk to you. I say give him a chance before one of them heifers get a hold of him." She laughed again. "Them cousins of yours and your Aunt Grace already talking about how they could do with some nice Jamaican ass. Now don't you think they wrong?"

Keisha couldn't help laughing. Aunt Grace was seventy-three. Aunt Grace was a lot of talk. "So what about you, Aunt Rose? I know you called to find out if the coast is clear."

"Now you wrong, Keisha. You wrong to say that, now. I was thinking about you, girl. But I can't say I never noticed what a sweet voice he have." She was cackling. Then she grunted. "Huh. I did. I sure did. But I know that you can't judge a man by his voice, and you said he done you wrong, and I believe that because they have some crazy-ass niggers all over the world. I know that. But he wants to talk to you, girl, I can't see no harm in that. That is what I was saying. I mean, you got that baby growing in you, and a man deserve to have a chance with his child. You know what I mean?"

"I don't have a number, Aunt Rose." Keisha was planning to travel to Illinois the next day. She didn't know where she could be reached. She was thinking about crossing the border into Canada after that. There was no method to her meandering. She moved with the randomness of someone who did not want to be followed.

"I told him that you didn't have no number, and that he was crazy to be asking us when he knew we were your kin and when we knew all what he had done to you," Rose went on. "But he's got the sweetest tongue, ain't he? Talking about how much he liked talking to us 'cause it gave him a taste of you, and how much he wanted to come to South Carolina to see us and see where we live. And he knew Ridgeway. Yeah, he knew all about Ridgeway and about the swamps and the highway and everything. I was listening to him and I was just feeling like we was kin or something. Hell, that man got some roots stuff in him, you know. He had me laughing and grinning away with him like me and him was, you know . . ."

Keisha laughed. She found it funny. Kofi had won over Aunt Rose. Drawn her into that world he knew how to create with his voice. A world of such intense privacy that a woman could feel as if she were the only person there. But that was an old Kofi. He had made her feel that way on the first walk in Columbia, and then when they first made love in New York. That was so many Kofis ago.

As Keisha had driven out of Maryland after her conversation with Rose, a slight drizzle misted everything. In the rental car she had picked up in D.C., she pointed her body northwest. She was eating pure junk. Hamburgers from

Burger King—something she had never eaten before. The unhealthiness of it was her indulgence. She ate the food as she drove, while Lauryn Hill contemplated the joy of her life.

She had given Leonora her e-mail address for Kofi, though she avoided the computer until today when she checked into a Days Inn outside of Bloomington. Keisha still enjoyed hotel rooms. The sense of adventure, the anonymity, the feeling that she owned herself. She indulged in all of it. This was the only time she ever watched pornography, her mind barely registering what she was seeing and hearing on the screen. She kept waiting for a story.

She plugged in her laptop and began to check her e-mail. Kofi had written her a long message. In the room, with the lights out, the night thick outside, the television flickering its images and the strange moaning of the bad actors on the screen, she was drawn into a place far from everything around her.

> Dear Keisha,
>
> I am in Peter Tosh's room—the same one. If you kept the number you could actually call me and ask for me. I gave them Peter Tosh again. It's true.
>
> I want to know if you still hate me so much, still want to put me through all of this. I am not sure what happened. We should be closer now. I love you. I need you. I want to be with you. For God's sake, you have my child in you. Your relatives seem to like me and some of them have taken to calling me. You know how women can like me. They do. (Smile.)

Keisha stopped reading. She wanted to delete the whole thing now. He was starting to play head games with her. There was something despicable about what he was doing. But she continued to read. Clicking on the scroll bar. The words unfolding on the screen.

*I feel myself falling into a new place that is not as familiar as I thought it would be. There is no language to speak it.*

*These days, "in love" has a face, she has a smell, a texture, she has a way of looking at me, a way of understanding me, a way of making me laugh, a way of making me grow sad, a way of making me flare with frustration and anger, a way for me to pray, a way for me to feel adequate, and a way for me to feel inadequate. She has a specific face, a delicately soft eye, wide, white with dark brown irises, a nose that turns at the bridge but is a flared tender thing, lips so evenly cut, so perfectly etched that I can feel a sharpened piece of lead making the thin line of definition along their ridges. I love a pretty woman, a beautiful woman with cheekbones, sharp and constantly catching light, eyes that brim with laughter— that is the way that I limit the words "in love." If I contemplate this again and again, I know that I will have to find other words to shape what I feel. So we search for other words. You are filling a need that is in me. If I don't find you, I will crumble, I will be devastated. I did not allow myself to miss you while you were with me. I made a mistake there. Now I miss you and I don't know how to live that. Hey, I know this sounds melodramatic, but I am pulling out all the stops here, Keisha. I am not going mad, just hungry for you. I want you to write to me.*
*Love,*
*Kofi*

Keisha finished reading the letter and felt a deep pain in her stomach. She started to cry. It was a simple, unconscious act, but the tears came. She did not want to go back to the place where they had started, and yet here he was charming her with his words. She was angry though. Angry at herself for starting to see someone else other than the man who spent all his time in Jamaica lying down on the cool tiles of the porch, staring blankly at the world, not talking to her, not reaching for her, letting her walk away, walk into the duplicitous machinations of Dorothy. He must have known that she would be hurt by Dorothy, but he had done nothing. She was confusing this desperate man with that man in Jamaica. She was angry at Kofi, too, for believing he knew who she was, what she was capable of.

She did not know the Kofi in the letter. He was resolute. He loved her.

Not like old Kofi, who kept singing, *"Is this love, is this love, that I'm feeling?"* with a too gleeful edge of cynicism in his voice. His answer was always, "I don't know, I don't know, I don't know." Now he said he knew. Still, she was running. She was running from the way things tasted in her mouth when she left Jamaica. She was running from her own anger. And she was running with this child in her.

She played with the television. The computer went to sleep. She knew that she would have to answer. She would have to tell him something. She had to deal directly with his question, his desire to see her. She had to be clear. The images flickered on the TV screen. She could not concentrate. She went to the window and looked out. It was growing darker, and it had started to snow again. The place had a glow about it. She decided to go outside. She had noticed a small used bookstore down the road and she was going to check it out. She wanted to be distracted.

She put on her coat and walked out into the lobby, and then, with a certain surge of energy, into the snow. Her chest felt tight from the cold as she spotted the store wavering in the drifting snow. *USED BOOKS.* The deeper in she went, the darker and more comforting the place felt. She was not looking for anything in particular, but she did find a book that could transport her from the traps her mind was setting for her. She realized now that this was what she wanted. She walked across the street to the hotel. She was now hungry, but she did not want to eat. She had to write to Kofi.

Back in her room, she went to the computer.

*I don't want to see you. I am afraid of the way you are turning me on. I don't like it. Find someone else. Forget me. That is the simplest thing. I don't know. I just feel right now that as I clean up my life, I am holding up the sky. I am afraid that it will fall again if I let you in. I can't afford that.*
*Keisha*

She sent it before she could change her mind. The computer muttered and then sent the message. She lay back in the bed and listened to her stomach churning, or maybe it was the baby moving, swimming somewhere safer.

# Chapter Twenty-Eight

When she woke, the red digital numbers on the clock radio read *1:45 a.m.* She looked at the computer. She wanted to hear what he had to say. She could tell that this was going to be a problem—the computer, him having her address, and her need to connect with someone.

His message was sitting there in the in-box. She opened it. It was long, hurried, tumbling.

*Dear Keisha,*

*You wrote. Jesus, you wrote. I am so glad you wrote. I wanted you to write. I really needed you to write. I imagined another story of me and you. You are married to someone else. But you still love me. You have two boys. Maybe one of them is mine. It is always about you.*

*I am making up stories in my head so that I can seduce you into wanting to keep hearing from me. There is that story of the Arabian Nights. The story of a woman captured, trying to distract her executioner with the tales of her people, with tales she makes up. How desperate she is, making tales every night to keep him from drawing the knife across her throat. I feel like her, wanting to make the stories go on and on. I know it is never enough, but that is enough, in its own strange way . . .*

She did not want to read the rest. She was afraid of it.

Had she read further, she would have known that Kofi was heading for South Carolina in a few days to search for her.

But Keisha deleted the message.

For most of the day it snowed. Keisha stayed in the hotel and stared at the snow or at the television. She was getting used to not moving. She did not look at Kofi's messages. They were piling up, but she did not want to see them. She got one from Joan telling her about the new job. Joan kept saying she was excited to have Keisha with her again—somebody who knows what a Philly cheesesteak is, someone who knows that riding a subway is an adventure, not a ritual of convenience. Keisha liked the attention.

# Chapter Twenty-Nine

To get to Columbia, Kofi flew into Charlotte from Newark. He had to wait for two hours in the Charlotte airport, where he passed the time wondering whether or not Keisha was even in Columbia. He had been writing to her, but was not sure where she was. Her aunts had told him that she had left Columbia a long time ago. That she was not even in the state. But they were lying. He could tell because their stories didn't gel with one another. But he knew they were lying to protect Keisha. They lied to him again and again. It was one of their ways of getting to know him. They were treating him like they would any new man entering the family through a relationship with one of the women. It was a sweet familiarity and he was growing comfortable with it. It flattered him, their attention—the way they had a definition of what a man was and what he was supposed to and not supposed to do, and what a woman was supposed to do for a man. They had rules, all of them, and they seemed determined to teach him these rules.

Leonora, whom he was talking to more than the others, was a divorced woman who had worked hard for what she had. She liked her life—most of it. She worked two and a half jobs. A daytime job at the university as a secretary, an evening job filing insurance forms at Blue Cross, and a weekend job typing and filing for a dentist. She made good money and owned a five-bedroom house in Ridgeway. She had furnished it nicely after her two sons left to live in Atlanta.

She was alone now, alone with a stray dog she called Blue who she had found nosing around her house one evening. She fed the dog and he stayed. He was a mongrel, black and unremarkable. She was not sentimental about the dog—he stayed outside—but she loved him. She would come back from her Blue Cross job at 10 p.m., point her black truck into the garage, and wait for the dog to come out to her, tail wagging.

She was also attached to the house. It was her own, not from her marriage—and she was proud of that. She lived mostly in the large living room, with its massive television fed by the satellite dish that she had gotten a suitor to set up outside a year ago. She had dumped him quickly. He was a fool and had no ambition, and she suspected that he sold drugs.

On Fridays she would either go drinking with her friends or stay home, light incense, take off her clothes, put on some music—something black, thick, and seductive, with a pulse like D'Angelo—and she would read a novel. She lived through the telephone, too. Her greatest love affairs were on the phone, finding the language to make orgasms in that large room, with music playing and smoke from the incense creating a haze.

Leonora wanted to see Kofi. He knew everything about her now. And she lied. She lied and told him that Keisha was still in town, and then she said that Keisha was not in town. She had made the mistake because she had forgotten her story. And he confronted her with such anger that she had cried. That was her last invented story.

Kofi did not know what to believe, but he was going to

find Keisha. He would start in South Carolina. He knew, too, that Leonora knew where Keisha was.

Kofi did not want anything to happen between Leonora and himself, but he could tell that the relationship was shaping into something of an affair. Their talks had become sexual. She did a lot of the talking. She told him about her husband, the terrible time they had in that year-long marriage. His abusing her, his inability to satisfy her. She told him of her first orgasm when she was thirty-five. She told him all kinds of things and he listened. And he knew that if he said the right things to Leonora, if he let her see him and talk to him and maybe embrace him, she would also tell him where Keisha was. But Kofi knew that he was not being as strong as he could. He could avoid Leonora altogether and ask someone else about Keisha. Yet he wanted to feel the comfort of being with a familiar person in this new town. It would take longer without Leonora. He could tell that. And Leonora would be offended. Maybe the whole family would be offended.

Besides, Leonora said she would pick him up at the airport and let him stay in her place. "Don't worry, honey. I won't jump your bones. I ain't so desperate. Listen, I really respect a man's wishes, you know." And she said all of this laughing. Laughing that full laugh that he now knew and liked.

He did not know what she looked like, but he expected her to be overweight, unattractive. And he was surprised when he saw her. She was Keisha's relative, but she looked nothing like Keisha. She was lighter-skinned, tall, and big-boned. Her hands were massive, and she carried her shoulders with a sturdiness that startled him. She was built firmly on long legs, but the effect was not masculine.

When they embraced, she held him tightly. He

embraced back. She spoke with charm and familiarity. This was not what he had expected. It was dark outside in the parking lot. The truck was waiting there. Inside he noted the expensive upholstery and the CD player. As soon as they pulled away, he looked at her thighs pumping with smooth skill as she shifted gear.

"You want to see more leg, baby?" she laughed, her voice delicately refined; somewhere near a soprano singing low. He looked away from her leg, embarrassed.

They were on the highway when she spoke again. "I was nervous, you know."

"About what?" He was relaxing. The music was nice. Hip-hop. He was not sure who, but it was right.

"About meeting you, honey. But you gave me a sweet hug. That was nice." She turned to him and smiled her impossibly big smile.

"It is good to see you," he said. The words got caught in his throat and came out like a mumble. His throat was dry. She smiled and continued driving. "So your man wouldn't have a problem with another guy in your home?" Kofi asked after a while.

"I told you that I have a man?" Leonora smiled fleetingly at Kofi.

"No. But you never say you don' have a man either. When a woman don' say nutting, it mean that something in something."

"Something in something." She repeated his words, mocking his accent.

"Exactly," Kofi said. "Now, I not trying to get into your business, but I just want to know the escape plan, you know. Know the lay of the land and when to tek bush."

"So why all of a sudden? You never asked me this on the phone."

"Yeah, but a man couldn' shot me on the phone. I don't want no trouble wid no Yankee madman. I always like to have a contingency plan."

"You hide in the closet, that is what you do." She was laughing.

"That is the first place that man gwine check. No, yuh not gwine ketch me like a punk."

"I see. Well, under the bed would be out, then—"

"*Your* bed?"

"Where else?"

"Oh, so you making a pass at me now."

"You set me up." They laughed. She drove on.

Then he spoke again. "So you have a man?"

"There is someone I see now and then. Nothing serious. Satisfied?"

"Now and then . . ."

"Now and then."

"A married man . . ."

"Now why you had to say something like that? You don't know me like that." She was still laughing.

"Intuition. It's true, right?"

"I won't say . . ."

"Well, at least I don' have to worry 'bout him then."

"I thought you were in love with Keisha . . ."

"You thought right. You thought right." He got suddenly cool after that. Leonora regretted bringing up the issue. Kofi stared out his window as they drove past the strip malls in the Cayce area.

Leonora had not told Kofi about her man because she told no one about him—he *was* married. She had been seeing him for ten years. They met three years after her divorce at a jazz concert in the 701 Gallery. Leonora had gone alone after work, and he was there alone, too. She had teased him about his trying to avoid his wife, and he said she was right. They began a relationship on the phone and on e-mail. It developed into something deeper. In a month they were sleeping together. After six months they had a routine. Twice a month he would come by her home. They made love. They talked. He remembered her birthday. He remembered the anniversary of their first love-making.

She had other men, but she never replaced this one. She made room for him twice a month. He talked to her about his marriage, about his wife's coldness, about problems that he had with his children. She listened, comforted him, fed him, and sent him home with a kiss and an "I love you." At first she hoped he would see that she was the one he really needed, but it didn't take her long to realize that what she had with him was not passionate enough, was not life-transforming enough to make him leave his wife. Still, she liked the routine and relied on the regular sex. Ten years. She knew that she could go on like this for another ten years. She worried sometimes that this thing made her far less willing to work hard at developing relationships with other men. But he made her feel special. And sometimes it was enough.

"Everybody has their own arrangements," she said to Kofi after a long pause. "I have mine. I don't make a big thing out of it, and I don't expect you to. Okay?"

"No big thing," Kofi replied.

"No big thing," she said, doing the echoing thing and smiling.

Kofi knew that she was again telling him more about herself than she normally would. He liked her. He had liked her on the phone, but now, seeing her, he liked her more. She was beautiful. It was a disturbing admission for him. He was not sure what was going to happen at her place, but it was not hard for him to imagine how easily a man could slip into Leonora.

She fed him as soon as they got to her place. She gave him some baked chicken that her mother had sent over. Leonora did not cook much—she did not need to. Her mother cooked for her. She was on a special diet. She suffered from high blood pressure and had recently lost thirty pounds on this new diet. She was feeling pretty, beautiful. She was wearing clothes she had not worn in a long time. She nibbled at fruit while he chewed into the succulent chicken. He was enjoying it. He looked at her and noticed how her breasts weighed down the low cut of her dress. She started to smile. Then she put her hand to her chest as if brushing something off. He looked away and continued to eat.

"Is Keisha here?" he asked.

"Keisha's gone, sweets. I told you. But we could find her. You really want to find her?"

"Yeah."

"I like how you look. Did not know you had so much hair." She smiled. "You got it like that all over?"

He chuckled.

"We got to go to Greeleyville tomorrow to see Keisha's aunty. She says she wants to see you. Okay? Then one of them cousins you been sweet-talking says she has a message for you from Keisha. Then I bring you back home. After that you can do whatever you want. This way, you get to do what you said you want to do. You get to see where Keisha come from. This is her country, you see." She spoke with her large hands rested in front of her on the table. "I think Keisha's crazy to make a man follow her like that and not let him catch her. A man like you. Now, you not crazy or anything, right?"

"No."

"I can tell. I can tell. Love just messed your head up a little bit. Made you sad. Did it to me, too. I know," she said. She touched his hand. "Oh yes."

He looked at her and startled himself with an effort to imagine what her face would look like during orgasm. He imagined it crumbling into character, creases, articulations of a history, maybe tears, and something like impatience in her eyes. He felt himself hardening, and tried to focus on the chicken. She was humming to Sweet Honey in the Rock. They were singing something holy, but she was making it sound quite unholy.

"You like the chicken?" she asked, leaning toward him again.

# Chapter Thirty

They drove across the Midlands the next day. There was much sexual tension in the car. Everything she did seemed to draw his eyes to her body, to the shape of her lips, to the way her fingers curled around the wheel, to the easy languid way she sat back and guided the truck, to the texture and shape of her legs, to her scent, a delicate musk that made him want to breathe her in. He fantasized about touching her as they drove, about the logistics of love-making in a moving vehicle. He kept imagining various moves, various positions, and eliminating them. The act of cataloguing was the sweetness. She would suddenly smile at him for no good reason as they drove, and then her mood would change quickly to a petulance that dripped with sensuality. Occasionally she would touch him as she talked. Her fingers were damp.

The night before he had gone to bed while she sat in the living room on the sofa, her legs stretched out, a glass of wine in hand. She was waiting for him to do something. He could tell. She was not smiling, but he could sense that were he to sit beside her, he would fall into her bosom. The incense swirled around her, perfuming everything. He wanted to stay. She had on a pair of black-rimmed spectacles that made her look so much more alluring to him. More vulnerable. If he knew he could have simply held her, sat with her and held her for the night, he would have. But he could tell that they would have made love, and then there would have been regret.

He left her there. Said goodbye, and she said, "Good night, baby, call me if you need anything." And she said it as a kind of plea, but with little irony.

He could feel the tension through the door. Heard her move around, turn off the television, and then listened as the bathroom sounds came through to him, the teeth scrubbing, the gargling, and the flushing. Then he slept. He dreamt of Leonora and not Keisha that night. He masturbated in the shower the next morning and was intentionally careless about cleaning up—hoping she might find a trace of him in the tub.

She said nothing as they drove out. They stopped and ate omelets at an IHOP in Columbia. She ordered first. He followed her lead.

"I dreamt of you last night," he said.

"Fuck you, baby," she said. He was not sure whether she was laughing. She said it softly, but there was a coolness about it. He decided not to continue and she did not bring it up again. Not for the entire drive.

That night, after they came back, he wrote to Keisha. He knew now that she was not in town. Leonora was at the university doing some paperwork. She promised to come home and eat a late meal with him if he could wait. All day she had been sweet, pleasant, but quiet. But she also seemed angry. He could tell that it had to do with the night before. He knew they were going to end up together somehow. He just wanted to see if he could prolong it enough to make it seem to himself like it was an accident that Keisha was not around. He was resentful and disappointed. Everyone was telling him that Keisha was done with him. They said it again and again. Rose, the old aunt of Keisha's who seemed to be closest to her, took him aside and told him that he should probably leave Keisha alone.

"I can't tell you what to do because I know what love is like, and you young people have some funny ideas, but you got hearts like everybody else, and I can't tell you to be a waiter if you are a looker, a hunter, a searcher. I can't tell you to fish if you prefer to go and steal chickens. But I can tell you that Keisha is running from you, son, and she could wreck your life 'cause she will keep running. You don't want to wreck your own life. Now, I love that girl, but she has learned that running is her only way to cope sometimes. You may need to look at that and cut your losses. But if you got the hunter's heart in you, and if that girl's spirit riding your back like this, then ain't nothing I can tell you to do, right?" She touched his face. "You got a honest face. Weak chin though. Weak chin. But a honest face. You could do right by a woman. Careful of that Leonora now. She will spit you out." She laughed and then led him back to the yard.

They told him to move on with his life. All of them. It was not him, they said. It was Keisha. She'd had a rough life and she could not hold onto relationships. He started to believe it. And Leonora, this woman, was guiding him and looking after him. She did so as if she was trying to assure him that despite Keisha, he was liked. Leonora looked after him.

He wrote to Keisha to tell her that he had seen her, seen her life, seen her relatives.

*Dear Keisha,*
    *Few things here succumb to time, though the old grow tender and die. That is what I thought when I drove through*

your family's town, Greeleyville. I know you are somewhere, somewhere where there are a lot of people. Somewhere where it will be impossible for me to find you. The scent of jasmine, a scent that I now know quite well and feel funny talking about. (Leonora has been kind to me. She has taught me dogwoods, wisteria, and jasmine—how they smell. You should be jealous of her.) And there is another smell. It is a smell I associate with Rose: the dank earthiness of this soil soaked by an old river. It reminds me of my grandfather's village in Jamaica—remember it?—where he is buried in a thick grotto of aloe vera and stunted coffee trees. You never told me that they were so alike. But maybe you did not think they were so alike, these places. You never said. I saw a ginkgo tree as we drove past a small town on the way there. It was glowing with yellow leaves. They say it came from China. I wonder who brought it here. All over the floor, yellow blossoms like a carpet. It reminded me of Jamaica when the pouis is in bloom. Rose said you played violin and sang in that church. I did not know you played the violin. She showed me the violin—your violin. The one you got from Night (?) . . . anyway, her husband. She is saving the things for you. I feel as if I am going through your things. I can smell you sometimes. You should be taking me on this journey. I know, you said you would and I did not seem interested. You are never going to forgive me, are you? To tell you the truth, I am afraid of this place, too. It makes me feel very far from you even as I feel closer. Sometimes I feel that if I did not know all of this, I would be better able to love you, without pain, without fear. Your people are into blood ties. I would never know this knowing you. How you used to talk about my family as if we were sick or something. You guys are worse. Maybe that is why it pissed you off so much, my family. I have a lyric for a song I am writing. It is simple: "This earth knows God, knows family, and blood ties." Sometimes I think Bob

*Marley is leaving me. He would never write a line like that.*
*Never.*
*Love,*
*Kofi*


He wanted to tell her everything about the trip. He wanted her to know that he had touched her life, her world. But he wanted to see her face as he told her these things. He was not sure how she would react. He would tell her about the drive with Leonora into the heart of South Carolina, the sun flaming everything beneath it. They rode Highway 15 through Manning toward Kingstree, listening to the bourbon-grooved voice of Lady Day on the sound system.

Leonora pulled the truck over and asked Kofi to drive. He was reluctant, but she insisted. At first she said she wanted to look at him while they talked, and then she said she was just tired. He moved to the front, stopping for an instant to stretch. It was now quite warm. To their left and right were stretches of fields—farmland. Further out he saw the pale gray façades of broken old structures that may have housed sharecroppers, or perhaps they still did. Rusty farm equipment littered the fields. The sky rose sharply beyond the flat line of the trees edging these fields. Birds turned in the open sky. He felt the surge of the truck as he gunned the engine.

Leonora started to fiddle with the tape recorder when a song ended. It was "God Bless the Child." She had to lean forward, as she had dropped the seat so far back that she was almost lying down while he drove. He looked across at her. The brilliant light caught her skin and flamed. He wanted to touch her. Her face had the look he expected to see when she was coming, but she was listening to the music. Her eyes were closed tightly, her lips open, mouthing the words. As soon as it was about to end, she would leap forward and punch viciously at the knobs, rushing the tape back to its beginning.

Finally, she let it play and it seemed she had fallen asleep with her hand on her left breast. He was not sure where he was going. He continued on the highway. Then she rose, pulling the seat up. She sat still, looking sadly out the window.

"I want you to make love to me tonight," she said quietly. "Wrong or right."

He turned to her. She reached and touched his face. He drove on.

She asked him to turn onto a side road, which he did. Then she asked him to slow down right beside a broken gate that opened onto a field rising slowly up a gentle incline. She pointed to a tree isolated against an indifferent blue sky.

"Like that," she said. "You see how that looks? Normal. Natural. Simple. That kind of thing makes me cry. It makes Keisha cry, too. You understand? We are very simple people. If you made love to me, if you made love to me and then told Keisha that you did because I saw that tree and cried, she would understand. She wouldn't get mad because she knows. Me and Keisha, we sat under that tree one time. I don't remember why, but we sat there, me and Keisha, and we ate chicken, and she was crying for no good reason. And I started to cry just looking at that tree. "

He glanced at her and saw the tears filling her eyes, then turned back to the road. She did not make a sound. Then he glanced again. She was wiping away the tears.

"She's seen a lot of shit, you hear me? You got to understand why she don't take no chances. She been through all kinda shit, man. Poor girl."

"What is that?" he asked.

Leonora's eyes were closed. He leaned over and kissed her. Her mouth opened to his. Their tongues moved lazily. Then he lifted himself, touched her face. Her eyes were still closed.

She drove for the last leg of the journey into Greeleyville, a town with one supermarket, one gas station, one elementary school, one high school, one bowling alley, one post office, and ten churches. Leonora was quiet. Waving to the line of bungalows, she said, "Our in-laws live there."

They crossed a bypass and headed down an avenue of dignified homes, modest as tarnished heirlooms, American-made cars lining the street.

"We all grew up here," she said. "And that house over there, a man lived there for as long as I know this place. He lived there all my life. He is now passed. He passed last week."

Through a circle of roads turning in on themselves, a whole society lay hidden away. Kofi could tell that this was the life that simply continued while the civil rights activists were marching around chanting, "Power to the People!" It was not the passing of time that made the place look normal to him. It was the fact that the world never did change. Never changed a bit despite all the natural and unnatural disasters and upheavals that spun around the fragile roofs of the houses.

Leonora talked on, pointing out places, like stations of Keisha's lives. She showed him her step-grandmother's home, the red brick house where they used to visit, through a wooded area full of sweet succulent plums, now a gleaming used car lot with no trees, nothing but asphalt and more asphalt.

When they visited the family "estate"—a series of pre-fab houses that formed a kind of village of relatives—Leonora remained silent while everyone else talked. ("These houses might be new, but this land been in my family since slavery days," she had said.) The conversation moved from mundane topics to petty quarrels about who talked too much and who was just showing off for this nice man. They laughed a lot. Leonora smiled, but she stayed aloof. She was easily the lightest-skinned person there, and this seemed to mean something. He understood the politics of skin color, but he was not sure whether they were showing deference or disrespect, a sense of difference. He could tell that something about her was outside. But he did not understand the family structure. He heard so much. Rose told stories, and so did the other relatives, or were they friends? There were no men. The men were not around, Leonora said afterwards. They just were not around. Kofi said that they must have been somewhere. She laughed and said, "Well, they sure staying there, they must like it over there," and left it at that.

There was nothing simple, Kofi was seeing, about Keisha's life. It had to do with history, the complicated intersections of history—the secrets. He was afraid of the secrets.

Kofi had eaten everything he was served—the soppy black-eyed peas, the syrupy sweet potatoes, the greens. But they loved him for coming back to the whiting fish, battered golden in corn flour. He ate the white flesh after soaking it in hot sauce. He ate about seven of the fish. Rose was pleased. She was pleased with him and forgave him for not eating more of the macaroni and cheese. Then afterwards, they sat in the densely furnished living room and started to remember. The mantra was the same:

"Alma begat Powie begat Okla begat Lynne begat Keisha."

Lynne was dead. She had gone to Atlanta to sing and she died. Got sick with pneumonia, but what killed her was drinking.

He wrote the names down. He wanted to sing them back to Keisha. Leonora stared at him. He was not sure what she was saying, whether she approved or not. But he wrote and then put the pen and paper aside. Leonora looked away when he was finished. She was ready to leave, he could tell. But she would not rush him. She would wait for him. Her silence frightened him.

Leonora said little as they began driving toward Ridgeway. The road was dark. She moved with force and speed. She was seeing things that he could not possibly see. He felt safe with her. He liked the assurance that she had, the way she handled the car. In the darkness, with the music playing, the silence was not as daunting as he feared it would be. It seemed to make sense that their heads would be in different places.

She started to sing softly with the music. He leaned his head back and closed his eyes. He was not sleeping, but he was drifting. It felt comfortable. He felt her hand rest on his thigh. It stayed still there.

"Tired?" she said.

"Yeah."

She patted his thigh, but kept her hand there. He was drifting.

"Keisha told you what happened to her, the man at the university who tried to force himself on her. She told you about that? She told you about her cousins? She told you about those? Her uncles. The men who were not there. She told you about those? And the thing that gets her is that nobody was there to protect her. She couldn't go to nobody. Those men looked at her and figured she had no one looking out for her." She grew silent. Then she continued: "Keisha says sometimes she don't even know who she is really and what she is feeling. You know, sometimes I feel just like that. That is why we get along. We get along good because we seen these things, and these things been done to us. It is like that."

He heard her as if from far. He heard everything. Keisha had said so little. The world was opening to him. Leonora stopped talking. He felt himself falling asleep. The hand was warm on his thigh.

When they got to the house, Leonora said goodnight. He stood there somewhat perplexed. He had been sure that something was going to happen. But she emptied some dog food in a plate, shut the blinds, turned off the lights, and went to her room.

He waited.

She did not come out.

He went into his room and lay on the bed. The door was ajar. He could feel the light from the street on his face. He drifted asleep as he listened to Leonora carry out her ritual. He slept. He was stirred by the sound of Leonora's voice and the weight of her body against him. His body slipped against her.

"Just hold me. Hold me. You don't have to do anything but hold me, baby." She moved against him steadily, her breath short and quick. She stiffened, then relaxed, coming tenderly into the night.

He held her.

# Chapter Thirty-One

That night Keisha called Rose, and Rose told her that Leonora had brought Kofi to see the family. Rose said that Keisha ought to call Leonora to find out what was going on.

"I am not calling them. I don't want to know what's going on with him, Aunt Rose. I really don't," Keisha said.

"Okay, honey. Look here, I got something on the stove. Take me a minute to be done. Give me the number where you're at and I'll call you back. No point raising up your bills."

Keisha gave her the number.

"You going anywhere far tonight?"

"No, Aunt Rose. Not going nowhere. I am done for the night. I'll be right here."

The phone rang thirty minutes later. It was not Rose but Leonora. Keisha was surprised. Leonora did not have her number.

"Rose gave it to me. Said I was to call you and get this all straightened out."

"No need for that, Leonora. Ain't nothing to be straightened out."

"Keisha, this guy's crazy about you. He is."

"Okay. So what do you think I should do about that? I mean, what are you saying?"

"I know how he feels."

"Oh, you do?"

"Don't get all funny on me now, girl. I am just saying, I talked to him, I know what he is going through."

"Well, since you are the damned expert on him, why don't you make him feel good with you? I know you want him, Leonora. If you haven't fucked him already."

"For somebody who don't care about the guy, you acting kinda jealous."

"Jealous. Oh please. Look, I just don't like you playing me for a fool or something. Talking about how you know what he feels. Leonora, you know you want him."

"Why you getting all bitchy all of a sudden? Hey, you said you don't want this guy. Now, I ain't saying me and him are having a thing, but you taking this to the street like me and you fighting over some man. Nobody told me that this was the deal, girl, so explain that to me. Why you getting all bitchy and jealous like that?"

"Oh, so I am a bitch now. That's what he said?"

"There you go again. No, I said you was a bitch 'cause you behaving like a bitch, all right? Sure, I like him. I like him. He nice and everything. He's a nice guy. That is how I see him. And yeah, if he wasn't so fucked up about you, maybe I could get something good going with him, you know? But he ain't studying me and my designs. His head is still way up in you. And I think you gotta let him go. I mean, if you ain't interested in him no more. That is all I am saying. I didn't call you to argue over nothing. I just want you to know. He ain't right, and that is 'cause you're killing him. Like you put some roots on him or something. You know what I'm saying? He thinking about you. Even when . . ."

"Even when what?"

"I am just saying that you on his mind."

"You fucked him, Leonora?"

"Jesus, Keisha. What—"

"No, no, you fucked him, didn't you? So who else fucked him? Tell me that."

"Ain't nobody fucking nobody, okay. Ain't nobody fucking nobody. Look how you got me cussing and stuff. You know I don't like to cuss, Keisha."

Keisha could not help laughing at this.

Leonora laughed, too. "He just want to know everything about you. Everything. Like you and him was married or something. That is all he is into. Now, he's going to keep looking for you, and I bet you Rose is going to tell him how to find your ass. That's all I am saying. I want you to talk to him, you know. Tell him it is done. Tell him proper. Give him a reason or something . . ."

"Then maybe you can get with him, eh?"

There was some good humor there. Leonora could sense it. "Aww shit, you on that again . . ." They were smiling.

"You know it's true, Leonora . . ."

"Now, I am not saying that I don't like him. I do. I like him. I like his ways. But I know what this is, you know. It is about you first. If I was to have anything with him now, it wouldn't work. Make me feel like leftovers, you know. He always thinking about you. Don't know what kinda roots you put on the guy."

"I ain't give him a thing." They laughed full-blooded laughs.

Then after a pause, Leonora spoke. "I miss you, Keisha. Miss you. You sure you all right?"

"Yeah, yeah. I'm all right."

"Like your head is confused, you know. Getting all crazy with me . . ."

"I'm, sorry, baby. I just felt really stupid when I started to think that maybe he just came to Columbia to . . . I don't know. Shouldn't be jealous or nothing like that.

I don't want him. Can't do a thing with him. His head is fucked up and mine is fucked up, too. When I think about him, I keep thinking ugly things. But I am all right."

"You going to write him?"

"Maybe. He still in Columbia?"

"Yeah . . . he still there."

"Where he staying at?"

"Some hotel, I don't know . . . You should write him though. You know, with the computer and stuff. Okay? I didn't mean to get you all upset now, Keisha. You know, you my cousin and all. You know that."

"Yeah, I know."

"I love you."

"Love you too."

The lie rested on Leonora's head like a weight. Nobody would know, really. Everyone was sure that Kofi was staying at a motel off the interstate. Kofi himself had said that it would be a mistake to tell Keisha what had happened, so he wouldn't be telling her where he stayed. Maybe someday she would know, but things were all messed up now anyway, and there was no point making it worse. No point making it worse.

She walked out to the porch and saw Kofi standing at the far end of the backyard looking into the sky. He was a beautiful man, she thought. Messed up, but beautiful. Something she could take into her home and look after.

Keisha turned on her computer and wrote to Kofi. She did not bother to read what he had written to her in the interim. She simply deleted those messages. Her message to Kofi was her way of finally letting him understand why she had left and why it wouldn't work with them. She felt able to explain that she just wanted to be normal, and any feeling of being normal with Kofi had lasted only a short while. She wrote the letter as if she was finally going to help him to see her, help him to understand why she was the way she was. This was her journey with him to Ridgeway, Columbia, Greeleyville. This was the journey he obviously wanted to take with her. After this he would stop, she was sure. He would stop.

Dear Kofi,

Your last five messages—I have deleted them without reading them. I know you want me to communicate with you. I just spoke to Leonora. I don't know what you are doing with my people, but I want you to know that I feel like you are trespassing on my life. I have to give you something to hold onto and then I want you to step away and leave me alone. I mean this. I really do. We just couldn't make it work. Not me and you. Maybe it was a lie I was telling myself when we started. I had a messed-up life before I met you and meeting you messed it up more. I'm not blaming you, but it's how things are. I can't look at you again and not feel sick with all of that. And you didn't do anything to try and help me. I am not mad at you or anything, but you deserve to know what all of this is about. Then you can leave me alone.

One day you asked me if I ever loved before. I lied. I said I did not know. I did. I loved. Loved someone with even more sickness than I loved you. I don't even think I loved you. I loved Troy. To love him, I gave him every single secret about me. I gave him everything of that part of me. I told him about my past, about my uncles. Things I never told you. I never told you how my uncles used to say, "We like to have that little girl Keisha around, 'cause she is like a woman already." I told him all this stuff because that is what lovers do. I told him about me and Blossom and what our uncles used to do to us in that closet. I wanted him to know me. In our rupture, nothing cherished remained precious—everything was like a weapon.

*Where I come from, black folks have learned the art of quiet. Everything seems old there. Only sometimes, when you listen, you hear this sobbing and a woman hissing, "Shit, shit, shit, shit . . ." When she sings at church, she knows the Good Lord understands it all.*

*Kofi, you are not in love with me. You are not following me around because of me or because of any love for me. You are following this idea of a child. And I would want you to do that. I hated your following me around, and yet when I thought about the child, I felt that you were at last doing the right thing. But Kofi, you can stop now.*

*I have been here for three days. I would have left two days ago. I got sick two nights ago. There was a lot of pain. Then I woke up with blood all over the bed. I went to the toilet and I kept bleeding. I went to a clinic. They say I have miscarried. I am sorry, Kofi, because I know that I will lose you for good. But it is better this way. I don't want your pity. In fact, now I know that you should stay away. It is clean.*

*You are not important to me, Kofi. It sounds harsh, but it is true. I don't want you to get in my way. I want to be happy, and you and all that happened in Jamaica and the way that you have come and set yourself up as part of my family feels like a lot of shit that I don't want to get myself in. And this child dying   it is best. It tells me that this is best. So I really want you to stop writing me and to leave me alone. I want you to get on with your life. I don't want to know how you are doing. It is not hard for me to say any of this because I don't love you. I don't. Stay out of my life. Please.*

*Keisha*

She sent it. A part of her wanted him to defy all that she had written and say, *Forget the child, I want you.* But she did not dwell on this. It was now over.

She did not shut down the computer.

Instead, she closed her eyes and waited.

Then the blip of new mail came, as she had anticipated it would.

She would open this one message and that would be it.

*You are hurting me. Why? Why are you hurting me?*

She deleted it and then deleted his name in the address book. She opened up her e-mail preferences and put a block on his address. It was over.

She had planned to start driving the next morning, at sunrise. But now she had nothing to wait for. She collected her bags, carried them to the parking lot, looked up into the sky, staring at the dizzying lines of snow. She drove slowly, the snow rushing at her in a blinding fury.

# Chapter Thirty-Two

Kofi got Keisha's message while sitting in Leonora's living room. He sat there and read it. He read it again. Then he replied and waited. Nothing. He wrote again and the message came bouncing back. He waited. Nothing. He could feel his chest constricting, and his whole body started to get that strange falling sensation he felt before he wanted to fly. She was going from him. He was feeling the panic rising in him, in his chest, in his blood. He did not know what to do.

He had not expected it to end this way. He was feeling so close to her, feeling that warmth and safety that he had cherished and desired so much. Then she pulled away. Then she killed the child. He was angry with her, but he was afraid.

Leonora stood at the door looking at him. She could sense what was happening, what had happened.

"She's miscarried," he said.

"She what?"

"She lost the baby—in a hotel."

"Jesus Christ! You sure?"

"Look."

Leonora read the section of the message that Kofi pointed to. "Oh man. Oh man."

"She don't want me go look for her," Kofi said.

"Maybe it is for the best, baby."

"What the fuck dat suppose to mean?" Kofi shouted.

"Sometimes God—"

"I said she lost my child. What could be 'best' about that?" Kofi was standing over Leonora.

"Hey, hey, don't get all ugly with me, okay? I was just saying—"

"Yeah, yeah. Sorry." Kofi walked across the room. He was confused. The moment he read about the miscarriage he had felt a strange kind of relief. And then he did not know what to do about Keisha. Now he regretted that reaction. Keisha without the child did not make sense to him.

"She thought it, and so it happened," Leonora said quietly. Her mind was traveling back to her own abortion—the guilt that had never left her.

"She doing this to screw me up, man," Kofi said.

"It happens. The body is a tough thing."

"Why she pushing me away like that? Why? I came to find her."

"You came to find the baby."

"I came for her!" Kofi shouted.

"You wouldn't be here if there was no baby, Kofi. Keisha knows that."

"You don't tell me how I am feeling, okay? I just heard that I lost my child."

"Sorry, baby. Sorry."

Kofi was starting to cry. His body was trembling. Leonora was worried for him, for herself. There was a sense of deep instability coming over him. She could tell. She did not want this.

"Hey, hey. It's all right, baby," she said softly.

Kofi stopped crying. He looked at her. There was something deeply lost in his eyes, but he was reading her. She could feel his eyes on her. His eyes all over her. She covered her throat.

"Come here," he said.

Leonora knew what was happening. She knew in that instance that what each of them was going to do had nothing to do with the other. She knew that he was going to use her to get something out of him, something off his mind. She knew that he would hate her afterwards. She even knew how it would be: impersonal, rough, and aggressive. She knew that her head would be so locked in her own body, her own desire, that she would forget who he was. He reached under her, opening her with his fingers. She breathed sharply. Then he took his hand from the wetness.

"Taste it," he said. "Taste it." He offered his fingers. She opened her mouth and tasted herself.

Then he was on her, his penis in her, and he was moving. Staring into her face and moving. He was angry. He was slamming hard against her and she could feel herself leaving him, leaving the room, imagining other meetings. She felt her orgasm coming on her quickly and without warning. She came loudly, hitting his back. He was still pushing, pushing hard against her, but she was fading now, and soon she was barely moving, trying to urge him on, but he was slowing. He was slowing until she felt his soft member slip from her. He pulled from her and sat down, staring at himself. She lay there, and then slowly pulled her dress over her legs.

"Sorry," he said.

Then he stood up and walked out of the room straightening his clothes. She sat there. She had come. She had come quicker than she had ever come before—it was like a fist, it hit her and then went. She was still stunned by it, but what she felt was not pleasure, just a sense of shock. He could not do it. He could not do it.

Kofi did not come back until after midnight. Leonora

waited up for him. She sat on the sofa in her dressing gown.

He walked in, looked at her, and then moved to his room. She waited for a few minutes and then followed him.

He was sitting on the bed. His eyes were red. His face was heavy.

"I have to go home. I think I am dying," he said.

She listened to him and sensed something breaking down slowly.

"I have to go to Jamaica, you know. People been trying to kill me in Jamaica, you know. Yeah. People a try murder me and I gwine fix matters in Jamaica. Kingston, you know." He spoke quickly. Then he stopped. He realized that he was not making sense. The world was closing in on him. He could feel his brain getting crowded. He understood that he had to be where he was safe, where he was able to fall into himself. "I need to go, get my medication, relax. Forget everything. You know?"

The shift from the confused, very Jamaican talk in his first statement to this clear request unsettled Leonora. She was puzzled by what he had said about people trying to kill him, about him needing to fix them. It did not make sense, and now he was back to the self she knew.

She nodded.

He stayed silent, his hands dangling impotently between his legs.

She sat beside him and pulled his head into her lap. She caressed his head slowly. He began to soften on her. She opened her thighs and let him fall softly into them.

"Yuh smell sweet. Like Keisha," he whispered. "I could live here, live with my face here, breathe you."

She let her robe fall open. He breathed deeply then groaned.

They stayed like that for the whole night.

# BOOK V

# Chapter Thirty-Three

I t is a brilliant day. There is no equivocation about the way the sun has imposed itself on the morning. It is high morning. The sun is startling. Everything is already white with heat. This is not dawn. This is morning. The time of morning when the city seems to slow down. In the residential areas, domestic workers start to appear with bundles of clothes to hang on the line. Gardeners are taking their first break to stare at the domestics. They will talk.

There is something private and strange about this time for a school child or for someone who works in the day. To be here to witness the rituals of midmorning is to be involved in something clandestine. There are people who have lived most of their lives without seeing these things, people who grew up going to school each day, rain or shine, sickness or health. They are people who then went on to work, and worked and worked and never took a break, never stopped to watch the rituals of the midmorning. There is a whole world lost to these people. There is a whole undiscovered existence that is out of their reach, outside their imaginations. In this place, something strangely magical is at work. Not for the ordinary person who lives in this place—the domestic, the gardener, the postman.

These are the denizens of this strange place in between dawn and noon. They are like sprites in an enchanted forest who have become so used to the strange happenings that they have no idea they are in a world of magic. But the stranger, the person who is off from work or out of school, the sick person—that person is seeing this all for the first time, and all kinds of things begin to happen inside. The reactions are never uniform, but they are extraordinary.

For some, there is an intense need to stay closed in, wrapped up in sheets, listening to the sounds happening outside, the laziness of the dogs' unconvincing growls, the clinking of the gate when the postman arrives, the voices of the people walking the streets, muttering like ghosts through the midmorning haze. Some must busy themselves in the room, keep it dark.

Others react by wanting to be out there. They walk into the sun as if they have never seen it before—not like this, not the way it makes the hedges grow mute in their greenness, the way there are no shadows on the ground, the way a dog seems to grow drunk and casual in its lazy movements across the porch. These people walk into the sun, sit in the sun. They hardly speak. They just sit hypnotized by the quality of light, the intoxication of brilliance.

Then others feel an uncanny need to be rebellious, to break taboos. They walk into every room they have never entered in their lives. They pull open drawers and read the private letters of lovers and wives and husbands. They stand naked in their rooms and look out through the louvers not caring that anyone can see them. They take baths instead of showers, and they linger in the water long after it has become tepid. They touch themselves to orgasms, again and again, not feeling the strain of each release. They want to call friends and tell them what they are doing, they eat food they have never eaten. They search the yard for fruit from the tree, pick ackees and breadfruit. They will go to the chicken coop to retrieve eggs, scramble them themselves, and then eat them slowly, slowly, as slow as each orgasm. They taste things for the first time. Their bodies and minds are consumed by everything around them.

But the most unusual are those who suddenly discover that they are someone else. They become other people. They understand equations they never understood before. They know why the world is as it is. Their minds are alert to anything that suggests itself in the wind. They transform themselves into people they never thought they could be.

Most clairvoyant people discover their gifts at midmorning. It is a proven fact. The same is true for most people who come to an understanding of their other lives. Some people are under the misapprehension that such revelations take place at night. Read the Bible carefully and you will discover that most revelations arrived to people not at night, not in dreams at night, but in the middle of the morning—during the apex of sunlight. And those we call mad really find their madness at this hour. It is simply the way the world has organized itself.

It may have been Keisha's final letter to him—its closure, the completeness of her desire not to see him, the death of the child—that unhinged him or made him bitter. It may have been his memory of their love-making, or perhaps the thought, which occurred to him, that she might have been with someone else. Or it could have been the morning that was causing him to feel as if he could fly, as if he could escape his uncertainty and pain. But his mind was turning, and Keisha was gone.

The ideas were coming to him so quickly that he did not have time to contemplate them. He was thinking about the logic of all of this, though. The logic of it came to him, and as the thoughts grew in him, he found that explanations came to him just as easily.

# Chapter Thirty-Four

Returning to Jamaica, Kofi had hoped he would be able to start again, get his life back on track. The guys in the band were not happy about his dropping out so suddenly, but when they saw him in New York, they understood. He was sick. He would have been a liability. They suggested he go back to Kingston and try and get his head together. He promised to do some work on the record while there.

It was night when he landed in Kingston. He felt the chokehold of heat when he stepped out into the night, looking at the dark shape of the Blue Mountains looming ahead. He did not feel a warmth of welcome. The heaviness was still on him.

Dorothy had sent a driver to pick him up. The driver had been instructed to take him to Ocho Rios. Dorothy's plan was to have him stay there until he felt better. But Kofi insisted to the uncertain driver that he be taken to Spanish Town, to the duplex. He would stay there.

The house was filled with a stale smell. Kofi opened all the windows hoping to air the place. But the air that came in was thick and humid, laced with the dank foulness of the septic gully behind the house. Kofi sat in the darkness. He did not want to turn on the lights, to see the roaches scurrying about. He was sure the place was a mess, but Dorothy had arranged for someone to come in and clean it regularly. Kofi slept in a chair in the living room for the entire night. His sadness was full.

He had tried to smile for Leonora the morning after Keisha's letter. She had come into the room to look in on him. She was concerned. She was dressed for work, a full black skirt suit with silver trimmings. Her silver earrings jangled.

"Honey, you want me to stay with you? I don't have to work today, you know. I could call in . . ."

"No, I am all right. Go to work. I will rest a little," Kofi said.

"You sure now?"

"Yes, yes."

"Okay, listen, I will leave the keys for the other car if you want to go into town, all right?" She walked into the room with unusual tentativeness and leaned over him. She touched his head. "You poor baby," she said. Then, falling to her knees, she put her arms around him and kissed him, looking into his eyes. "I know your head is with Keisha and I know all of this is a lot of shit you don't need, but you was nice to me. You didn't have to be, you know. But you was real sweet, and I can't forget that. You hear me? I won't forget that."

She kissed him softly on the lips, stood up, and walked out of the room.

Kofi drove into Columbia that morning. He found the address of a Caribbean grocery store in the *Yellow Pages*. He found it tucked in behind a retaining wall that supported the elevated car-wash hut of a gas station. He walked into the dusty store that was owned, apparently, by Koreans. He picked up some yams, two cans of ackee, some salt cod, hot peppers, tomatoes, fresh bulbs of sorrel, and a bottle of jerk seasoning. He then drove to the mall sprawled out at the far end of Two Notch Road. He walked into Sears and spent a long time in the women's clothing section. The women were helpful. He showed them Leonora's dress—the sunny yellow one that he finally found tucked into her basket of dirty linen. He described Leonora, but suggested that the dress would do a better job. They showed him dresses. They indulged in this activity with greater and greater amusement and pleasure, the more helpless he seemed. He picked an elegant dress, black with carefully embroidered lace at the throat. It flowed down, falling loosely into a generous split just about where the middle of her thigh would be. They helped him with the crimson underwear as well. He felt too distant to be embarrassed by what he was doing. He wanted her to be happy. He wanted to thank her.

He left the mall and stopped at a grocery store to get the chicken, some more seasoning, rice, fruit, and some vegetables for the salad. Then he drove back to Ridgeway, the car moving sluggishly along the highway, far below the sixty-five-mile-per-hour speed limit.

That day he cooked. He skinned the chicken, saving one stretch to be used for moisture and flavor. He soaked the chicken in jerk, added bits of pimento, onions, green onions, and thyme. He left it soaking for several hours. Then he wrapped the meat and the strip of skin in foil and put it in the oven to bake. While the chicken roasted, he prepared the salad and broke the cod fish into tiny strips, which he soaked in water to drain it of as much salt as possible. He sliced red and green bell peppers, hot peppers, garlic and onions, and placed them in a lightly oiled frying pan along with the fish. He emptied both cans of ackee into the pan and let the mixture simmer. He dropped in a little coconut milk, and the aroma filled him with deep nostalgia.

He worked steadily, his entire body moving with the effort. This was a meal he wanted to share with Keisha. But it would be Leonora's gift. It would be his last gesture before he left. The meal cooked slowly, and he sat staring into the yard while the aromas filled the house. By the time Leonora arrived at 5:30, the yams were soft and almost slippery, the plantains were fried and in the oven, and the jerk was browning slowly in the oven as well.

"Oh, sweet Savior, you cooked!" Leonora could not stop smiling.

He served her each morsel of food. She ate slowly. He watched her eating, smiling at her. Her hands kept waving in front of her, her body moved by the pleasure of what she was eating. He was happy, but his mind was so far away. Yet he tried. He cut a mango in two and offered the half with the seed to her.

"Just bite into it," he said when she looked at him questioning. "Bite, and enjoy it."

"It's sweet. It's so good." She ate with relish. He watched her. He smiled. She smiled back. "My mouth feels like a riot is going on in there. I want to sleep now. I want to stretch out and sleep and feel all of this food happening to me."

He got up and brought the box to her. On it was a small card.

She read the card out loud. "*I have come to depend on the kindness of strangers. You have been a sweet stranger. Thank you. I hope you liked me too.*" She looked at him. She was full. "I do, baby. This is sweet. You want to see it?" she said shyly.

He nodded.

She came into the room and stood before him. She looked beautiful. Her feet were bare, her breasts filled the cloth.

"You like it?"

"It is nice. It fits. How did you know?"

"Everything fits?"

"Everything." She walked over and sat beside him. She leaned on him and drew him close. "Thanks, sweets. Thanks."

"Thank you," he said.

He left the next day. Leonora was sad, almost impatient with him, with everything. She promised to keep in touch. On the way to the airport she called everything "fucked up." He knew what she meant. But his mind had gone now. He was in Kingston already. He was far from her. He was trying to find some kind of peace, some order.

Now, back in Jamaica, he did not feel the calm he had hoped for. He wanted to find a way out of this uneasy feeling.

# Chapter Thirty-Five

The dreams began because of the heat. He was afraid of himself, of what he was becoming. He knew in his head that falling in love was a decision. Most people described it as a thing that happened to them. But he knew, years ago, that falling in love was like falling into his madness, falling into that place of wanting to fly. He knew that the misting of the world around him was a decision, a way to cope with the pressure. He could feel the thing coming on him while the cars—shining, loud, uncontrolled—made chaos in his head. He could feel it beckoning him while he stared into faces, people talking to him, trying to get him to understand them. He knew the sensation of wanting to fall into himself, into the fogging of the light, making everything mute, gentle, tender. He would then decide whether to walk away, or whether to allow the leaping logic of his madness to rationalize everything into a manageable disorder. Falling in love was something that he had decided to do while he was in South Carolina. He thought he had fallen in love before that, but he had not. Not until that night in Leonora's living room, reading Keisha's words on the screen, slipping into his mind, slipping under his skin— not until then did he suddenly realize that there was a door open before him, asking him to come tumbling in. And he did. He knew he could not afford it, but he still walked in. And as he walked in he started to feel the salty flooding of his whole body, his mind and his heart. This heart where all the chemicals and nerves of passion clustered. He was in love with Keisha—he had fallen for her the instant he knew he had lost her.

In Jamaica again, the heat was around him. He was sick. He could tell. He could tell that his whole body was giving up on him. He was limping now, and he could feel a pain in his toe. His right toe was black with some ailment that he could not understand. He did not go to see a doctor. He watched the blackness grow, and then he felt the rest of his body give way in this slow manner.

At night he would lie in bed and wait for the dreams to come. They came on him slowly, taking shape like images in a film, growing in color and texture. He would speak to himself, trying to urge the narrative into greater focus. The world that he dreamt became as compelling as the weary days he spent in the house in Spanish Town, sweating naked in the heat, the room in constant darkness, the smell of his neglect saturating the place.

America had been hard. Keisha had kept running. He was alone. He had missed Jamaica. He missed the taste of the air, with its dust and stench of dead things. He missed eating an orange, pulling on the tart sweetness, and sucking on guineps, the tiny cups of green skin scattered around his feet along with the carefully stripped seeds, white with only the barest hint of pink flesh on them. He missed the sun on his back, the way the heat would come on him. After a few months in America, he had begun to feel pale. He felt as if he was losing himself in the mute gray of New York. He hated it. He had spent most of his time there indoors, in the studio, pretending to be writing songs, making jokes with the other musicians from Jamaica. But he was in mourning. That is what it felt like. Like he was in mourning.

Now a Jamaican morning was upon him. The radio was chattering. And he looked out into the slight mist and he felt that he was dead, that he was in another world. He walked onto the porch and looked out at the hills. The hills looked back at him. Then he walked down into the grass and made his way across the lawn in the backyard to the cluster of berry ficus trees.

He sat among the roots and felt his body going back into a sleep again. The sun crawled across his skin. He was home. But everything was falling apart. Everything was uncertain.

He slept a lot. When he had done this for a week, when he could tell now that his hair was finding its own path of unruliness, he made plans to leave the country.

In this midmorning of regret, he dreamt.

He dreamt of Keisha. In his dream Keisha was someone else, a darker woman, a woman who looked at him as if she had been looking at him for centuries. The landscapes he dreamt were so real to him, so complete that he would wake and still see the glow of color around him even though he was wide-eyed, awake, and listening to the chattering radio. The talk shows, the talk of blood, of chaos, of bullets, of corruption, of the dead, of hopelessness, all this talk was supposedly his reality, but the glow of his dreams would not go away.

Kofi felt that something had woken him, but he was not sure. The pain in his stomach came on him gradually but irrevocably. Then came the pain in his head, in his limbs, deep inside his stomach. It was the pain that had awoken him.

As he lay there, the pain creeping across his ribs, filling his head with an intense pulsing, he began to think hard of flying from everything, of going somewhere else. He was drifting.

# Chapter Thirty-Six

She placed the slab of red beef on the wood board. She could smell the rawness, the fresh scent of game. She began to part the flesh with the silver edge of a huge knife. The knife was sharp and cut through the meat smoothly, evenly, with vicious ease. She tossed the tiny cubes of beef into the pot, her fingers reddening with the blood.

Then she washed the board. Washed it carefully with soap, her hands gleaming with the warm water.

Her mind was growing blank. The weight of the child in her seemed distant as she ritualized the preparation of her meal. It could happen anytime—the sharp pain, the water, the blood, the birthing. But she did not want to think about that, about the growing impatience she was feeling for this thing to drop. Even the prospect of the pain of birthing seemed bearable in the face of her need to feel free again, to feel her body as hers again.

Her fingers pushed the tomato forward as she cut into the slippery flesh with the knife. The chunks of tomato glowed in the sharp light of the kitchen. She liked her apartment in this high-rise building in Toronto. She had festooned the room with plants, large plants that she imagined to be tropical and herbs that she grew in the kitchen. The lemon grass gave the room a sweet lemony scent that she enjoyed. Each morning she would brush the bush so that the aroma filled the place. The light from the window above the kitchen was always startling with its angled grace. She would stand in that sunlight naked, letting the brilliance warm her body, touch her skin, tickle it into a sense of being alive. She was walking around naked more and more these days.

Joan had arranged for her to do most of her work at home, and now she could feel freer, the clothes no longer so constricting. She was standing in this same light now, cutting carrots, onions, fresh bulbous green onions, and cracking sprigs of thyme into the pot. She gathered the vegetables and poured the flamboyant handful of color into the pot of meat. She then shook a wash of soy sauce into the pot and watched it darken the food with a musky shade. She turned the stew around with a wooden spoon, inhaling the aroma of the raw meat and fresh vegetables. She poured black pepper into the pot, added some salt, then a few drops of strong red wine vinegar. She then reached above for an elegant rectangular bottle wrapped in thin strips of dried grass. She held the open mouth of the bottle to her nose and relished the scent of the extra virgin olive oil. She poured a little more than she needed into the pot. Then, in a splash of indulgence, she poured a cup full of bloody red wine. Finally, she peeled five small potatoes and diced them, placing the pieces in a plastic bowl beside the sink. She covered the bowl.

She turned back to the stove. The frying pan was deep, with a sturdy black base—a pan that Joan had given to her as a welcome gift, saying, "This thing has cooked some of the best ethnic dishes in the world." Keisha did not know what *ethnic* this Anglo woman was referring to, but she trusted the worn, darkened, and used look of the pan. She poured some more olive oil into the pot and waited for the gas flame to heat it. She moved her fingers slowly through the meat, pressing the flesh, trying to massage as many of the juices into each slice of meat as she could.

The pan sputtered with the clash of water and oil. She grabbed handfuls of the meat and opened her palms over the pot. The piping oil pricked her hands, but she squinted and continued to drop in handful after handful of the mixture.

The room filled with the savory smell of meat browning, the pungent scent of onions, and a strange sweet smell of honey. Keisha was expecting Joan at 8:00. The dinner was Joan's idea and, typically, she had gotten Keisha to do the cooking and the hosting. Yet this was Joan's treat. It was therapy. Keisha had been complaining that she was depressed about the impending arrival of the child. She wanted to see a therapist.

"That is always a good idea," Joan said. "I like them, the attention. You are sitting there and talking and they have to listen to you. I like that. You should try my friend—she is a woman, beautiful tall superwoman with three children, and she is good. She will be perfect for you."

Keisha was reluctant to make arrangements with Joan's friend. She liked Joan, and in many ways Joan had rescued her when she reached Toronto in such a bad state. She had not thought that the final separation from Kofi would affect her like it did. It had come down on her as she crossed the Canadian border somewhere in Ontario. It was a brilliantly sunny day and the snow was startlingly white. Keisha had felt full, very full, as she showed her papers at the border. Driving into Canada, however, she began to cry. It made no sense. There was nothing permanent about crossing such a porous border, but she felt that she was entering a new life and putting Kofi and all that mess behind her. By the time she made it to Toronto, she was a wreck. She was tired, uncertain, and already itching to call Troy in South Carolina.

Had Joan not been there with her whirlwind of excitement, Keisha would have found herself curled up on a bed, speaking in that thick low tone that she assumed when she spoke to Troy.

Joan distracted her by talking about the job, the stupid people that she had to put up with in Toronto, about the lack of excitement in the place. Then she began to outline the research project that would soon completely occupy their time. They were in Toronto because Joan wanted to be away from New York and distractions. Joan was planning, on the side, to put together a really hip book on sexual proclivities around the world.

"*Sex around the World* is what I might call it," Joan said. "But that is not sexy enough. I mean, it needs to be sexy. This is not a serious research book. I told my agent that I wanted a book that people could use when they were traveling. Like a *Traveler's Guide to Sexual Dos and Don'ts from Antigua to Zanzibar*. Yeah. I'll be sticking in all that crap about aphrodisiacs and male prostitutes and holes in blankets and that kind of thing. There's some really funky, sick material that I could just put in the book. It will be a hit. We got all these sex tourists, man, these sick midwestern men who tell their wives they're going off to Malaysia for a business trip, when all they are doing is going to jack up some preteen kid in Kuala Lumpur or Bahia, or Georgetown, where they say the sands are nice and golden and the children are tender and precocious. Getting their sick jollies off on the hapless natives."

It was hard not to find Joan funny, and harder not to be infected with her enthusiasm. Joan lived a life that sometimes puzzled Keisha for its emptiness. But Joan was quite clear about it.

"I have been married three times and I am barely past forty. I have lived. I have lived. I don't have children—that is my only regret—but I have had to mother three screwed-up men and I am sick of it."

Joan was good for Keisha. Joan found the apartment for her, and crowded it with plants. In this world, Keisha felt far from some of the pain she wanted to leave behind. She was growing away from the mess.

When Keisha began to dehydrate from the persistent morning sickness, Joan came in and stayed with her. She brought the office to the apartment—that and far too many herbal brews. The brews were for the nausea, she said. And one thing worked: the mint tea that she made from a mint and lemon bush plant. Joan also came with music. Most of it was rhythm music from the Congo—the sweet falsettos of the Congolese singers would fill the apartment. She also liked the Vinx, David Murray, Wasis Diop with his alluring baritone, the Neville Brothers, and anything with that quality of percussive, infectious blues-flecked music. When Joan was in the apartment, the place was a different world, an oasis. Joan would strut around the place with barely any clothes. She argued, cussed, shouted, and laughed raucously into her cell phone with people, it seemed to Keisha, from all over the world.

Joan was a blanket for her. She made food a constant point for discussion, which suited Keisha fine, as her whole mind seemed to be centered on managing the nausea. They ordered from the Thai restaurants downtown, from the Greek restaurant nearby, and from the Queen of Sheba, a small Ethiopian restaurant.

Keisha was comfortable. She had some money, she had

a job, she had a baby growing in her. Her habits were new ones, and they seemed healthier. Kofi was far. Ridgeway was far. Greeleyville was far.

Joan had arranged for her to see the therapist—it would cost Keisha nothing, as the insurance Joan had arranged for the job was good.

After the first visit, Keisha was disappointed. Joan wanted to know what had happened.

"She gave me these exercises to do. *Cognitive distortions*, she calls them. You make note of situations which arouse the emotions and behavior you are trying to get rid of. Thinking about my life and what stupid mistakes I have made, I told her. She said I need to write them down. Write them like automatic thoughts, and the mood they put you in. Then you write down the cognitive distortion and any rationale to support such distortion. After this, you write any rationale against the thought, so that you come up with a balanced thought. Along with this, my homework is to look at people and smile, and if possible, say, 'Nice day.' So here is my smile to you, Joan, thanking you for all your help." Keisha smiled the most plastic smile she could muster.

"It sounds like a good session, Keisha."

"I don't think this is going to work for me, but we'll see. I was hoping that she would just give me a pill and make the problem go away, but the pills, she said, only blunt the problem. So I wanted to tell her that what I want is to blunt the problem. What was she thinking? Anyway, she said the pills would not be good for the child. So we will see how that goes. I'll keep you posted on my progress, if any, since you are so interested."

The therapy sessions did not last long. But Keisha kept writing down her reactions to events in her life. The process gave her a greater sense of control over things, a sense that she at least knew what was happening with her. Little else. But everything helped.

The last meal that Joan had convinced her to prepare was to be a kind of ritual act of healing before the arrival of the child—and a celebration. The baby was due in a week, which meant that it could come any time. Joan wanted them to have a meal, to drink some non-alcoholic wine, and to find a name for the child. She was going to arrive for dinner in a little while with a few books she had bought for Keisha with baby names.

The beef had browned enough. It was still uncooked inside. Keisha emptied the contents of the pan into a crock-pot. She put the potatoes in the fridge. She turned on the crock-pot and covered the lid.

She then focused on the seasoned rice, sweetened with a handful of fresh raisins. She half filled a pot with water and poured in three cups of rice. She allowed the rice to come to boil and dry out slightly, and then she drained all the water out and poured the half-cooked rice into a dry frying pan. She covered that after yellowing the rice with a hint of saffron and placed it in the refrigerator.

The broth she prepared was a light one made with beef stock. She simmered the stock in a pot that gave off the delicate smell of the green onions floating in the broth like water lilies. She shook in several drops of soy sauce, along with a healthy sprinkling of fresh black pepper. Several leaves of lemon basil topped it. She covered the pot and let the sweetness linger.

As she worked, she could feel the inevitable fatigue creeping into her limbs. Her body was not her own. She wanted to finish the meal before Joan arrived, but it did not look at all likely. The child was now kicking fiercely at her side and she was trying to soothe it with gentle words. The child did not take heed and she had to sit down to calm the kicking somewhat.

That evening they ate heartily. The rice was delicate— Keisha had waited for Joan to come before she fried it in its own oils, gently stirring until it glistened yellow with fullness and the flavor of the raisins and saffron. The beef in the crock-pot was tender and seemed to melt when approached by a fork or any other implement. The natural juices, flamed by the seasoning and the tablespoon of deep, almost wet brown sugar that Keisha spilled into the pot near the end of the process, gave the meat a rich variety of tastes. Keisha boiled the potatoes before adding them to the stew near the end of the process, so that when they were cut, they remained white as bone against the dark brown of the stew. Keisha sliced open a few potatoes as she served the meal in bowls.

Joan loved the meal. She had brought wine and some candles and, oddly, arms full of copies of the *Globe and Mail* and the *New York Times*.

Groans and moans at the table were typical of Joan, but she outdid herself that night. Keisha ate with her and smiled at Joan's enthusiasm.

"You are not calling her anything like Keisha or LaQuisha, Keisha," she said, staring with her sharp green eyes. "I mean it. Your parents made their mistake but you don't have to do the same. This child needs a sensible name, something with roots. And, by the way, I am its godmother and there will be no argument about that. None of that Shaquisha crap, okay? I know you are going to get upset with me, but I am going to mention Kofi's name. Throw stuff at me now and get it over with." Joan looked earnestly at Keisha, who did not respond. Joan continued. "Okay, I just think that if it is a boy, Kofi should be one of the names that you consider."

"Kofi is a day name," Keisha said. "This child has to be a boy and has to come down on Friday. Today is Saturday, he is dropping on Tuesday, Wednesday at the latest . . ."

"You know this for a fact?"

". . . which means that he can't be Kofi. I am not giving him that last name, Pollard. I don't want much to do with that crazy family. So, can we now rule out all of that Kofi stuff? He is out of my life now. He hardly even tried to come and see me."

Saying this made her realize that she had been suppressing her anger at his habit of acquiescing to her. She had told him to stay away, it was true, but he did so without a fight. No resistance. Other men would have insisted on coming to see her, made an effort. Other men would have stalked her—at least that would have been a sign of concern, of desire, sick as it might have been. There was a fine line, she knew, between the madness of love and the sickness of obsession. Kofi had never dallied with that line. Kofi listened to her, did what he was told. It was how he made love. He took her instructions, did what she wanted, was gentle, perfectly kind . . . and she resented this in him. And she hated herself for resenting it because she was sure that her sickness came from Troy, the man who made her drop to her knees and fellate him while he stood there telling her what a slut she was. She had done it, done it hating him, and yet had done it nonetheless. But it was the persistence that she wanted. That sense of someone caring enough to make a fool of himself. Kofi was not like that.

Kofi did not try hard enough. He could have been in Toronto, he could have been at the door every day, and he could have pleaded with her to take him back. But Kofi had stopped caring when he knew that the child was dead. She had suspected that he would, but she was still disappointed.

Keisha could not explain any of this to Joan. Joan would understand, but it would make Keisha look bad. She hoped that Joan would leave the issue alone. And she seemed to. She collected the newspapers from the sofa and brought them to the table.

"Okay, we will start with famous names," she said, opening to the world news section of the *New York Times*. "Famous names. Historical names. You know what I mean. I think we can start there and then we can find our way to something significant."

"There is some dessert, Joan. Just relax."

"No, not now. Okay, here we go. Slobodan."

"He would be the first black child with that name."

"Well, you never know how things will work out with the guy. He may be famous. But I am not attached to Slobodan, okay? A little too ethnic. There are others. Well, there is Bill or William, but you can see the obvious pitfalls there. Where have all the heroes gone?"

"This is so silly."

"Ah, ah. Here we go. Nelson."

"Too nerdy. Kids will laugh at him."

"But he is a black guy. There are not many on the list, you know. Okay, what else do we have . . ." She continued through the list. "John, too common. I was thinking about going back, though, you know, to guys who might not be in charge or might be dead. Like—well here is one: Kwame."

"Nice name, but another day name. Saturday."

"Ahh. Jomo? Great guy, that Jomo. Okay, you don't like Jomo. Too ethnic, right? What about Idi? Now don't rush to judgment. I mean, his record is not the best, but Idi is a sweet name—it is kind of unisex, so if it turns out to be a girl . . ."

Keisha had stopped listening. She was drifting again. She did this a lot now—gave herself permission to ignore people, to become engrossed in herself.

Joan noticed and went quiet. After a few moments, she spoke again: "Keisha, I think that at some point Kofi will have to know."

"At some point," Keisha said quietly. "At some point."

"What if it's a girl?" Joan said, changing the subject again.

"Alma. It means soul. My ancestor wore that name well. Alma."

"You think it will be a girl, don't you?"

"She has to be. The story makes no sense otherwise."

And the conversation was over. Joan put away the newspapers, served herself some ice cream and thick mango juice, put on some music, sat cross-legged by the large windows, and slowly ate as she watched the city glimmer beneath her.

Keisha stood behind her, looking through Joan's eyes into the city. Keisha's reflection in the window, a flowing expanse of yellow, blooming like a flower, filled Joan's eyes. There was something calm about Keisha, something calming.

# Chapter Thirty-Seven

I t took two days for Kofi to start to understand that his weakness may have had something to do with his hunger. The radio was still going. The world outside was defined by the radio. Voices chattering, images of faces looming over him and then disappearing. He kept returning to his dream, which was no longer a dream but a narrative. But the narrative was being interrupted by voices, by the sound of the telephone, by the increasingly anxious messages that were being left by Dorothy, by people he was not sure he knew.

Kofi was hungry. He felt the hollow inside of him. It no longer hurt. It was a dull pain. He was not dry. He had been drinking water from the tap. He would walk to the bathroom, cup his hand under the tap, and drink until his stomach hurt with the pain. Then he would go back and lie down and wait for the idea to come to him. He was dreaming of Keisha. Keisha was lying on a table, her legs apart, and a man in a mask, a man with tendril hands that looked uncannily like those of Pedro, was leaning down between her open legs and doing something to her. Kofi could tell that the man was feeling deep inside her for something, and when he seemed to have it in hand, he was grimacing with the effort of moving it, pulling at it. Keisha was in pain, howling, twisting, there was blood underneath her, spreading. The light in the room was blue.

Kofi opened his eyes. The abortion. He was sure she'd

had an abortion. But his head was unable to grasp the idea. He closed his eyes again. His most peaceful moments were those that came on him gently and sent him back into a dream state.

No one came to rescue Kofi. He lay there for three days, his body growing weaker and weaker and his mind traveling to memories and snippets of conversations that kept him locked in a state of uncertainty. He wanted to fly. He wanted to fly so much. But he was anchored. The anchor held him in the room, in the heat, in the smell of his body decaying.

The phone rang.

This time he reached for it. When he heard his own voice he was unsure of what to make of it. It sounded strange. He kept focusing on that voice as it echoed back and forth in his head. It took him awhile to realize that someone on the other line was trying to cut through this echoing of his voice. It was Leonora.

"Kofi, her boss Joan called, baby. Keisha is in the hospital. She is having the child now, baby."

Kofi had trouble understanding what was being said. Keisha had had an abortion. He had seen it happen. It had happened in his head while he was lying there. He had seen it.

"Kofi, baby? You there? You heard me?" Leonora raised her voice.

"I thought . . ."

"She was lying, baby. She was lying. I knew she was lying, but she wouldn't come out with the truth. She is having the baby, Kofi. Your child."

"You sure 'bout this?" It was not an abortion—it was a miscarriage. He remembered the letter now, the details: *They say I have miscarried. I am sorry, Kofi, because I know that I will lose you for good. But it is better this way.*

"Joan said she is having the child. She said it was best I call you." Leonora was excited. It was clear that she had just heard. A child had come back from the dead. She was excited.

"I don't know . . . I . . ."

"Kofi, listen to me . . . You there?"

"Yes, yes." The echoing continued.

"She just went in this morning. She could have it anytime. She is at the Queen Anne Hospital in Toronto. I don't have the number, but they are listed. Toronto. Ask for Obstetrics . . . You heard me?"

"Yes, yes . . ." He waited for the echo. It did not come. His voice was flat.

"Baby, you all right? I was worried. I've been calling you. You got my messages?"

"I've been sick . . . I am okay. Is Keisha all right?" He could feel the cloud clearing.

"She's all right, but she's going to have your child now, baby. You could call her, you know?"

"She doesn't want me to call her."

"Well, you better get that crap out of your head. That ain't got shit to do with nothing. Okay? You should call her. It ain't got shit to do with her. It's about you." Leonora's voice carried clean across the lines.

"Okay, okay," he said.

"Yeah. You okay? I miss you," Leonora said, her voice softening. "I miss you, baby. But I got to go. Call her, hear?"

"Yeah. And thanks." He hung up. He closed his eyes. He felt the falling again. But he did not fall. He waited. Nothing happened. He sat up. It was getting light outside. He stood and felt his body's incredible weakness. He was hungry. Very hungry.

He wanted Keisha. He wanted to live.

# Chapter Thirty-Eight

I n the birthing room, the purest light from the brilliant day spilled through long windows overlooking a city determined to bloom in spring. It was midday, fresh and slow in the hospital, before the madness of night emergencies, before the chaos of other births. Keisha liked the cleanness of light in the room.

When she realized it was time, Keisha had been cooking. She did not want to rush. She stood in the kitchen and finished the stew peas and rice she was preparing. Then she packed her bag, making sure to include her Walkman and a copy of the novel *The L-Shaped Room* by Lynne Barnes, which she had been saving for the time in the hospital. Only then did she call Joan.

She was sitting on the curb outside her building when Joan came. She was in pain, but she managed to keep her head upright. Her slender neck, the glow of her short-cropped head, the large earrings, the dramatic largeness of her stomach above her firm gleaming legs suggested a sculpture, a woman from somewhere else.

For an instant, Joan expected to see this cityscape of steel slick cars, asphalt, and concrete transformed into a village, an open kraal with the occasional hedge of hibiscus bushes to mark out each compound.

But it was Keisha in labor, sitting there waiting in the middle of Toronto, no plains, no open fields, just the dull gray of the pavement and the drab and sullen shades of the buildings. She sat with her bag beside her, her eyes tired from concentrating on calming her body. They walked in the sun through Keisha's bright contractions to the parking lot at the back.

"Take your time," Keisha said to Joan. "Not too much shaking, please."

Now Keisha was propped like a queen on white cushions. The midwife, starched to severe purity, commanded the ritual of birthing, ignoring Joan's attempt to be in charge. With firm reassuring hands, the nurse orchestrated the proceedings.

Soon the room was all light for Keisha, a swirl of silver and bright steel instruments, and the sensation of prodding, feeling, squeezing, looking.

*Push . . . now . . . push . . . now . . . push . . . Wait.*

*Push . . . You're not breathing, girl . . . Bear down! Wait!*

And Keisha floated in a cloud of white pain until the howl shattered the room, announcing the coming down of everything wet, everything flowing river-wet, down.

It was a girl with a head full of hair.

They swaddled her in white and named her softly, named her for an ancestor.

*Alma, Alma, Alma.*

Keisha dreamt of clouds and more clouds swimming in the brilliance of this white room. And as she slept, she took flight, alighting on the land of her birth. She was coming home to the Midlands, back to thick green and the soil enriched with the bones of old travelers, deposited on that soft earth, where the water settled so close to the surface and where you could smell the dank and feel the chill. She was returning to all the tears, all the songs of lost homes, all the libations poured to broken gods, to the memory of the tender village, the dance of the mothers in the sunset: Alma, Powie, Okla, Lynne, Rose, and Leonora.

These women whose blood tied them in mythic oneness as if they were age mates in a village. And when she got worried, when she remembered her own horrors, she was settled by the gaze of a black woman burdened with age, walking the darkly meandering roads of this low country, always smiling, always singing. It was Alma the matriarch. She comforted Keisha. Keisha knew that this was all the home she had. In the dream she arrived in the low country, to the thick green mellowness of tobacco fields in the fallen sun. She breathed in the dank of memory: home, home.

Kofi was standing at the door looking down on Keisha when she woke. At first she was sure she was dreaming him. But he spoke.

"I came."

And she knew. "You came for her."

"I came for you. I just didn't know how to come for you . . . I—" He stopped talking. Keisha was staring at him, but he could not read her expression. "I have seen her. She is beautiful," he said.

Keisha did not smile. But she nodded.

"Keisha, I am sorry."

Keisha turned to the window.

"I have been dreaming about you," Kofi said, still standing at the door. "That you came to rescue me; you and your family came to rescue me. I was dying. The place smelled of death and everyone was giving up on me. Then you came to rescue me."

"Very forgiving of me," she said without looking at him.

"Your Aunt Rose said I was dreaming life not death. She said everything I dream is the opposite because I have that kind of brain."

"Aunt Rose getting old, you know."

"She said if you came to rescue me in my dream, then—"

"You should come and rescue *me* . . ."

"No, no. That I should come to be rescued," he said.

"Cute, cute." She was smiling now.

"And you looked good, in the dream. You had hair though." He smiled, hoping she would feel it.

"Sorry to disappoint you," she said.

"No, no, no." The weight of his words convinced her. "No."

She was afraid to look at him now. She imagined the way his eyes would pierce her with their desperate need to assure her that for him she was everything, everything. He spoke again.

"She is beautiful. You did good."

"She is beautiful," she repeated, daring to look at him. She noticed the gaunt weariness of his face. He looked darker, more serious. His shirt hung loosely from his body. "Starving yourself?"

"Love," he said, smiling.

"You should fall in love more often. It looks good on you."

"Keisha, I am sorry."

"You know things are different, right?"

"I know."

"Okay." She looked out again. "You see that?"

It was the sunset. Dramatic, impossible colors filled the sky, and the sun, a clean ball, was dropping slowly. The glow fell on her face, tinted the sheets around her, flamed her skin. He felt full of her.

"I see," he said. "I see."

Then he dipped into the black bag hanging from his shoulders and retrieved a wrinkled brown paper bag. He walked toward Keisha with the gift.

"I had to tell dem lie at customs. *Nothing to declare.* But I bring in some illegal substance." He put the bag on her lap and then leaned forward and touched her forehead with his lips. Her scent was sweet—like fresh milk. "You smell nice."

She smiled, then took the bag and pulled out a smaller plastic bag filled with tamarind balls.

"I mek dem myself. Put a little sweat and other things in there." He grinned.

She opened the bag and dipped in, pulling out a ball of sugar and sour. She bit into it, anticipating the secretions in her mouth, the tart taste of the fruit. The warmth of the tamarind ball flushed her chest and face. She looked at him.

"Thanks, Kofi. That's real sweet of you. Sorry I can't offer you any. Have to make up for the months without this."

"No problem, loveliness. No problem."

# Chapter Thirty-Nine

They drove for fifteen hours, stopping only for her to use the toilet. She sat for most of the time in the back of the car, cradling the child, changing her, singing to her, while Kofi drove. He never felt tired, never dozed off. The excitement of being with them was enough to keep him fully alert along I-95. The landscape changed gradually, grew unruly, rugged, the colors more and more vibrant. Along the highway as they drove through North Carolina, the kudzu flaring in the sunlight and the regal purple of wisteria catching the corners of their eyes. It was Sunday morning when they reached Florence, and the streets were empty and quiet.

Kofi kept looking at Keisha, staring at her face, the way her skin smiled softly with the sun. There was a calm in her, in the simplicity of her hair, low and tidy on her head. He kept reaching across to her to touch her arm. Behind them the child was making sounds.

They were driving into her past, taking that journey that he knew he had to take with her before they could even think about returning to Jamaica. She suggested that they travel to South Carolina to bury old things, to make ready for new things. She said it like that, as if she was speaking a poem. He had dreamt of them there, walking through Greeleyville, touching the cotton trees, feeling the heat, smelling the muggy stench of pig manure, slowing down to the dictates of the climate. She wanted him to take her home and remind the place somehow of their presence, of the new presence. She wanted her child to see the grave of Alma, to feel the hands of the women on her head, to be blessed by her home.

Kofi had been here before, but it was different now. The mountain of clouds rising above the highway as they crossed the border into South Carolina struck him. He was entering a world that would define them. The rough parcels of open acres, a solitary barn in the distance, and the ubiquitous dwarfed bushes of tobacco. He had grown accustomed to the flatness of the land, the clean horizon.

"There are dead bones in the soil," she told him.

She told him that the paths scarring the fertile earth sometimes whispered the magic of sorcery at nightfall. She said this to him when they had parked by an old abandoned grocery store just outside of Greeleyville where they sold fried whiting battered in corn flour. He bought two plates of food. Each had four whole fish and a mess of green vegetables soaked in Thousand Island dressing.

She leaned on the car and ate the fish with her fingers, soaking the flesh with hot pepper sauce from small plastic packets.

She was nervous about going home, but she wanted him to experience it with her.

Soon, she walked away from the car. He was still eating.

She stood at the edge of a tobacco field with the baby bundled in a stark white cotton cloth, and stared out into the failing light. He looked over at her, at his woman and his child, and he felt both close to them and very, very far from them.

"This is how I will put it all away," she said.

Kofi could feel that familiar instinct to withdraw, to

create a shield of mood around him to protect himself from what could happen with Keisha in South Carolina. They had not spoken about whether she was going to go and see her ex-boyfriend, but he could tell that coming there had something to do with that man, with how she was going to put him away. He was not going to ask, but he knew that he had to fight the desire to carry his mood like a shield to protect him from the distance of their language.

Driving on, they said little, rehearsing the uncertainty that her sadness caused for both of them. The bare landscape outside the car was perfectly balanced, the weight of an old oak on the right tilting the sharply angled bland sky upright again.

Keisha took Kofi to the grave of her mother. Leonora had not taken him there. She had taken him to the church graveyard, but not this one just on the outskirts of town.

"They buried folks here who had not made their peace with God," Keisha said, leading him through the thickly bushed uneven field. Keisha's mother was buried under a full-bodied live oak tree, sturdy, unmovable.

"She was a runner. My mother was a runner. She ran and ran and then she had to stop. She stopped right here."

Keisha spoke of her mother as if she were talking to someone who knew the details, the small things of dates and the names of places. But he didn't. What he got from her was a mysterious tale of this woman who still haunted Keisha. She called her "Old Mama," but it was clear to Kofi that Old Mama had not been very old. The liquor had destroyed her.

As they stood at the grave, they looked up to a sudden howl and stared at a swooping jet circling the base.

"Leonora says I walk with Old Mama's limp, favoring my right ankle," Keisha said. "Maybe she just says that to make me feel like my mother was real or that she was part of me. Leonora likes to do that."

It seemed the kind of lie that Leonora would tell.

"Leonora said Old Mama twisted it when she ran from a white man's stallion when she was a little girl," Keisha said. "I wish I knew her a bit, you know."

Another jet swooped across the sky like a diving hawk screaming.

"Kofi," Keisha said to him quietly.

"Yes, sweets."

"You came because of Alma, didn't you?" She would not look at him.

"Keisha, when you tell me Alma was dead, I had nothing else on you, baby. It was like nothing else for me to hold onto . . ." Kofi stopped talking.

Keisha had convinced herself that if Kofi did come for her, she would send him packing. But now she found herself open to his arrival. She found herself softening to him—not blindly, but with a calm willingness to accept what seemed right. He did not try to lie about his fears, about how he had failed her. He admitted that they both had a lot to work out and that it would not be easy. But he wanted to be with her, wanted to be with Alma—there were few things he understood as clearly as this.

Keisha was surprised at how she found this to be enough for her. Enough for the moment at least. "I see," she said after a long pause.

They were silent. Her doubts lingered. But he was there. Maybe that was enough.

And eventually, it is what we come to. A jet heading for home, a jet training to drop bombs on buildings with careful precision, two people who cannot be seen from so far up, standing with a child between them and a twisted story behind them. From this far up, the story is nothing.

Somewhere, Keisha knew, women were standing with shawls on their heads contemplating the burnt-out buildings of their lives. Bombs had fallen, children had died. They were sweeping—the dust on the ground, the residue of destruction—and that was what was most important then, nothing else. That simple act of sweeping, despite it all, was what was most important. She held her baby, cradled the girl to herself, and carried her as if she were the broom—nothing else remained.

So much to place on one small infant.

A third jet swooped across the sky like a diving hawk screaming.

The new church was planted twenty yards away from the burnt-out ruins of the old sanctuary. Kofi remembered the spot well. He had stared at the crows hopping around the broken remnants of the place, his mind on Keisha. The new building was a modest façade of brick and aluminum siding. A simple white wooden cross rose at the top of a small steeple on the angled roof. Everything was painted white. A cluster of large trees sheltered the building and it stood there as a symbol of resilience, strength, and defiance. Kofi parked the car on a grassy slope just off the road.

"They rebuilt it," he said. "When I was here, it wasn't there."

"Yeah, they rebuilt it."

They walked into the church. People looked at them with only a hint of interest. They sat near the back. The preacher, a tall black man with hands that looked massive even from where they stood at the back of the congregation, wrapped his body over the pulpit, his voice worn, deep, sonorous. His gray hair was a tangle of uneven brush. He spoke slowly, the music of his voice filling the church. It was the voice of a man whose language was birthed in the low country but reshaped by years of travel, years of taking on the cadence of people he had heard during his travels. He had the look of a man who had journeyed, seen things, understood and felt things. He spoke with his hands, with the sway and dip of his body, and with his eyes. It was easy to forget the room, forget the faces around, forget the circumstance of one's presence in that place at such a time, and simply be carried away by this man. He was reading, but he barely looked at the page. He knew the words. He spoke them like a man taken by the story.

> *I slept but my heart was awake . . .*
> *Listen! Listen! My lover is knocking: "Open to me, my sister,*
> *my darling."*
> *My lover thrusts his hand through the latch-opening;*
> *my heart began to pound for him.*
> *I arose to open for my lover,*
> *and my hands dripped with myrrh,*
> *my fingers with flowing myrrh,*
> *on the handles of the lock.*
> *I opened for my lover,*
> *but my lover had left; he was gone.*
> *O daughters of Jerusalem, I charge you—*
> *If you find my lover, what will you tell him?*
> *Tell him I am faint with love.*

When he was finished, he stood straight and breathed deeply.

"*Behold, I stand at the door and knock.* You hearing me? *Behold. Behold.* Folks, he ain't gonna stand at the door forever. No way. Now, that is what he is out there saying.

Jesus is out there knocking, getting his hand all cut up and bleeding trying to break inside. *Open the door! Open the door, people.* But what are we going to do, people? We going to lie down there in the bed, feeling nice in ourself, knowing that he always coming back to the door, 'That Jesus, why he always wanna come when I am trying to get me some sleep. Why he always on my case?' You know how we talk. You know how we get on sometimes. But you got to be careful, 'cause you could come to the door and ain't nobody there. Ain't nobody there. It would be a sad day. You might have to go out there in the cold, in the wet, calling out, 'Jesus! Jesus! Jesus! Where are you, Jesus!'"

The preacher wiped his face. An electric current burnt across the air. Keisha and Kofi both understood the swelling of bodies and hearts in the church at the same time.

"Many of y'all know that my wife passed ten years ago. Y'all knew her. That woman taught me the taste of love. I loved that woman. Now, I ain't saying we did not go through a whole lot. I gave that woman a hard time, but I will tell you this, I will tell you that there came a time when I realized that I had to start talking about love. It come that one day I wanted to marry her all over again. This time I wanted to marry her because I knew I could never live without her. I knew that it would be the darkest thing in the world for me to be without her. One day she said, 'Baby, I am thinking of going, of leaving you.' And that changed me. The darkness I saw before me. Love is weakness, people. Love is knowing we need. Need. I needed her. I needed her so bad. And I told her, 'Let me marry you again. Let me marry you again, baby, and this time, this time, you won't even have to knock. I'll be at the door every night waiting for you to come. I'll be standing at the door waiting. That is what I'll do.'

"She's gone to see her maker now. But I still think about her. Still smell her, 'cause I can't get rid of none of her things. Now, people say it ain't healthy, but I am eighty years old, so what feels good is healthy to me. I ain't marrying another woman. I just know what I have tasted and loved. Maybe all y'all young folks might find it kind of sick to hear a old man like me talking about all this loving and stuff; so I ain't gonna do it. But what I got me here is a serious gospel message. This thing with the bride and the beloved, that is me and you and the Lord. And I say Jesus is knocking at the door, knocking, knocking, knocking . . .

"These days I talk to people like I'll be going down the road soon to a new place to live and I know that they must come there sooner or later. All I keep saying is that when I see someone I like, I say, 'I sure hope I will see you again.' I surely hope so, 'cause I am going off soon, that's right, and I'll be looking out for a lot of people. So if you want to see me over on the other side—and I sure hope you do—I want you to come down to the front here so we can make some arrangements to meet up. I want to make sure I got your name so when you get up in there, I can come up to you and say, 'Hey Pedro, hey LaQuanda, hey Jerome, hey Colin, hey Betty, welcome, baby!' And you can come to the gate and shout, 'I am looking for a guy named Clarence! Where Clarence at?' and folks will say, 'Clarence right here, he been waitin' on you!' Hallelujah! So, come on down here and we can make plans to meet up yonder, 'cause I promise you, I'll be there."

A fat organ sound filled the vacuum, flooding the chapel. A woman wearing a red dashiki with spindles of yellow emanating from the middle stood with her huge twelve-stringed guitar and began to sing in a rich contralto.

*Just as I am without one plea*
*That thou thy blood was shed for me*

The old man stepped from the pulpit and it became clear how old a man he was. He was stooped over as he walked across the altar with a shuffling gait, his worn Bible clutched against his chest, his face beaming with smile, his hair a mad white jungle. Were he to stand fully upright he would have been at least a foot taller. He sat down on one of the two ugly wooden thrones flanking the altar. The seat was too low for him and he was all legs.

The woman kept singing as people began to walk to the front and fall at the altar.

*And as thou bidst me come to thee*
*Oh, Lamb of God, I come,*
*I come.*

Keisha and Kofi stood up and, without discussing it, stepped out of the pews and made their way to the door at the back of the church. Kofi turned around and peered at the old man, who seemed to wink. They stepped into the sun, and the child started to cry, sharply, loudly.

"She's hungry," Keisha said, taking the baby out of the carrier and placing her on her shoulder. Kofi took the baby seat, and then started down the stairs.

"Children," said a deep voice behind them.

They turned to see him standing on the small landing just outside the church door. He was smiling broadly. His right hand gripped the railing.

"That baby wants a blessing now. We don't baptize them here—that is for when you get old enough to know. But it don't hurt to bless them. So I am saying that we can do that right now and you all can go on on your journey and God will take care of the rest."

Kofi looked at Keisha. She nodded without understanding why.

"We ain't got to do it in there. Too much confusion in there right now, anyway," the man said. "Let's get under them trees over there, right under that nice dogwood where things look like God made the light."

Several others had come out to see what the old man was doing. They followed the procession under the tree. It was a little garden area with a massive live oak tree and two smaller dogwoods that were now fully green with those lemony leaves that tinted every bit of light filtering in. The ground was covered with a thick growth of soft grass.

In the shade, the old man took the child in his arms. She stopped crying as he held her. "What you call her?" he asked Kofi.

Kofi hesitated. He had forgotten her name. Keisha looked at him.

"Her name—" Kofi said to Keisha. Then remembering just as Keisha began to speak, he said, "Alma." And they said it together.

"Ah, the soul. The soul. Sweet Alma. In the name of the Father, the Son, and the Holy Ghost, and in the name of Jesus, I anoint you, bless you, and plant richness, beauty, peace, and a life of sweet kindness into your heart, my child. Sweet Jesus, bless these two who hold the child, show them things they have never seen before and give them power to see themselves as bigger than the smallness of this world. Amen." He lifted the child to his face. "Sweet Alma, me and you have a lot in common. You get that way after all. Ahh, you like the gray hair, eh? That is the splendor of age, Solomon says:

*My heart is not proud, O Lord,*
*My eyes are not haughty;*
*I do not concern myself with great matters*
*Or things too wonderful for me.*
*But I have stilled and quieted my soul;*
*Like a weaned child with its mother,*
*Like a weaned child is my soul within me.*
*O, my people, put your hope in the Lord*
*Both now and forever."*

He handed the child to Keisha, then touched the child's cheeks with his huge dark finger. He turned and started to walk away. "Drive carefully. Love each other. Watch that child. Alma. Sweet soul."

The other church people touched them and patted their backs and smiled and ushered them to their car. They spoke blessings and they spoke of the beauty of the child and the sweet strangeness of their pastor and of time, and of the times.

Kofi and Keisha accepted the blessings and drove off with the cadence of that man's voice and the sweet contralto of the woman in their heads. Alma was awake but so intent on her own sounds that she did not seem to care that she was facing the sky behind them and looking back at the paths that they had already taken as the car sped southwards. The sun cut a sharp line across their faces, across the dashboard, and across their lives.

The sun stood full and round at the end of the highway. Its perfection was startling. It was massive. Kofi breathed and reached over to touch Keisha. She hummed softly. The car moved into the wash of light that filled the air.

Had they been people blessed with the language to speak of grace, to speak of faith, to speak of purity and holiness, to speak of hope, they would have said more than they did in the car that day. But they stayed silent and listened to the sounds made by their daughter, a sweet baptism of hope in the brilliant light of a new day.

# Also from **AKASHIC BOOKS**

**JOHN CROW'S DEVIL by Marlon James**
A finalist for the *Los Angeles Times* Book Prize
and the Commonwealth Writers' Prize
232 pages, hardcover, $19.95

"A powerful first novel . . . Writing with assurance
and control, James uses his small-town drama to
suggest the larger anguish of a postcolonial
Jamaican society struggling for its own identity."
—*New York Times* (Editor's Choice)

**IRON BALLOONS: HIT FICTION FROM
JAMAICA'S CALABASH WRITER'S WORKSHOP**
edited by Colin Channer
282 pages, trade paperback, $14.95

*New stories by: Kwame Dawes, Elizabeth Nunez,
Kaylie Jones, Marlon James, and others.*

"[Channer's] story comes at you with hurricane
force and an irresistible title, 'How to Beat a Child
the Right and Proper Way' . . . a big breath of a
piece, and something of a tour de force, spoken in
various registers of Jamaican English."
—*New York Times*

**BECOMING ABIGAIL by Chris Abani**
A selection of the *Essence Magazine* Book Club
and Black Expressions Book Club
128 pages, trade paperback, $11.95

"Compelling and gorgeously written, this is a
coming-of-age novella like no other. Chris Abani
explores the depths of loss and exploitation with
what can only be described as a knowing
tenderness. An extraordinary, necessary book."
—Cristina Garcia, author of *Dreaming in Cuban*